COCKY BUTLER

ANNABELLE ANDERS

ANNABELLE
ANDERS

COCKY BUTLER

Edits and proofing by Tracy Mooring Liebchen and Laura Dickey.

www.annabelleanders.com

❀ Created with Vellum

A DUKE PRETENDING TO BE A BUTLER...

... and a very suspicious spinster realize that choosing love isn't as easy as one might think.

"The loser must perform butler duties for the winner throughout the Season this spring."

The Duke of Blackheart should never have accepted the wager. A foolish drunken night of games had led to an uncomfortable promise, but after considerable planning and a good deal of delegating, he'd found the charade almost too easy...

Or so he'd thought, until Lord Greystone's spinster cousin arrives, lips pinched in disapproval, eyes filled with suspicion, with the potential to spoil everything.

Miss Violet Faraday had come to London for one reason only —to assist in launching her niece into society. She did not come in hopes of landing a husband for herself, nor had she expected to come face to face with her tragic past.

Most of all, she had not planned on becoming extraordinarily fascinated with Mr. Cockfield, her cousin's charming, arrogant, and ridiculously good-looking butler. He is a servant and she is a lady... anything beyond a mild flirtation can only lead to heartbreak...

ARRIVING IN LONDON

"I remembered Knight Hall being much larger than this," Lady Posy Marsden announced after stepping onto the pavement.

"You were only ten years old the last time you were here," Miss Violet Faraday said. She herself had only come to London a few times in the years since her debut in 1821—nearly a decade ago—and she'd intentionally kept those visits short.

Exceedingly grateful to be at the end of their journey from Yorkshire to London, Violet assisted her aunt out of the ancient carriage and then twisted side to side, stretching and enjoying the open air. The drive had involved far more stops at inns than ought to have been necessary.

That was because dear Aunt Iris, who was nearing her eighth decade, had insisted she could endure no more than three hours of riding in the carriage per day, and since the vehicle belonged to her, as did the luggage coach that trailed behind them, Violet and Posy hadn't any choice but to yield to the older woman's wishes.

1

Which, of course, they would have done anyway.

Violet glanced around, surprised that none of her cousin's servants had stepped outside upon their arrival. Although they'd arrived considerably later than intended, she had sent word last week to let her cousin's housekeeper know.

Had the servants given up hope for their arrival altogether?

"Where the devil are Greystone's manservants?" Aunt Iris groused, her lips pinched as she stared at the closed door. "I'll not have my nephew taken advantage of by his staff if I've any say in the matter. He is a marquess."

"Yes, he is, Aunt, and I'm sure he is not being taken advantage of by his servants." Violet smiled weakly, already exhausted at the prospect of having to apologize for her aunt, who said precisely what she thought, while also keeping watch over Posy, who *did* precisely what she wanted. What with keeping these two out of trouble, the spring promised to be a trying one indeed. "Besides, Aunt, we are arriving nearly a fortnight later than we originally promised. You did not expect the household to keep watch at the windows for eleven days, did you?"

Just as Violet uttered the rhetorical question, she glanced up to see the door to Knight Hall open. A small, youngish-looking woman stood partially in the shadows inside—and that woman was embracing a gentleman.

Dressed in almost all black, he wore the apparel usually reserved for butlers—black tie, white waistcoat, black jacket, pristine white shirt, and dark gray trousers—no gloves. This man's ebony hair, however, was far too unruly for any self-respecting manservant to consider proper. Even as she watched, an unruly lock fell along his jaw.

The gentleman was most definitely not Greystone.

Confused, Violet tipped her head back and studied the windows flanking the terraced facade of her cousin's perfectly symmetrical four-story limestone manor. There was the same number of windows on each side, each decorated with the familiar arched headers and framed with molding that resembled Grecian columns.

Confident that this was, indeed, Knight Hall, Violet returned her attention to the couple standing at the threshold of the partially open door.

The man was of similar height and coloring to her cousin, the Marquess of Greystone, but the likeness ended there. Whereas Greystone was a proper and fashionable gentleman, this man wore his uniform with a casual nonchalance. He possessed more of an athletic, cat-like build—like one of those tigers she'd once seen at the Tower exhibition.

Violet looked on unashamedly as this… *person* standing in Greystone's entrance dispatched what looked to be a purse filled with coin into the young woman's hand and then squeezed her shoulder. Such a transaction could not be payment of wages as the girl was dressed too well to be a servant. Surely this gentleman wasn't Greystone's butler making such a spectacle on the front steps of Knight Hall?

The lady tucked the small drawstring purse into her reticule, and the man then leaned forward to press a kiss on the young woman's forehead.

He lifted his gaze and pinned it on Violet. One corner of his mouth twitched. Was that a smirk?

Annoyance at his insolence rolled through her. Her irritation increased when he showed no inclination to hurry along with his business.

Without acknowledging Violet, her aunt, or her niece, the gentleman bid his lady visitor farewell, disappeared for a moment, and then returned to step outside, followed by a small army of uniformed manservants.

And strolling behind them was her cousin, dressed in an evergreen superfine jacket, olive waistcoat, and tan breeches.

"Aunt Iris! Either you were set upon by highwaymen, or you stopped at every inn between here and Blossom Court!" Greystone approached with the familiar cordial smile Violet associated with her childhood. He placed a kiss on their aunt's cheek and turned to Posy. "Look at you, all grown up. What a breath of fresh air you'll be to all those young bucks this spring."

Posy wrinkled her nose but hugged Greystone back, her escaped curls bouncing. "I'm only here because Aunt Iris and Violet didn't allow me a say in the matter."

"My favorite cousin didn't wish to visit me?" Greys feigned offense, laughter lurking in his gray eyes.

"I'm your *only cousin*, second cousin if accuracy matters. And I suppose visiting London is not all bad." At nine and ten, Posy possessed the ability to act childish one moment, and the next behave like a woman older than her years. Violet was going to need to keep a close watch on her this Season. Aunt Iris took some interest in Posy's upbringing but was far keener to insert herself into as many games of parquet as was humanly possible.

Greystone placed a kiss on Violet's cheek. "Posy has all but denounced marriage," Violet informed him. Although, a London Season was sure to turn this around. Ensuring Posy's future was Violet's priority—if not for Posy's sake, then for Posy's mother's.

For Adelaide's sake. The memory of Violet's older sister never failed to sting—even after all these years.

Making up for their own mother's lack of interest in

parenting, Violet's sister had stepped in and provided all the motherly care Violet had needed. Adelaide had been twelve years older than Violet, but they had been very close. And although Greys was Posy's legal guardian, responsible for managing Posy's financial affairs, it had seemed the most natural thing in the world for Violet to raise her sister's daughter.

Taking over the care of Posy had somehow… saved Violet.

"She'll be breaking hearts left and right." Greys sent the younger girl a warm grin.

"Quite right." Exactly what Violet was hoping. Well, not the breaking of hearts part, but that Posy would have several suitable offers to choose from. "And for the record, we did, I'm quite certain, stop at every inn between here and Yorkshire."

Her cousin laughed sympathetically, and Violet's chest loosened at the sound.

Defying their aunt's low expectations, Greystone had taken an active part in his duty as Posy's legal guardian and made visiting his ward at Blossom Court at least twice a year a priority. And furthermore, he'd not once failed to respond to Violet's letters when she'd sought his advice or opinion.

As cousins, she and Greys had spent a good deal of their childhoods together. And despite Violet living in Yorkshire and Greys spending most of his time in London, their shared history ensured a comfortable familiarity.

"Aunt Iris, you're looking as handsome as ever." Greystone offered his arm. "How is it that you appear younger than the last time I saw you?"

"Flatterer. You, on the other hand, are looking positively ancient—" Aunt Iris studied him critically, "—for an unmarried man, that is."

"In that case, you'll be happy to know that I'm of a mind to marry this spring."

Violet's brows shot up at hearing this. Nearly thirty, the Marquess of Greystone was one of London's most sought-after bachelors. As such, details of his life—usually comments on his fashion sense—even made it up to Yorkshire, thanks to the *Gazette* and the dependability of the English mail.

But that he was considering marriage was news, indeed. "Who is this young woman who has done the impossible and caught your eye?"

Greystone glanced down the sidewalk. "Why don't we all go inside and have this discussion once you've settled in—in the privacy of my drawing-room." He grimaced. "Where not all of Mayfair is privy."

Violet jumped when a hand landed on hers, which was gripping the handle of her small valise. She didn't need to look up to know that it belonged to the insolent man who'd been hovering in the doorway.

"Allow me, Miss Faraday," he said in a cultured voice, provoking a… fluttering in her belly.

She hadn't eaten much before leaving the inn that morning. Tea—she would have some tea after washing up.

"Violet, this is Mr. Cockfield, my new butler." Greys gestured, and she met the man's gaze. His eyes were black—no, not black, but dark navy—midnight blue.

Violet gripped her bag more tightly than she had been before.

The man who was comforting the woman on Greystone's front steps is the butler?

Did her cousin realize what sort of questionable activities his butler was up to?

"Miss Faraday?" The butler cocked a patient brow, apparently having remembered his duties.

"What happened to Mr. Tuppenwiser?" Violet asked, turning back to her cousin. She barely remembered the elderly fellow from when she'd visited in the past.

"Suffered a fall last winter. And, as he was nearing eight decades, when I offered him a small house near the ocean with a stipend, he accepted.

"He has retired?"

"It was high time. Lucky for me, Mr. Cockfield was available for hire." Greystone seemed a tad overly enthusiastic about this fellow, and Violet slid the man a skeptical sideways glance.

And, of course, Mr. Cockfield was watching her. But this time when she met his gaze, he smiled graciously, all innocence.

If Greys approved of his butler, Violet grudgingly admitted to herself, then she must as well. Perhaps the little scene she'd witnessed a few moments ago was not as it appeared.

Although... what else could it be? Had this Mr. Cockfield fellow been paying a former employee her wages? Or perhaps the young woman was there to collect a charitable donation.

Neither of which explained him kissing the woman on the forehead—or that the woman had embraced him.

"Miss Faraday?" Mr. Cockfield's voice sounded amused as he flicked a meaningful look at both of their hands still clutching her valise. While she'd been contemplating all the different explanations for what she'd seen, the others had entered Knight Hall, leaving her standing alone with her cousin's butler.

She nodded with a jerk and relinquished the bag that contained her knitting. "Thank you."

"I can show you to your chamber as well, since Mrs. Hambletone is seeing to your niece and aunt." He gestured for Violet to precede him inside, and she did her best to ignore the prickly feeling on the back of her neck as she did so.

Why would Greystone hire such an unsuitable man for his butler? Butlers were supposed to be quietly dignified in a manner that brought comfort to the household members.

Butlers were not supposed to smirk at guests nor allow their gazes to silently laugh while greeting newly arrived visitors.

Inside, Violet strode toward the elegant staircase that led upstairs. Even though she'd not visited in years, she was quite familiar with the house. She lifted her skirt to take a step and glanced behind her.

Was Mr. Cockfield ogling her behind? She scowled at him. No one had ogled her behind since—since… she did not know when!

He met her gaze, a blank expression on his face. She had imagined it. Of course, she had imagined it.

SIMON COCKFIELD, the Duke of Blackheart, rubbed his fingers together, frustrated that he couldn't use his eyepiece to present a subtle set-down to Greystone's pretty but strait-laced cousin.

Miss Violet Faraday was as starchy as spinsters came.

He'd met her only once before, at some affair hosted by Greystone's grandfather, and that had been years ago. But she did not remember him. No, she was far more concerned with what he'd been doing with Lucinda when the carriage had arrived.

Lady Lucinda—one of his younger twin sisters, who had only recently made her come out and who'd had her pin money lifted by a pickpocket on Bond Street earlier that day.

Miss Faraday, no doubt, had conjured all manner of nefarious reasons for him to be giving money to a young woman at her cousin's door. The woman's face revealed her every thought, and Simon had required a healthy dose of self-restraint to keep from laughing out loud.

Two weeks had passed since he'd begun the charade as Greystone's butler. And although he'd been a fool to enter such a wager, making good on his loss wasn't as troublesome as he'd first imagined.

Hopefully, he'd feel the same by the end of the Season.

He'd agreed to the bet nearly two months earlier, at a late winter house party at Westerley Crossings. Simon had wagered that his good friend, the Earl of Westerley, would have no difficulty convincing the daughter of Daniel Jackson, the visiting American Whiskey King, to marry him. Simon had bet that the earl could secure the chit's hand within twenty-four hours of meeting her.

Who wouldn't accept an offer from one of England's most sought-after noblemen? Miss Jackson—that was who. The stubborn chit had kept Westerley cooling his heels for a few weeks.

Simon had lost the wager.

And the stakes? He'd been mad enough to wager his services as Greystone's butler for the entirety of the Season if he lost. Mad with drink, that was. If he'd been sober, he never would have bet against the marquess.

Upon reaching the third-floor landing, Miss Faraday

glanced back at him. Again, Simon smothered his mirth to see her looking at him so suspiciously.

"To your left, Miss Faraday." He modulated his tone to that of his position. Her only indication that she'd heard him was a stiffening of her shoulders and an almost military pivot in the direction he'd indicated.

Not even Lydia and Lucinda's governess had shown as much starch as Miss Faraday exhibited. He couldn't help but feel a little sorry for her niece.

"Here you are." Simon reached around her to open the door to the Rose Room. Not that it was nearly as elegant as the name implied; it was named because the walls were painted a soft mauve color. Although the maids had prepared all of the guests' rooms for their arrival, that had been over a week ago, and the air inside wasn't as fresh as it ought to be.

Simon cracked one of the windows open and, crossing back to the door, made a mental note to have fresh flowers brought up. He'd send one of the footmen over to Heart Place to raid his own greenhouse.

And that reminded him of a few maintenance issues he'd been informed of earlier that required his attention there.

It went without saying that he could not, in fact, set aside his ducal responsibilities. But he was finding that with a little delegation and careful planning, he could manage two entirely different staffs and effectively fulfill all of his responsibilities. It was merely a managerial juggling act.

No matter that he rarely got four hours of sleep or that he was missing out on squiring his newly come-out sisters about town. Lucas, his younger brother, was on leave and had been more than willing to take over in that regard.

Performing required duties as both the Duke of Blackheart

and Greystone's butler was challenging, but it was also satisfying.

"Will this be to your liking, Miss Faraday?" Standing in the open doorway, Simon watched as this tightly wound woman drifted across to the window. As a spinster, she was the one category of woman he didn't fully comprehend.

He shoved his hands into his pockets and slouched against the doorframe. Most women wouldn't choose spinsterhood willingly. They were usually forced into it due to a deficit in looks, or finances, or both. But that was not the case with Miss Faraday. As Greystone's cousin, she would have had a substantial dowry. And although her chignon was too tight and the collar of her dress too high, anyone could see that she was an attractive woman.

And, if he remembered correctly, as a young girl, she'd been quite a delight—until she'd lost her fiancé.

Fate had not been kind to Miss Violet Faraday.

In addition to the apparent drawbacks of spinsterhood, Simon supposed, there must be certain benefits. At the moment, however, he couldn't imagine what those might be.

"The marquess knows I like watching the mews." She was being polite. "There is something comforting in hearing the comings and goings of the household."

Simon jerked himself away from the doorframe to cross the room and join her at the window, which, indeed, provided an excellent view of the tidy stable and carriage house.

"Most women prefer a view of the park."

"Yes, well, I am not most women." She backed away from the window, which incidentally moved her away from him, and then hugged her arms in front of her. "That will be all."

Simon blinked a moment and then bit the inside of his

mouth to keep from laughing. By God, she was dismissing him.

Greystone had deigned to do the same on only a few occasions, and he'd mostly only been joking, but this woman was firmly putting him in his place.

Clasping his hands behind his back, he bowed. "Very good, madam." He could hardly remember when a woman had charmed him more.

Not for the first time, Simon mused to himself that this spring might prove enjoyable after all.

GETTING TO KNOW THE BUTLER

After spending the first night settling in, Violet woke and dressed bright and early the next morning intent on meeting with Greystone. In addition to finalizing the plans for Posy's coming-out ball that Greystone had promised, Violet needed to go through the various invitations to select which affairs would be best suited for a debutante. Once she decided on their calendar, she would go right to work finalizing Posy's wardrobe.

No lady could embark on a Season without at least a dozen gowns made up by Madam Chantal. While making plans in Yorkshire, they had, of course, ordered several dresses from London's most sought-after modiste. But those gowns would require alterations—for which Violet needed to schedule appointments. With any luck, the famous dressmaker would be able to get them in without delay.

When Violet burst into her cousin's study, she was more than enthusiastic about getting to work.

"Good morning—" Her smile faltered when she realized Greystone was not alone.

Mr. Cockfield—the butler—was seated across from her cousin, reclining, actually, with one foot resting on the opposite knee.

"You're up early this morning," Greys greeted her.

Both men rose.

"Greystone," she acknowledged her cousin. And then, "Mr. Cockfield."

Violet lowered herself into a second chair facing Greystone's desk, expecting the butler to excuse himself.

He did not.

"You are a sight for sore eyes, Vi," Greys said as both men lowered themselves back into their seats.

Keeping her gaze locked on her cousin but aware that Mr. Cockfield was watching her, she shifted and straightened her spine. "I don't wish to interrupt if the two of you are discussing household business."

"Not at all," Greystone answered. "I suppose you'd like to go through the stack of invitations I've been ignoring."

"That and the guestlist for Posy's ball." She appreciated the reminder of why she'd come. And since Mr. Cockfield showed no indication of excusing himself, she addressed another concern. "I also wanted your opinion on Posy's prospects." Unfortunately, she wasn't nearly as familiar with society as most sponsors were, and she'd need to rely on Greystone's judgment.

Her cousin shook his head. "If it was up to me, I'd steer her clear of all of them." He frowned. "But I suppose that's not an option."

"She is nearly twenty," Violet reminded him.

Her cousin exhaled loudly. "I know."

Violet had wanted to bring Posy to London two years ago, but Posy had been reluctant, and Greys had indulged her.

"Anyone, in particular, she ought to avoid?" Violet opened the small book she liked to keep notes in, pencil poised.

"How much time do we have?" Greys chuckled.

"Perhaps it would be easier to list the names of those you approve." She slid a dismissive glance in Mr. Cockfield's direction. In answer, the man reclined and recrossed his legs.

He was either obtuse or purposely ignoring her, and she'd wager her favorite hat on the latter.

Greystone had opened a drawer and pushed a stack of envelopes in her direction. "Trouble with separating them like that, my dearest cousin, is that all the bachelors happen to be male. And knowing how they think, I'm inclined to withhold my approval perpetually."

"Not all males are animals," she said. "There must be a few decent ones."

Violet drew the collection of invitations toward her, casually flicked through the envelopes, and frowned. The names were familiar as the same families had made up the *ton* for as many years as it had existed.

However, as to their on-dits, she wasn't nearly as confident in deciding who was and who was not appropriate for Posy to mingle with.

But before she could voice her concerns, the stack of envelopes was plucked out of her hands. Mr. Cockfield began flicking through each of them one by one, building three separate piles.

"What—?"

"Trust my butler in these matters, Violet," Greys said. "He's a better handle on *ton* affairs than both of us put together."

"Lady Ravensdale finalized the guest list last week," Mr. Cockfield said. "As to the invitations, Posy shouldn't miss these…." He sifted through the stack, tossing envelopes one by one onto the desk. "Send your regrets to these." He pointed to a second pile. "And leave these to her own discretion," he tapped the third pile.

Which, Violet realized, effectively cut her out of the decision-making process altogether.

Mr. Cockfield leveled his gaze on her. "Avoid an introduction to Lord Tempest's brother, Mr. Gilcrest. Other gentlemen to steer her clear of are Viscount Trident, and the Marquess of Lockley if he is in town. They've always been troublemakers."

Violet wanted to appreciate his opinions, only they didn't sound like opinions at all. They sounded more like orders!

"I am in full agreement," Greys said.

Violet wrote down the names and, feeling more than a twinge of exasperation, turned to face Mr. Cockfield. "And which gentlemen should she encourage?" Violet asked, not bothering to tamp down the sarcasm in her voice.

"Aside from the names I've provided, whoever she fancies."

"But there must be someone…"

"Miss Faraday. To set your sights on one or two potential husbands for your niece would be an exercise in futility. Why don't you simply wait and see who she likes? When one of them catches her eye, we will vet his suitability then."

"But…" This wasn't at all how her family had handled such matters. In fact, it had been Adelaide who had introduced Violet to Christopher, the man she'd become engaged to. And what did he mean, *we will vet*? "With all due respect, Mr. Cockfield, I cannot imagine you have much experience in this area. A lady requires a guiding hand. And Lord Greystone and I will be the ones to provide that."

She turned to her cousin, but Greys, who'd gone back to

reading the paper in front of him, provided no assistance whatsoever.

Mr. Cockfield studied her with eyes that seemed to know more than they ought. "As you wish," he said, rising from his chair.

"I do wish," she grumbled beneath her breath.

She wished this butler would learn his place; that was what she wished.

"BUT LORD SHORTWOOD seemed so sweet, Posy, and his estate isn't all that far from Yorkshire," Miss Faraday reasoned, not convincing her niece in the least. And then she added, "those spots on his face will fade as he gets older."

Simon resisted the urge to smirk when Miss Faraday set her knitting aside, obviously exasperated with her niece.

"Perhaps *you* ought to marry him then," Posy returned. "Aunt Iris and I agree that you ought to look for a husband for yourself. Where is she this afternoon, anyway?"

"Another game of piquet with Lady Sheffield." Simon winked at Lady Posy as he lowered the tray of tea onto the table.

"Really, Aunt Violet. It couldn't hurt for you to put yourself out there while we're here."

"I had my chance, and it was not meant to be," Miss Faraday answered, shifting in her seat. "Besides, it's not your concern."

"But you'd be setting an excellent example." Simon couldn't help but toss fuel onto the fire.

"This isn't your concern either, Mr. Cockfield."

"Of course." He stared at her innocently.

"I am content as I am," she protested—perhaps a tad too vehemently?—which meant that she was not.

Content, that was.

"Buy some new gowns, do something with your hair, practice fluttering your lashes." He dared suggesting before handing her the plate of biscuits.

She was staring at him with her mouth half-open, dismayed, no doubt, at his audacity. He resisted the urge to stuff one of the biscuits between her lips.

With large, expressive brown eyes and thick hair that was only slightly darker, she was a very pretty woman.

If she'd allow herself to be.

"I smile." She stared down at the dish with a grimace. "And my gowns are perfectly fine."

"Of course they are," he responded. "Is there anything else that you require right now?"

"What's wrong with my hair?" She all but ignored the sweet bread in front of her.

"Nothing at all, Aunt Violet," Posy chimed in. "If you're trying to look like a governess."

"Or a vicar's wife." Simon teased with a grin as he closed the drawing-room doors behind him. More and more, he enjoyed these little run-ins.

Strolling back to his office, he chuckled that he'd gotten a rise out of her this morning. Because as much as Violet Faraday pretended to be happy as a spinster, Simon suspected otherwise. She was too resigned, too strait-laced. Greystone ought to have noticed and done something about it the day she arrived.

But since that wasn't happening, Simon would challenge her himself—with a little flirtation, a little teasing. And this morning, he'd achieved just that. Because just before he'd closed the door to the drawing-room, Simon had caught Miss Violet Faraday staring down at her hands and pinching her mouth together.

But she hadn't hidden her smile completely. And that, he decided, was progress.

SUSPICIOUS BEHAVIOR

"Good morning, Aunt Violet, Uncle Greys," Posy mumbled in a very un-Posy-like manner as she dragged herself into the morning room.

"Good morning, Posy." Greys barely flicked his gaze up from the paper he was reading.

"You look tired today," Violet offered, remarking on the dark circles etched beneath Posy's eyes. "Please tell me you did not stay up late playing chess with Mr. Cockfield again." At Posy's innocent look, Violet turned to her cousin. "Your butler ought not to be fraternizing with your ward, Greys. Can't you speak with him?"

"Don't be such a stickler, Auntie. And I'm not *fraternizing* with him. I'm getting walloped at chess. Mark my words, though. I will beat him at least once before we return to Yorkshire."

There were so many things wrong with her niece's words that Violet hardly knew where to begin. "First of all, if you would only go a little easier on the gentlemen you've met, you wouldn't need to return to Yorkshire—not permanently anyhow." Violet inhaled a calming breath. Despite having a successful come-out ball by all accounts, and attending all of the most sought-after events in the month since they'd arrived, Posy had made very little progress in securing a husband thus far. This wasn't because she hadn't attracted any worthy gentlemen, however, but because Posy had done nothing whatsoever to encourage any of them.

Because, apparently, her niece was only interested in frittering the Season away with Greystone's butler.

"I told you—"

"But you haven't given any of them a chance." Violet cut off Posy's objections. She had heard them all before. Lord Tibbons was too old and boring. Mr. Spencer was too intent on his music. And Sir Frederick's breath was foul.

Besides all that, Posy complained that she didn't want to have to move to another shire, nor did she have any desire to manage her own household, forced to host parties for her husband while acting hoity-toity. And—a point she was most adamant about—she didn't want babies.

Violet dismissed such complaints. Surely, her niece would feel differently when she met the right gentleman?

Because those were the very things a proper lady did. If Posy didn't achieve all the accomplishments of a lady, it would mean that Violet had failed Adelaide.

It would mean that she, Violet, had failed, period.

"If spinsterhood is good enough for you, why isn't it good enough for me?" Her niece could be relentless in her objections.

"Greystone, would you say something?" Violet begged.

Greys finally glanced up from his paper for more than two

seconds and then set it aside, pinning his gaze on Posy. "Even I haven't been able to best Mr. Cockfield at chess. I wouldn't get my hopes up if I were you."

Violet closed her eyes, but before she could argue with either of them, Aunt Iris's voice sounded from the door.

Rather than utilizing her cane, her normally independent aunt was allowing the butler to assist her to the table. "Thank you, Mr. Cockfield. I cannot imagine where it could be. I'll have to speak with Gwen about leaving it within my reach."

The cane, Violet was quite certain, was resting in its usual spot between her aunt's bed and the small table beside it. And if her aunt couldn't locate that one, she kept a spare by the door of her private sitting area.

Violet pinched her mouth together. Everyone, it seemed, was enamored with Greystone's outrageous butler.

She, of course, was not so easily fooled. Because something was off. She didn't know what, but she was sure of it.

Violet met his gaze from where she sat with narrowed eyes, trusting him less now than she had the day they arrived.

Not because he didn't perform his duties, and not even because of his all-too-often inappropriate comments. No, she distrusted him because he managed everything a little *too* well and was, perhaps, a tad *too* popular with the staff.

Not to mention that he was a little *too* charming—a little *too* handsome.

Furthermore, he continued to receive lady visitors who were neither servants nor her cousin's guests. The same lady who'd come the first day had since returned, and others as well. And they all seemed to be looking to him to solve some sort of problem. Fellows made visits as well—not servants and not gentlemen of quality, but men of business.

On Saturday the week before, she'd spied him returning to the mews… riding a *white Arabian.*

She'd asked him about it the next day, and he'd told her he was borrowing it.

Butlers, most assuredly, did not *borrow* prize-winning horses.

"Are you unwell, Miss Faraday?" he asked. "You're looking as though your tea is brackish this morning."

Was he smirking at her again?

"The tea is perfectly fine, Mr. Cockfield," she said through clenched teeth. "As am I."

He, on the other hand, looked far too chipper for a man with a sprained wrist. Two afternoons prior, he'd returned sporting a bruise on his cheek and his arm wrapped in a sling.

She'd asked him how it happened, and he'd winked and told her it got caught in a door.

He had winked!

At her!

Dreadful creature.

It was a well-known fact that those who took up the vocation of butler henceforth put their employers' needs and comforts above their own. How could Mr. Cockfield achieve this, let alone all his own nefarious goings-on, with one arm out of commission?

And of course, those goings-on must be nefarious, because why else would he conduct them secretly? And what proper reason might there be for him to be doling out money?

Perhaps what confounded Violet most of all was that she neither her aunt nor Greystone were willing to protect Posy's virtue and reputation from him. And since they both failed to recognize the problem, Violet was going to have to deal with the situation herself.

Aunt Iris leaned back in her chair and allowed Mr. Cockfield to pour her tea, looking thoughtful before turning to Violet. "I hesitate to mention this, but if I don't tell you, you'll hear it elsewhere."

Violet stiffened.

This comment captured both Greystone's and Posy's attention.

"Hear what?" Posy asked.

"What is it?" Violet braced herself. Such a caveat before an announcement never indicated good news.

"Lord Percival has died," her aunt announced.

She hadn't heard that name in... years.

"The Marquess of Coventry's younger brother?" Greystone asked.

Iris nodded.

"Why would this concern Aunt Violet?" Posy asked.

Mr. Cockfield reached over Violet's shoulder and refilled her cup of tea.

"He was Captain Donovan's father," Violet answered, feeling an odd combination of weakness and determination come over her. The very last thing she wanted was for the details of her engagement unearthed.

"Your dead fiancé?" Posy asked. Violet never brought his name up if it wasn't necessary, but Aunt Iris occasionally mentioned the engagement.

"Lord Percival was a good man. I'll make sure to send my condolences to the Duke of Coventry."

"And he is...?" Posy asked.

"Lord Percival's brother." Christopher's uncle.

Lord and Lady Percival had doted on their son, who had been an only child, but Christopher had resented their interference in his life—even if that interference had been needed. In the end, Christopher had reminded Violet of Icarus, daring and exciting but also reckless. Oddly enough, it had been part of his charm.

But it hadn't been necessary for him to join up. There'd been no good reason for him to sail off and take part in an imperialistic war. Violet knew that now.

She'd considered him terribly heroic back then.

"Lady Percival passed away two years after Christopher's disappearance. I don't think she ever got over losing her son." Saying his name ought not to chill Violet's blood as it did— nine years had passed—and yet doing so summoned feelings she'd fought long and hard to extinguish.

Anger. Despair.

Shame.

"Disappearance?" Posy swiveled her head from Violet to Iris. "I thought he was killed."

"He was. That is, he was pronounced dead, but his body was never recovered. The army officially lists him as missing." Violet lifted her cup to her mouth, grateful to see that her hand was only shaking a little.

Mr. Cockfield stood across the room, his midnight gaze pinned on her. Violet dropped her gaze to stare at her tea and blinked, not at all comfortable with the idea of being pitied.

Again.

"WHERE DID HE DISAPPEAR FROM?" Posy asked.

"India. Just after the Maratha War." He ought not to have gone missing. The skirmishes had come to an end. His unit, the entire army, had achieved a major victory.

"Details best left in the past, Posy. I believe we've made your aunt uncomfortable. My apologies, Violet." Greystone frowned across the table at no one in particular. But he was right, and Violet sent him a grateful glance.

The room fell into an awkward silence until Greys spoke up again.

"What adventures do you ladies have planned for today? Anything exciting?"

"I do." Posy sat up tall. "Mr. Cockfield has promised to escort me to Bond Street. There is a particular bookstore he's told me about that I've been wanting to visit." Her niece then caught, and *held*, Mr. Cockfield's gaze as though they shared a secret.

"Absolutely not." Violet could only handle so much. "Madam Chantal requires you for another fitting. She's expecting us today." She forced a brightness into her tone, hating that she always came across as the spoilsport. "Greystone may accompany us if he is free."

"Eh, I'm happy to leave that privilege to Cockfield. Have you purchased anything for yourself, Violet, since you've been in London?" Was her cousin so oblivious?

"But that is not at all proper." Violet glanced around the room at three curious pairs of eyes. Oddly enough, Mr. Cockfield's gaze wasn't as smug as usual. In fact, if she didn't know better, she'd think he appeared almost sympathetic.

She straightened her spine. "Ladies do not have butlers as escorts. A debutante most certainly does not. Please, take no offense, Mr. Cockfield. I-It's just that—" Not one of them was nodding and agreeing with her. Did her aunt and cousin not comprehend how inappropriate it was for a male servant to chaperone a lady?

"Greystone has a prior engagement, and Mr. Cockfield will provide excellent protection." Aunt Iris lifted a jeweled monocle to her eye and stared hard at Posy. "For both of you." She turned to Violet. "And you will order some new gowns. I insist."

Posy was obviously disappointed at the change to her plans for the day. Greystone turned to Violet, looking perplexed.

"Surely, with both of you present, there will be no appearance of impropriety," he said.

Posy frowned. "Mr. Cockfield can take me to the bookstore afterward. Aunt Violet needn't be inconvenienced."

If Violet clenched her teeth any more tightly, they would shatter into a thousand pieces. When had it become acceptable for a butler to consort with his employer's impressionable young ward?

"I have nothing else planned." If Posy was going to be gallivanting around London with Mr. Cockfield, then Violet would most definitely be going along as well. "I'm always happy to shop for books."

"That reminds me. Lady Chaswick has invited us for dinner this week. Purchase something new, Vi—something with a little lace and color. You're falling behind in your fashion," Greystone teased.

SIMON DID NOT GIVE in to the pleading look Lady Posy sent him. Nor did he express even an ounce of dismay that Miss Faraday would be joining them. Because he was not—dismayed, that was. And although he had hoped to tend to a few other matters while out, needling Miss Faraday for a few hours promised to be amusing.

Lady Posy was simply going to have to undertake her mission another time—the minx.

"Our appointment with Madam Chantal is at two. We can go to your bookstore afterward." Disapproval dripped off Miss Faraday's tongue. She directed her comment to Lady Posy, quite intentionally ignoring Simon.

He suspected she did that to remind herself that he was a servant more than anything else, because she obviously sensed that all was not as it ought to be.

He cocked a brow at Greystone. It didn't feel fair, keeping Miss Faraday in the dark like this, but the circumstances were beyond his control. If Simon were to tell her who he really was, he'd forfeit the bet, the same if Greystone chose to do so.

Simon exited the room, other concerns already crowding in. He'd tell one of the footmen they could clear away the morning meal, and then he needed to speak with an investigator over another matter. After that, he ought to have enough time to go over the household accounts with Greystone's housekeeper, Mrs. Hambletone, and read through his own steward's reports before ordering a carriage in which to escort the ladies to Madam Chantal's.

Or perhaps he'd order up the barouche—if the rain held off.

Every last member of her family was pushing Miss Faraday to improve her wardrobe, and most of her gowns were, in fact, out of fashion and somewhat matronly. And yet Simon doubted she would.

The woman was far too restrained for her own good. It was as though she wanted to be invisible. And that... was a travesty.

Making a quick decision, in addition to tasking himself with eliciting smiles from the lady, he'd find some way to show her how to have fun.

The fact that he considered it nigh impossible made him even more determined to accomplish it.

FASHION... AND OTHER SENSE

"Now, don't be mad at me." Posy tugged Violet toward the tall brick building, which, contrary to what most people expected a French woman's dress shop to look like, was surprisingly discreet.

"Please don't tell me you've turned down another offer to go driving?" Violet braced herself for bad news as they entered the hushed interior of the dress shop, Mr. Cockfield right behind them.

"No. Nothing like that, you goose. I've changed my appointment." Posy smiled. "Tell her, Mr. Cockfield. Tell her she needs new gowns."

"Posy! Don't be ridiculous." Violet gasped.

But the butler was already inspecting her person, causing Violet's blood to run cold and then hot. A woman's wardrobe was a very personal matter. It was not something one discussed with strange gentlemen.

Violet sent him what ought to have been a withering glare, and the corner of his mouth twitched.

Impertinent man.

But before Violet could reprimand either of her companions, the dressmaker herself, a short, curvy French woman with curly red hair, bustled into the room from behind an evergreen velvet curtain. "Good afternoon, my lady." The stout woman addressed Posy before turning to inspect Violet. "But we are to dress you today, *non?* It is Miss Faraday who requires many beautiful gowns for the remainder of the Season?"

"Oh, no!" Violet held out a hand.

"She most certainly does, Madam," Mr. Cockfield interrupted, speaking from behind a newspaper. "The Marquess of Greystone insists she be fitted with no less than five ball gowns and seven day dresses." The dratted butler spoke with such conviction that Violet doubted any person within one hundred miles would be willing to step up and challenge him.

Except for herself. And she would have—challenged him, that was—*if* he'd not invoked her cousin into the situation. She could not very well contradict Greystone's instructions. Not when it meant this lady's business and her employees would benefit from the purchase.

"Very good." The esteemed dressmaker circled Violet, eyeing her as though she could take her measurements by sight alone. "Such a lovely figure. You will be a dream to dress if you don't mind my saying so, Miss Faraday."

"Nothing too elaborate, please—"

"The marquess insists on the latest fashions," Mr. Cockfield asserted.

"Oh, but no," Violet protested. "Please, I'm only a chaperone."

"Oh, *but yes,*" Posy interjected. "My *uncle* insists."

"Step up here, Miss Faraday. Lady Posy and the gentleman may have a seat and wait, if they wish. Or they can go. It matters not to me." She pointed toward a settee across the room. "The Season is well underway already, *non*? We haven't any time to waste." Madam Chantal's smile was a uniquely French one, her lips curving but her eyes looking rather stern.

Before Violet could summon any further protests, she was standing on a short pedestal in the center of the room feeling considerably self-conscious. Two assistants appeared from behind the drapes and began taking all manner of embarrassing measurements while the other held various swatches of fabric near Violet's face.

"The *demi-gigot* sleeves, I think. Gauze," one of the assistants declared, whereby Violet realized a third young woman had entered as well and was taking notes. "Let's avoid the full *gigot*, but with such a lithe figure, *a la giraffe* will not overwhelm her."

"Please, I far prefer simplicity," Violet said. She hadn't completely bought into this puffed sleeve trend, but she knew that *a la giraffe* was a ridiculously ornately styled sleeve, with several bands affecting a series of puffs from her shoulder to her wrist. "I'm too old for those—"

"And as to fabrics…" The woman flipped through a collection of fabrics organized like a rainbow. "This one?" She pointed to a burnt umber. "Autumn colors."

"No," a deep voice inserted, "no autumns." The room fell silent at Mr. Cockfield's contradiction. "Miss Faraday's complexion demands cooler tones—peacock or cyan—with small prints. She'd also be beautiful in a rich indigo or juniper, I think. But keep the size of the sleeves within reason. The lady is a rather industrious person and would never abide feathers in her puffs."

Madam Chantal blinked in Mr. Cockfield's direction and then curtsied. "I didn't realize it was you, Your—"

"But steer away from warmer tones."

"But of course... er..." Madam Chantal looked unusually flummoxed.

"Mr. Cockfield," he supplied.

The dressmaker had *curtsied* to a butler, lending even more of the absurd to this outing.

Violet stared at him, dumbfounded. Posy, of course, gazed at him adoringly—an expression that was coming to be all too familiar and could only mean trouble for Violet's innocent niece.

Ladies did not allow themselves to become infatuated with servants—not even those who seemed infallible—who exhibited impossible arrogance and possessed an abundance of charisma along with a penetrating gaze that sent shivers down a lady's spine.

In fact, those were precisely the sorts of manservants a proper lady ought to go out of her way to avoid.

Not that she'd ever come across a servant quite like Mr. Cockfield. Not only did he speak with more knowledge than any butler ought to have of ladies' fashion, but most astonishingly, she feared he was right.

Because Violet could not, in fact, suffer sleeves that required feathers to keep them from collapsing. That would drive her positively batty.

"A vee-styled bodice for the ballgowns—off the shoulder, showing varying degrees of décolletage," he instructed.

"*Oui, monsieur.* You have an excellent eye for fashion."

Violet considered protesting but held her tongue instead. Arguing would be somewhat hypocritical of her, because she had admired that particular style on Lady Chaswick earlier that week...

"Lady Posy." Another seamstress had appeared. "If you'll

follow me to the back, I can adjust the fit of your canary muslin. It's nearly finished."

"I would be delighted." Posy hopped up, tossing a grin in Violet's direction. "I'll return shortly, so don't even think of trying to escape."

Violet shuffled her feet, feeling guilty. She very well might have attempted to do just that but doubted Mr. Cockfield would allow it.

How had this happened?

Madam Chantal eyed Violet up and down and then stepped backward. "I've several fabrics newly arrived from France. They are *magnifique*, but dear." At Mr. Cockfield's nod, she added. "I'll return shortly with samples for you."

"Of course, thank you, Madam," Mr. Cockfield answered for Violet.

As quickly as the gaggle of dressmakers had appeared, they disappeared again, leaving Violet feeling awkward where she stood on the pedestal, but also afraid to move lest she jostle one of the pins and get a poke.

So instead, she stared at herself in the giant looking glass, trying to appear as though all of this was perfectly normal. Her flushed cheeks from all the fussing, however, gave away that it was not. She reached up to repair the tight coiffure she'd twisted her hair into earlier and caught Mr. Cockfield watching her in the reflection.

Although his long legs stretched in front of him, hands folded and resting on his abdomen, Violet sensed that he was alert to everything going on around them.

"I had no idea Greystone had such strong opinions regarding my wardrobe," Violet murmured. She ought to have allowed for that, however, as Greys was somewhat obsessive regarding fashion in selecting his own apparel. Had her gowns been an embarrassment to him? That must be it, and she'd embarrassed Aunt Iris as well, and most likely Posy.

Violet cringed at the realization.

"Your cousin doesn't, really." The butler didn't even blink.

Wait? What? "Are you saying that Lord Greystone doesn't have strong opinions about my wardrobe? But—"

"It was not Lord Greystone who insisted you order new gowns." His cocksure demeanor demonstrated that he experienced no regret confessing his falsehood. This man was utterly shameless.

"Don't tell me this is because Aunt Iris—"

"No, although she'll be pleased when they're delivered."

"Posy?"

He shook his head.

"Then why would you say such a thing?" she asked.

"Because you are cousin to a marquess and ought to dress the part." His gaze stayed pinned to hers in the mirror. "And because you would not submit to a fitting otherwise."

Violet blinked.

"You'll find, Miss Faraday, that I am quite devoted to the well-being of my employer and his family—which includes you."

"And you believe new gowns will affect my well-being?"

"Yes."

That single word seemed to reach inside her chest and squeeze it.

"I—" Violet searched for something to say but came up empty. "I am fine. I look after my own well-being."

But Mr. Cockfield, it seemed, had other ideas.

"Then there will be two of us."

It was true that part of a butler's duty was to put the needs of his employer above his own. It was why butlers never married or had children. They dedicated themselves to their careers in exchange for spending their lives in a beautiful home with an abundance of security.

Mr. Cockfield, however, was going about it all wrong.

He was right in that she ought to have ordered new dresses for herself at the onset of the Season. Her cousin was not just any marquess, either, but the *Marquess of Greystone*, for heaven's sake. She'd been so concerned about Posy's success that she'd failed to consider the image she presented.

And this dratted manservant was also correct about amber tones. They did absolutely nothing for her complexion. When had she stopped caring about those sorts of things?

He cocked a single brow. "You need someone to shove you back into the world, Miss Faraday. You've been hiding, and I consider that a damnable shame."

MISS FARADAY STARED BACK at Simon for all of twenty seconds before visibly rallying her composure and twisting her mouth into a scowl. He was becoming quite familiar with that particular expression on her, where she lowered her brows and pursed her rosy lips just so...

"I'll ask that you watch your language, sir."

There she is.

She'd been unusually compliant this morning and he far preferred seeing that flash of spirit light up her coffee-colored eyes.

Even if it was laced with scathing disapproval.

"My apologies." He dipped his chin, satisfied to see that her cheeks had pinkened up as well. Simon wondered if he was the only one of them who'd watched the color drain out of her face when her aunt brought up Lord Percival's death.

That the subject was an unpleasant one for her had been obvious.

Had she been madly in love with Captain Christopher Donovan? Was that why she'd settled for spinsterhood?

"I appreciate your concern, but might I call attention to the fact that you seem dedicated to at least a dozen other individuals as well? Individuals who have nothing to do with my cousin's household," she pointed out. Because, of course, her surveillance of his activities had been quite thorough since the day she'd arrived. She'd caught both of his sisters visiting him, his steward, the housekeeper from Heart Place, one of his solicitors, his sisters' governess, and a few other persons he employed.

Miss Violet Faraday would make for an excellent spy.

"I protect those who are loyal to me."

She flicked a glance to his arm. "Is that how you injured yourself? Protecting one of them?"

"Yes." No need to dissemble. Simon stared down at his hand, where it rested in a black sling. Straightening his fingers, he winced.

Not so much at the pain of it but that he'd failed to prevent the attack on a friend's life. All had ended well, but he ought to have realized who had been behind the attacks to begin with.

"Be certain it's completely healed before returning to normal," she surprised him by saying. "One of our neighbors failed to do so a few years back and ended up losing his hand."

"You do care for me," Simon teased.

"I don't wish such an affliction on anyone." Her mouth twitched.

"*Touché.*" He nodded. "You'll be relieved, then, to know that I am under the care of a most excellent doctor. He's assured me it was only a sprain, and I'll have full use of my hand in a matter of weeks."

She dropped her gaze to the floor. "You injured it the same day Greystone and Viscount Manningham-Tissinton showed up looking as though they'd gone at one another with fisticuffs. I do wish gentlemen could resolve their differences without resorting to violence."

"I quite agree, Miss Faraday," Simon said. "But there are times when a man has no choice but to fight."

Her frown reminded him that her betrothed had disappeared after a not-so-necessary military skirmish.

"I suppose that a man who wants to fight will always find a reason," she said.

Simon stilled at a tight sound in her voice —not quite bitterness, nor pain. Her betrothed had chosen to travel to distant lands to wage battles on behalf of the East India Company. He'd decided to leave his family, and to leave her, to fight for a cause that could only be viewed as greed.

And he'd died.

"True," Simon agreed, and she glanced up at him in surprise.

Cynicism. That was what he'd heard. She stared at him with eyes that didn't quite trust and carried a tension in her shoulders as though continually expecting the worst.

How had he missed that before?

"These, I think." Madam Chantal breezed into the room carrying a batch of swatches ranging in all the colors he'd suggested, and her assistants followed with large books under their arms.

Satisfied the dressmaker and her staff had Miss Faraday's

styling well in hand, Simon turned the page of his newspaper with every intention of catching up on the latest headlines. He read, undistracted, until—

"It's gorgeous!" Lady Posy's announcement had Simon looking over the *Gazette* to see Miss Faraday step out from behind a privacy screen.

"I've never thought to wear this color." She was smoothing a turquoise skirt past her hips.

"But this gown might as well have been made for you. It's stunning." The seamstress assisting her was obviously pleased.

Simon lowered the paper a few more inches so he could peruse Miss Faraday from head to toe. *Violet.*

A flowery name for a lady who seemed anything but—on first acquaintance.

So why was he so distracted by her?

Taller than the average woman and almost waif-thin, Greystone's cousin wasn't anything like the ladies he'd been attracted to in the past. And yet...

Simon stared at the long wispy hairs daring to escape her coiffure, the delicate curve of her cheek, and very nearly caught his breath. Posy had the right of it, because at that moment, anyhow, Miss Violet Faraday momentarily took his breath away.

She was, as the assistant had said, stunning.

And yet, she wasn't, was she? Her dark hair wasn't quite mahogany, and her skin wasn't creamy enough to be alabaster. Freckles dotted along the backs of her shoulders revealed by the gown, and her figure lacked the voluptuousness he usually preferred.

What was it about this feisty spinster that charmed him?

Was it merely because she was the least appropriate

woman in the world for him right now? At the very worst time?

To make good on the lost wager, Simon must convincingly perform the duties of Greystone's butler without disclosing his identity.

If he failed, Greystone would win the privilege of selecting the woman Simon married—the next Duchess of Blackheart. That could very well turn out even more disastrous than this stint he had to play as a butler.

Furthermore, Simon was very much aware of the side bets his cohorts had placed. Chaswick, Spencer, and Mantis had bet Westerley and Greystone that he would succeed. If Simon botched it, the three of them would be compelled to sprint naked through Hyde Park. Greys and Westerley would be obliged to do the same if he succeeded.

Simon smirked. Greys and Westerley had a rather undignified run to look forward to because there was no way in hell that he'd fail. And watching their bare arses dashing across the very public lawns would almost make up for Simon's current predicament.

Which brought him back to his improper thoughts regarding Miss Faraday.

Simon clenched his good hand into a fist.

As a manservant, *as a duke pretending to be a manservant,* dallying with a gentlewoman of the house, his employer's cousin, a lady—would be reprehensible—especially one as unsuspecting and naïve as Miss Faraday.

Simon had been a fool to make the bet, but he'd be an even bigger fool if he failed to fulfill the agreed upon terms.

"Don't forget your reticule, Posy." Miss Faraday clucked around the room, much like any spinsterish aunt would be expected to do. She'd already repaired her coiffure, so tightly it tugged at the corners of her eyes.

Of course, he wasn't really attracted to her. Too much time had passed since he'd ended the affair with his last mistress, Cara. That was all. And without the usual privacy afforded him, he'd barely kept up his relationship with his own hand.

"Please send for the carriage, will you, Mr. Cockfield?" Miss Faraday ordered, doing her best to keep him in his place.

So, why in God's name did he find that sexy as hell?

"...*P*roficient enough at the waltz to step in. Ah, there you are," Greystone called out to Violet just as she reentered the ballroom.

She'd asked every manservant she could find, and, unfortunately, not a single one of them knew how to waltz. With only Greystone and Chaswick to partner Posy and Chaswick's sisters, one of the girls would have to sit out, and they'd hoped to simulate dancing at Almacks as authentically as possible.

The three girls—the elder Miss Jones, Miss Diana Jones, and Posy—made up a pretty sight, and it really was a shame that they wouldn't be able to make up a trio of couples.

She couldn't partner one of the girls herself as she would be playing the pianoforte.

But since she'd gone on her search, a third gentleman had joined them—Mr. Cockfield. She'd intentionally not asked the butler, and ever since their visit to Madam Chantal's, had done her best to avoid him altogether.

And despite all Violet's warnings, Posy had done the

opposite. Not only did she disappear with him whenever Violet's back was turned, but her niece had taken to polishing silverware, dusting vases, and assisting the butler at whatever other task he happened to be performing at the time.

"Mr. Cockfield has agreed to partner Lady Posy," Baron Chaswick announced, looking pleased.

No butler should be allowed to waltz with the lord of the manor's ward—for practice or otherwise—especially not a butler as unpredictable as Mr. Cockfield.

Violet glanced toward her niece, who looked far too pleased with this turn of events, and then over at Greystone.

"If you are quite certain, Greys." She waited for her cousin to change his mind. "Greys?"

"Even with only one good arm, Mr. Cockfield will suffice as a partner."

Violet closed her eyes in resignation but opened them again in time to see Greystone's butler execute a perfectly noble bow over Posy's hand. While the other dancers assumed their positions, Violet lowered herself to the pianoforte, frowning. Of course, it wasn't unheard of for a servant to step in under such circumstances. She'd looked to the manservants herself, but...

Mr. Cockfield was not just any servant. He was an overly familiar, impertinent, and arrogant one.

Violet shuffled through her papers, donned her spectacles for reading, and then set her fingers to the keys. She had to concentrate most of her attention on her playing but was able to peek over her glasses occasionally to watch the dancers. Miss Jones and Lord Chaswick seemed to be joking with one another, and Greystone, an expert dancer, moved like a dream with Miss Diana.

Violet's gaze didn't linger on those couples, however, as it was her duty to keep watch of Posy.

And unfortunately, as she watched Mr. Cockfield dance, she grudgingly conceded that Greys had been right. Because even with his right arm immobilized in a black sling, the dratted good-looking butler effortlessly steered Posy through the dance.

Violet might have found the slightest satisfaction if only he'd bumped into Chaswick or Greystone once or twice—or one of the potted plants at the edge of the dance floor.

If she were inclined to pettiness, that was—which she wasn't.

She was, however, relieved to see nothing untoward in his manner with Posy—nothing that even hinted at anything inappropriate.

Violet glanced down at the keys to keep from embarrassing herself by missing some notes, annoyed for feeling even the slightest attraction to a servant. It wasn't right. It wasn't at all proper. Hearing her niece's laughter, Violet glanced up again and pressed her lips together.

Posy had already been allowed to become far too caught up in this—whatever it was—with the butler, so much so that she seemed to have lost all interest in the eligible bachelors she met at any of the *ton* festivities they'd attended.

And seeing as Greys and her aunt had turned a blind eye to the situation, Violet was going to have to take matters into her own hands.

She would speak with Mr. Cockfield, appeal to his sense of honor. And if that didn't work, she would simply insist he keep his distance from her niece.

She might threaten to have him sacked if he did otherwise.

Violet pounded out the ending notes of the waltz with

more enthusiasm than was necessary. And after playing the final note, her skin pricked with awareness. She didn't need to look up to know that he was watching her; it was as though he could read her mind.

Heat flushed her cheeks—from her exertions playing, of course—and despite her efforts, she failed to keep herself from glancing up.

She had not been mistaken.

SIMON RELEASED Lady Posy and then escorted Greystone's guests out of the ballroom to the front foyer, where he then waited, along with Chaswick and Greys, while Lady Posy confirmed plans to go shopping with the baron's sisters later that week.

But Simon's thoughts were elsewhere as he contemplated the expression he thought he'd seen on Miss Faraday's face while she'd played.

And after closing the door behind them, rather than return to his small office where he had steward's reports to go over, Simon made his way back to the ballroom.

When he arrived at the open door, he didn't enter immediately. Instead, he looked on as Violet Faraday fussed with her belongings at the pianoforte.

If not for that blasted bet, he would put the poor woman out of her misery. She was quite convinced that he was dallying with her charge and, believing such, her disapproval was not misplaced. No servant of his would ever be allowed such liberties—no self-respecting servant would dare to take them.

Besides that, both of his sisters knew better than to fraternize thusly with any of the members of his staff. If he ever observed so much as the suggestion of impropriety, he'd put an end to it immediately.

Mainly because such a relationship was not at all fair to the subordinate. Friendship, common courtesy, and respect were one thing; anything beyond that became problematic.

Unfortunately, as matters stood, Miss Faraday would have to remain in the dark as to his true identity.

Because not only did he have his own secret to keep, he'd promised Posy he would keep hers as well.

Miss Faraday must think they'd all gone mad.

Simon stepped inside, and as the door closed behind him, she nearly dropped her stack of papers. Then, fumbling nervously, she tucked them against her bosom and met his stare.

The spectacles she'd balanced on her nose made her eyes appear even larger than usual, and he couldn't help but grin.

She scowled back at him.

There was something rather enchanting about a lady who, while attempting to appear stern and proper, instead exuded a sort of adorable befuddlement.

"Did you forget something, Mr. Cockfield?" She met his gaze over her spectacles and then hastily swiped them off her face.

"No." He crossed toward her. "But I got the feeling you wished to speak with me." The woman wasn't all that good at hiding her emotions.

Most of them, anyway.

She carefully placed her belongings on the bench beside her and then slid off to rise and face him. "I don't know how you do that, but you're right."

"How I do what?"

"Read my mind. Is that something all butlers learn while training for their vocation?"

She truly was a delight. "Indeed. Right after we learn how to realize someone is at the door before the bell is rung. Was there something you needed from me?"

"No, not at all. I mean, not in that sense. But there is something I wish to discuss with you." She was wringing her hands now. "I... I need you to please keep your distance from my niece."

She stilled her hands, raised her chin, and met his gaze, daring him to deny this request. For a moment, her brown eyes appeared proud and almost... magnificent. She was by no means a mousy woman, but he'd not seen her so determined as of yet.

He rather liked the look on her.

"I do not seek her out, Miss Faraday," he said, which was the truth.

"I am aware of this." Her gaze darted around the room. "But I would ask that you make excuses to avoid her. You're a busy man. This oughtn't to be difficult. She is impressionable and, I think, not as mature as most ladies her age. She's spent her entire life in the country, you see, and I fear she's forgotten her place. The affection she's developed for you cannot be comfortable for you, either. It places you in an awkward position, I understand, and it is most improper. She's so very young, and even as a manservant, you seem to be very much a man of the world."

"Affection?" he queried.

"It's obvious she's quite taken with you."

"You mean, romantically?"

"That is precisely what I mean."

Simon only barely kept himself from laughing at Miss

Faraday's conclusion. Apparently, dear Aunt Violet did not know her niece as well as she believed she did.

This woman, it seemed, was the naïve one.

"You've nothing to worry about," he assured her. And yet again, that pinch of guilt pricked at Simon that he couldn't tell her the truth. It would be so much simpler if Greystone would simply allow his cousins in on the bet.

"You will avoid her, then?"

Unfortunately, he'd already promised Lady Posy that he would assist her in a rather delicate area.

"I cannot do that."

"But—but—" He ought not to have found her outrage so beguiling. Rather than attempt to convince this woman her niece was perfectly safe with him, he took the conversation in a very different direction.

"Surely you aren't jealous, Miss Faraday?" He stepped closer.

If possible, her eyes widened to look even larger than they had when she'd been wearing the spectacles.

"Of course not! Why would you say such a thing?" She glanced from side to side, not meeting his gaze.

"I've assured you that your niece is in no danger from me, and yet you do not seem all that relieved. Are you interested in pursuing me for yourself?"

"You—I—But…"

He was not mistaken.

Her cheeks flooded with a most delightful pink, and her jaw dropped, leaving her mouth open, her lips slack and soft.

They were rather full-looking when she wasn't pinching them together.

And inviting.

∿

"ARE YOU MAD? I really must go..." Violet went to step backward but in doing so, the back of her legs hit the bench, and she dropped onto the seat.

Mr. Cockfield reached out with his good hand. "Are you alright?"

Was she alright? Would any lady be alright after being accused of setting her cap for a servant? And then she realized he was referring to her most inelegant fall onto the wooden bench. She stared at his hand for a moment before taking it and allowing him to assist her up again.

"I cannot imagine why you would arrive at such an absurd conclusion." But was he right?

Her voice sounded breathier than normal. Likely due to the tingling in her fingertips at his touch and his unusually intimate proximity.

Her lungs half-numb from shock, she dropped his hand and stepped sideways, away from him. He was an overwhelming sort of gentleman even when one wasn't standing so very close to all of his... maleness.

"You've been watching me." The corner of his mouth twitched.

"But that's only because of Posy—"

"You want the attention I've allotted for your lovely niece?"

"Don't be—" Violet halted her protests. Something in his words... *"attention I've allotted for... your niece."* His free time was finite, the same as other mortals, and if some other person took up those moments, he wouldn't have any left for Posy.

Therefore Posy could realize the folly of giving her attention to such a man and seek affection elsewhere. With Lord Shortwood—not with Captain Edgeworth—or any of the other military gentlemen who persisted in showing up everywhere, but… there was always Mr. Tibbons…

Violet envisioned her niece driving through the park with a very proper gentleman—a gentleman of her own station—a man who could protect her, who would not forsake her…

Good lord. What was Violet contemplating? Would it even work? It would be foolish for someone like her to think she could attract such a gentleman as Mr. Cockfield—a rakish butler, of all things! Wouldn't it?

And for what, exactly, an innocent flirtation? A not-so-innocent one?

How far was she willing to take this outlandish scheme?

But the most troubling question in her mind sent a shiver through her: Was Posy really her only reason for considering it?

The answer wasn't one she cared to examine.

"Miss Faraday? Are you well? You're flushed." His fingertips landed on her elbow.

Violet's heart raced. The most she could imagine was a tantalizing flirtation. An affair was out of the question. Wasn't it?

Of course, it was.

"I'm fine," she answered, still thinking.

He did seem to enjoy teasing her. Surely, that was something she could take advantage of. And long ago—very long ago, before Christopher—she'd known how to flirt.

Gathering all her courage and feeling more than a little foolish, Violet licked her lips and met his gaze. "What if I did?"

Both brows raised, he merely stared at her. Was he reading her mind again? Did he comprehend her strategy?

"Wish for my romantic attentions?" The disbelief in his voice meant that she was going to need to be more convincing.

Violet lowered her lashes and made the most of her nervousness. Because if she were making such a confession, she would not truly have been capable of making it with a good deal of confidence.

"I know it must seem silly to you." Her lungs squeezed. Even when one was only pretending to confess to… *feelings* for another person, it was difficult.

"Why would it seem silly?" He didn't sound wholly unconvinced—only partly.

Violet turned away. She could do this so much easier if his spicy, leathery scent wasn't overwhelming her senses. "As you well know, I've been on the shelf for some time now. And I have no intentions of ever marrying." This was true. These things were easier to say knowing they were not lies.

He didn't move or speak, and so Violet continued.

"But a lady, a woman…" She faltered, suddenly recalling far too many nights lying in bed, aching for sensations—experiences—denied to ladies such as her. Nights when she'd touched herself while imagining… And then later, afterward, feeling unsatisfied but swamped with guilt for daring to try…

Which hadn't been at all fair. Not when she'd never quite succeeded…

"A woman…?" he encouraged her.

Violet raised her hands and fidgeted with the lace around her collar. "A woman has certain needs. *Companionship*," she blurted before he misinterpreted her proposal. "The attention of a handsome gentleman, perhaps a kiss or…something, before she wakes up and it's too late."

"What is it you're trying to say, Miss Faraday?" He was

standing very close to her again. She'd not been wrong that first day, thinking of him as some sort of exotic cat. "Are you saying that you fancy a fling? With me?"

His voice sounded gravelly, and deeper than normal.

Violet lifted her chin and held his gaze for the first time since she'd begun this charade.

And, staring into the depths of this man's dark, navy-blue eyes, she conceded that her confession wasn't entirely for Posy's sake.

Because a small percentage of her—a very tiny, almost minuscule part of her—was jumping for joy at the idea of being the object of a handsome gentleman's attention—of *this* gentleman's attention.

Mr. Cockfield—her cousin's butler.

"Perhaps." But the word came out little more than a rasping whisper. She cleared her throat. "Perhaps."

His fingertips moved from her elbow to her chin, exerting the slightest amount of pressure so that she couldn't look away.

"Why, Miss Faraday. I do believe this spring just became a good deal more interesting than I'd imagined it."

COULD SHE?

*I*nteresting?

"Interesting?" Violet echoed in dismay. That wasn't at all the response she'd expected.

What had she expected? A polite refusal? Laughter? Mockery?

Had she anticipated that he would gather her into his arms and declare he'd wanted the same thing all along?

Anything might very well be better than…

Interesting.

Violet swiped his hand down and turned away.

"Only because I find *you* interesting, Miss Faraday." His voice halted her. "And you've surprised me. That's rare."

Was he complimenting her?

She turned back to face him. "You surprise me too," she admitted. No wonder her cousin didn't treat this man as an ordinary butler.

Because he wasn't an ordinary butler—not even close to it.

Caught up in the magnetism of his person, of his character, she realized how dreadfully important it was that she kept Posy away from him.

Everything about him screamed danger. Not that he was dangerous in a physical sense, but in the sense that while wholly unsuitable, he could persuade a lady such as herself to contemplate going against her own inclinations—without so much as even a kiss.

But he hadn't been the one attempting to persuade anyone. That had been her!

Posy hadn't stood a chance.

At least she, Violet, wasn't a complete innocent. She had been engaged once, and she had allowed her fiancé liberties that she ought not to have.

She had far less to lose than her niece did.

"It surprises you?" she asked. "That I am not dead inside?"

"It surprises me that you admit to not being dead inside."

Violet stared at his mouth. It was not the first time she'd wondered what it would feel like to be kissed by him.

But then a cold, ugly feeling twisted in her belly. Had Posy wondered the same things about him? Violet hadn't considered that in distracting Mr. Cockfield, her niece might experience feelings of jealousy—possibly even betrayal.

But it was for the best. Nothing could come of any sort of relationship between her naïve and trusting niece and this man.

Nor, really, could anything come of a relationship between Violet and this man—nothing proper, that was. Furthermore, whereas Posy stood to have her heart broken, Violet didn't have a heart left to break.

Hers had shattered into thousands of tiny pieces all those years ago when Christopher had disappeared. Even though she had managed to piece some of it back together, it wasn't whole enough that it could ever be broken again.

"And you?"

A man as charismatic and dashing as he was most likely had a mistress tucked away somewhere.

Likely, he had ladies, beautiful and sophisticated proper ladies, married ones as well as widows, who were more than willing to take him into their beds.

Was he laughing at her?

"I am not dead inside, either." That corner of his mouth jerked up. But he was not laughing.

His gaze flicked downward. "I like that color on you."

She was wearing one of the gowns that incorporated all of his instructions. A dark turquoise linen with modestly puffed sleeves. She'd tucked a lace fichu into the bodice, which was cut lower than she was accustomed to.

She ignored the compliment.

"Do you have mistresses?" She had to ask. Perhaps if she knew this, and could tell Posy about them, that would be enough to save her niece from his charm.

"Not presently." He continued studying her, and she frantically tried to mask her thoughts from him. "Are you applying for the position, then?"

How had this gone from a mild flirtation to…?

"Of course not!" She jerked her shoulders back. "I simply wanted…" What? What had she wanted? And why couldn't she make any sense of the words racing through her head?

Every rational thought fled as she stood frozen in his gaze.

"Would you like me to kiss you, Miss Faraday?" His thumb and first finger holding her chin moved gently to massage it. His injured hand, tucked in the black sling, nestled between them.

Before she could answer, however, footsteps sounded outside the door, nearing. And then voices. "We'll want to check for any scuffs and remove the pitchers of water."

It was the housekeeper and at least one of the maids. Violet went to step back, but his grip tightened.

"Mr. Cockfield," Violet protested.

"You didn't answer me."

Panic thickened her throat, partly at the fear of being discovered but also from her reluctance to answer his question.

She needed to think. And to do that, she needed away from him.

Acting impulsively was most unusual for her. And she was embarrassed to tell him the truth.

Because, yes, of course, she wanted him to kiss her.

The part of her that was physical, the instinct that required she have food and air and sleep and water—that part was screaming for him to kiss her.

Her brain, however, the rational and cerebral part of her, understood that this was likely the most reckless endeavor she'd ever considered.

Even more reckless than that night in the garden with Christopher.

She would do well to end this now, beg Greystone to order Mr. Cockfield away from Posy. And if that wasn't effective, she would insist they return to Blossom Court.

But no. This could also very well be her last opportunity to fulfill that other need. She wasn't ready to walk away. She needed to know...

"Perhaps."

She jerked away from him and, when the door flew open,

was gathering her belongings, fully intent upon making her escape.

Two maids had entered, both looking startled to find that the room wasn't empty.

"I'm sorry, Mr. Cockfield. We thought the lessons were finished in here. We can come back later, Miss Faraday."

"No. The lessons are over." The butler answered for them both. And then he sent Violet a most inscrutable glance. "For now."

BACK IN HER chamber and pretending her hands weren't shaking, Violet reorganized the stack of music that she'd dropped earlier.

He'd nearly kissed her. What if she'd told him no?

What if she'd told him yes?

"Here you are, Aunt Violet." Posy peered around the door without knocking. "That was surprisingly fun! I believe Mr. Cockfield might be a better dancer than Greystone, wouldn't you agree? He somehow makes waltzing tolerable."

Mixed feelings pestered Violet as her niece threw herself onto the bed. Half of Posy's outrageous curls had already escaped the coiffure Gwen had twisted them into earlier that morning.

"I don't think anyone dances the waltz better than Greystone." What would it be like, though, to dance with her cousin's butler?

What would it be like to waltz with Mr. Cockfield?

Violet shook her musings off. Regardless of this flirtation —diversion—distraction—whatever it was—that she'd initiated today, the one thing she would never do with Mr. Cockfield was dance with him.

He was a servant, and she was the cousin of his employer, who happened to be a marquess.

"You need to leave Mr. Cockfield be. He has work to do," Violet told Posy for the umpteenth time, feeling guilty and a little... sordid.

"He doesn't mind."

"Of course, that is what he would lead you to believe. He won't deny requests made by his employer's family. Surely, you understand this."

Was that how he viewed Violet's suggestion? As a duty he must perform to sustain his employment?

Violet snapped the case of music closed and moved across the room to stare out at the mews. Her insides were all jumbled up. Likely because they wavered somewhere between disgust with herself and a most improper excitement.

"He isn't like that," Posy said, staring up at the ceiling.

More guilt. What sort of woman made such inappropriate suggestions to the gentleman that her own niece felt an affection for? But he was not a gentleman.

Violet clenched her teeth together. What kind? A woman who wished to protect her niece, that was who.

"Come sit here." Violet gestured toward the chair in front of her vanity. "Let me repair your hair before we go down for tea."

"It won't stay up." But Posy climbed off the bed and took her seat there anyway. "Why don't you ever dance?"

Violet met Posy's stare in the looking glass. "One must be asked first."

"You're never asked because you don't smile at any of them. I imagine they're afraid of you," Posy said. "You do the opposite of everything you've told me."

Violet had worn a few of her new gowns to the last few

events, and then promptly found a seat safely tucked away behind the other mothers and chaperones.

Lords and ladies of the ton did not throw grand balls so that ladies of eight and twenty could be entertained. They were for the debutantes. Violet had had her turn as the belle of the ball. She'd landed her fiancé long ago. It was the younger ladies' turn to secure their happy ever afters.

"You might be asked if you stepped away from the old ladies you seem to prefer to keep company with."

"They aren't old ladies."

"They are much older than you, Aunt Violet."

Rather than belabor the point, Violet went to work corralling Posy's hair into some semblance of a dignified style.

"Mr. Cockfield says I ought to cut it. He seems to think my hair is well-suited for the shorter styles that are becoming popular this spring."

"Mr. Cockfield isn't right about everything." Blasted man. Violet stuck a pin into one curl, satisfied that it was staying, and then watched as one on the other side of Posy's head fell out.

Perhaps he had a point. That was part of the trouble with him. It was very difficult to oppose a person who was right about everything.

Not everything. He was not right to think that he could run around with her niece without it harming Posy's reputation.

She reminded herself of his fallibility as she followed Posy downstairs to the drawing-room because she was going to have to face him again. It was his duty to serve afternoon tea.

Perhaps if she could recall all the trouble he was making, she wouldn't feel so flustered in his presence. The last thing she wanted was for either Greystone or Aunt Iris to suspect that she had improper ideas where the butler was concerned.

Violet smoothed her gown as they entered the drawing-room.

"Do stay seated, Greys. Isn't Aunt Iris down yet? Should I go back up to help her?" Depending on their aunt's arthritis, the woman was either stubbornly independent or ridiculously needy.

"She sent for Mr. Cockfield, and he went up a few moments ago," Greys answered, looking dapper in a maroon velvet jacket and mauve satin waistcoat. "She's quite taken with him."

Aunt Iris wasn't the only lady who was half-smitten with the butler. The thought was an irritating one that also sent heat flushing up her neck.

"Feeling all right, Violet?" Greys crossed one leg over the other.

"I'm fine." She resisted the urge to press her hands to her cheeks. What must Mr. Cockfield think of all of them? Swooning in his presence, and herself, all but begging him to kiss her.

The idea she'd rashly come up with that afternoon was a horrible one. She needed to abandon it. Tell him she'd been joking. It was a mistake. She was a foolish, foolish woman.

The sounds of her aunt and the butler approach should not have caused her insides to jump the way they did. Rather than acknowledge his presence, Violet reached down and took up the knitting she kept in a basket beside her usual seat.

"Thank you, my dear Mr. Cockfield. I feel much safer descending the steps on the arm of a strong fellow such as yourself, rather than my wobbly little cane."

Greystone met Violet's gaze and grinned.

"My pleasure, my lady," Mr. Cockfield answered. "I'll return shortly with tea."

Ignoring her resolve, Violet glanced up from her yarn and needles.

"See if Cook has any of those raspberry biscuits, will you?" Greystone called out. Was her cousin smirking?

If he was, only she seemed to notice it. Even Mr. Cockfield went about his business without so much as that corner of his mouth twitching.

But as he turned to leave the room, his gaze landed on her. "Do you have any special requests, Miss Faraday?"

Why did he make that sound so very suggestive?

Violet's imagination was getting out of hand.

"I'm fine, Mr. Cockfield." She pinched her mouth shut. "But thank you." And this time, the butler's lip did twitch just so, as though he found considerable amusement in watching her squirm.

She was not squirming. Never in her life had she *squirmed.*

"You're looking unusually pretty for tea, Posy," Greys addressed their niece.

Aunt Iris settled herself in the tall wing-backed chair that she preferred.

Mr. Cockfield bowed to her aunt and then quietly left the room. Why was it that Violet's gaze wasn't the only one staring at the door after it closed behind him?

Violet stabbed the tip of her knitting needle through the next loop, determined to maintain her composure.

"Since no festivities are planned for tonight," Posy announced, "Mr. Cockfield is driving me to Lady Isabella's." And before Violet could argue, she added, "He has errands to perform and says it's just as easy for him to take me as ask Coachman John. Even you cannot argue against a visit with

Lady Isabella. She's invited me to view some of her paintings."

"I didn't realize you were interested in painting," Greystone said.

"Oh, but I am."

"Posy shows considerable talent," Violet said.

"You ought to take her, Greys. Have you spoken with Lord Huntly yet?" At least Aunt Iris was showing some interest in Posy's reputation. But...

"You wish to speak with Lord Huntly?" Violet glanced back and forth between her cousin and her aunt. "Do you intend to court Lady Isabella?"

"I'm considering it." Greys turned to Posy. "Mr. Cockfield needn't take you when I'm going there myself."

"Excellent," Aunt Iris announced. "I would join the two of you as well, but I promised Lady Sheffield I'd join her for dinner and cards."

Posy frowned, and Greystone looked as though he was pondering one of the mathematical equations he enjoyed. Or was he pondering marriage? Violet remembered he'd danced with Lady Isabella on a few occasions, but she hadn't noticed anything particularly... *special* between the two of them.

But if he was genuinely considering embarking on discussions with Lady Isabella's father, pondering was a good thing. She'd hate to see her favorite cousin make a mistake when it came to selecting his wife.

"Do you fancy her then?" Violet asked just as the door opened and Mr. Cockfield, followed by a young and pretty maid carrying a second tray, entered quietly.

"I barely know the gel," Greystone answered. "And I'm happy to keep it that way for now."

Mr. Cockfield gestured for the maid to set her tray down,

flicking a disparaging glance toward Greys. "There's one gamble I'm not willing to take," he said.

Aunt Iris shook her head at the butler's audacity, and Greystone grimaced. "No one is asking you to."

"It's the way these things are done, Mr. Cockfield," Aunt Iris explained with a tolerant smile dancing on her lips. "I'm certain you wouldn't understand the nuances involved in an aristocratic marriage."

Greystone caught his breath and then bent over in a fit of coughing.

"Can't you speak with her father another time?" Posy piped up.

Mr. Cockfield handed his employer a glass of water, and Violet rose to serve the tea. She rather prided herself on fixing it precisely as everyone liked.

"Might as well get it over with," Greys said when he'd finally caught his breath. "No need to drive Posy tonight. I'll take her," he addressed his butler.

Which, Violet realized, meant she could spend a rare evening at home alone.

Violet bent over the tea tray at the exact moment Mr. Cockfield reached down to uncover one of the serving plates. "Terribly sorry," she apologized for colliding with his arm. "Forgive me." And then, heaven help her, she nearly apologized for apologizing.

"My fault." He lifted the lid off the tray, and the sweet aroma of sugary confections mingled with his musky scent. "Cook just removed these from the oven."

Violet was doing all she could to keep her wits about her.

"Thank you, Mr. Cockfield." Good lord, she sounded breathless. She was grateful for Posy's argument for once in that no one noticed her lack of composure.

"But of course." Mr. Cockfield's breath warmed the side of her face. "A person needs to splurge now and then; would you not agree?"

Violet turned to meet his mesmerizingly navy-colored eyes, and her knees nearly gave out beneath her.

Because she was almost positive that he wasn't talking about pastries.

TEA WITH THE BUTLER

*L*eft to her own devices, rather than imposing on the servants to serve her in the dining room, Violet ordered a small meal sent up to her chamber. At home, in the small village near Blossom Court, she did her best to keep busy, visiting neighbors and even heading up the Ladies' Charity Guild. But even so, she spent most evenings at home with her aunt and Posy.

Violet wasn't at all accustomed to the schedule they'd maintained since arriving in London: staying out late every night, ensuring Posy was introduced to the right people and then making conversation. Never one to sleep in, the late hours were catching up with her.

And providing that she'd not get many evenings like this in the weeks to come, Violet intended to take full advantage of the quiet solitude.

After changing into her night rail and a modest dressing gown, Violet enjoyed a meal of cold meats and cheese while sitting by the empty hearth reading an adventure book by

Holden Hampden, a new author she'd recently discovered, suggested to her by Lady Chaswick.

When the words began to blur, Violet removed her spectacles and rubbed her eyes. The tapers she'd lit were nearly burned down to the nub. She stretched and set the book aside just as sounds of male voices rose from the mews. Was that Greystone and Posy returning?

She padded to the window and barely made out the figure of a man speaking to one of the stable workers and then turning toward the servant entrance.

Not Greystone, or Posy, or even her Aunt Iris, who must have gotten caught up in a rousing game of piquet.

The gentleman, whose arm was in a sling, was Mr. Cockfield. But there was something different about him tonight. He didn't appear bosky, but his shoulders were slumped, and he looked… sad. Had something happened?

She lifted the branch of tapers off the table and hurried out her door, through the corridor, and down the stairs.

"Mr. Cockfield?" She held out the light to see him better. "Are you hurt? Is everything all right?" He'd opened the door to his small office and chamber, but at the sound of her voice, turned and leaned against the wall.

He stared up at where she stood, four steps from the landing.

"Mr. Cockfield?"

"You look like an angel," he murmured.

"Are you…?" Violet descended two more steps. "Foxed?"

He answered with a derisive chuckle. "Unfortunately, no, Miss Faraday, I'm not."

And yet, this wasn't the man she'd come to know. Mr. Cockfield wasn't a person to show signs of defeat. "I thought you were running errands. Did your business not pan out?"

"My brother. I was with my brother." He rubbed a hand down his face. "He's on leave. We haven't talked much since he's returned, but hearing some of the stories… the thought of him going back…" For once, Mr. Cockfield's eyes weren't all-knowing. They looked bluer than usual—they looked…sad. "I can't protect him while he's gone." He shook his head and grimaced. "Even worse, the woman he's fallen in love with wants someone else. I hate to think of him returning to the front feeling dejected. I shared a few drinks, but I… stopped. I tend to do stupid things when I drink." He frowned and then inhaled. "I'll be quite myself again in the morning. Did you need something?"

For some reason, the fact that this man had a brother—one he worried about—suddenly added a humanness that she hadn't considered. Worrying was something with which she was all too familiar.

"No." Violet came down off the steps. She hated to leave him alone like this. "Yes. I mean. Tea would be lovely."

"Of course." He straightened.

"I wasn't asking you to make it for me. I was asking if you'd like to join me."

He was closer to her now, and his proximity changed the air in the foyer. It caused her nerves to stand up in attention.

"Tea?" He tilted his head, some of that teasing light back in his eyes.

"Tea is always a good idea," she said.

"It can't hurt." He gestured for her to go ahead of him. "Let's see if Cook left some water on the stove, then."

Violet nodded and when he took the taper from her, she followed him through the corridor.

Together, they descended the stairs to the kitchen, where

embers still glowed in the stove. Cook had indeed left a pot sitting on the hot surface.

"You sit." She indicated one of the wooden chairs at the work table in the middle of the room.

Feeling comfortable with having something to do, she easily located two cups and the box of tea. This wasn't the first time she'd come down to the kitchen late at night. She refused to wake a servant to do something she could easily do for herself.

Mr. Cockfield made himself comfortable, watching her.

"You must be proud to have a brother who serves." Violet wondered if he might want to talk about his concerns.

"He's a Lord Major," he said.

Violet blinked. That wasn't... "Surely not a *Lord* Major?"

Mr. Cockfield straightened. "Of course not. Good Lord, he's a major."

"Ah…" She smiled. "But a major. That is, indeed, impressive." Only the bravest and most talented of enlisted men could ever achieve such a rank.

"Weak or strong?" she asked as she poured the water into the teapot and then added the tea.

"Stronger, if you don't mind. No cream or sugar."

"That's how I like it too. Strong, that is, but with sugar. But, of course, you know that."

Violet smoothed her hands down her dressing gown, stupidly wishing she had a prettier one, while she waited for the tea to steep.

"Did my return wake you?" he asked.

"I wasn't asleep." She shouldn't have come downstairs knowing they'd be alone. But there was something about him…

He leaned forward, resting his chin on his hands, his elbows on the table.

"What keeps you awake, Miss Faraday?" The kitchen suddenly felt much smaller than it had a moment before. She shouldn't have taken the seat beside him.

He was the butler.

And she, a very proper lady.

He reached out with his good hand, pinching the end of one of her long braids. "I like your hair—the color." He was staring at the tip as though he'd never seen brown hair before.

Was he going to kiss her while they waited for the tea to steep? And why couldn't she bring herself to move away from him?

He dropped the braid and jerked away. "It should be ready." He was on his feet, going to pour the tea, but having the use of only one hand, faltered. "Blasted thing," he grumbled to himself.

Violet rose as well and helped him filter the tea leaves.

Bringing the two of them closer to one another than they'd been before.

Feeling as though all the air had been sucked from the room, Violet removed the filter and then added sugar to one of the cups. "Where is your brother stationed?" She would make normal conversation.

She ought to take her tea upstairs with her. Return to her chamber.

Only... she didn't want to.

"The Ashanti Coast. He's awaiting new orders." Did his voice sound lower than usual? Mr. Cockfield had a life away from Knight Hall—away from his employment here.

Violet was acquainted with some of the family members of

her aunt's servants. Most were nearly-impoverished country folk.

"Do you have any other siblings?" she asked, curious to know more about him.

He hadn't returned to his seat but remained standing—so close that she felt his heat all along her side.

"Two sisters. My brother swears they are keeping out of trouble, but I ought to be there for them more..."

"But you are providing for them," Violet reminded him.

"I ought to be there," he repeated.

"You aren't by chance the oldest, are you?" She couldn't imagine him as anything but.

"Are you saying you think I'm bossy?" He tugged at her braid again.

It was odd to see him like this, so relaxed and... unguarded.

Until that moment, Violet hadn't realized how guarded his demeanor normally was. As flippant and arrogant as he could be, he kept an invisible barrier erected around himself.

"A little. Why did you decide to become a butler?" Violet went to sip her tea but then lowered it to the table when she realized her hand was shaking.

The air had grown heavy around them.

She was so tired of being... alone. But she wasn't alone. Was she lonely?

"You certainly have a lot of questions." His head tipped forward, and the scent of whiskey and tea teased her nostrils.

It was not unpleasant.

"Are you going to answer them?" Violet teased. Perhaps she hadn't forgotten how to flirt after all.

He simply stared at her. She stared back, shadows dancing around them.

"I'm not here by choice." But he still hadn't moved. "I have duties, not the least of which concern my brother and sisters. I will always do what is necessary to uphold them."

His tone of voice sent a chill down her spine.

This man was no ordinary manservant.

"And your career allows you to fulfill those responsibilities."

"Some of them." His gaze hadn't left her face for even a second, and an unfamiliar force had her wanting to lean into him.

"I'm going to kiss you, Miss Faraday." It was not a question, but she knew that if she told him not to, he would heed her request.

Mr. Cockfield was not the sort of gentleman who would ever lack a willing woman. Besides being handsome and intelligent and charming, he possessed an abundance of confidence. All of that together was…

Sexy.

"You want to kiss me?" Her voice came out thready… needy.

"Who would not wish to kiss you? A beautiful, willing woman." He was leaning even closer.

She parted her lips and could almost taste the whiskey now. She lowered her lashes. "You would be surprised." Her answer held all the self-derision she'd fought over the past decade. He had not kissed her earlier that afternoon—not even after she'd essentially propositioned him.

For Posy's sake.

Don't be a hypocrite. Violet chastised herself. If this had been for Posy's sake, she would have returned to her chamber ten minutes ago.

Alone.

"It's late. We should go to bed. I should go to bed. And you should go to bed. Both of us—but separately." She stepped backward, caught by his gaze and feeling as awkward and silly as she had with Christopher nine years ago.

Mr. Cockfield's gaze softened, and both corners of his lips tilted up. "Not quite yet." He followed her, dropping his good hand to her waist, his other remaining trapped in the sling. And then he dipped his head, not quite kissing her but close.

Very close.

He hovered so closely that a feather would barely fit between them.

Later, Violet might question her actions.

But for now, wild horses couldn't stop her from sliding her hands up—one to his shoulder and the other over his injured wrist. "Does it hurt?" she whispered.

At the slight shake of his head, she moved her hand up farther and wound it around his neck.

Pressing up on her toes, Violet closed that last fraction of an inch between them so that her mouth was touching his.

And she kissed him.

SIMON WASN'T FOXED. He'd only had a few drinks, and that had been much earlier. But, knowing his brother could be called back to the front at any time, and also learning that Lucas was nursing something of a broken heart, he'd returned feeling not quite himself.

The last thing he'd expected upon his return was to find Miss Faraday waiting for him.

She tasted like tea—sweet tea. She surprised him with parted lips—and again when she ventured to taste him as well.

The kiss she bestowed, her embrace, enveloped him in a deep sense of well-being. He felt as though he'd returned home after a lifetime of travels and the temptation to lose himself had him forgetting where they were, who they were. All he knew was that she fit, and that she felt…

Perfect.

But that was the opposite of what this was. She wanted pleasure, she wanted affection. What had she said? *Before it was too late?*

It didn't matter who he was.

Simon checked himself from gathering her closer, which, unfortunately, was made easier by the throbbing in his wrist.

But that didn't keep his good hand from exploring the curve of her hip or deepening the kiss, memorizing her taste.

He suspected she'd gone quite some time without kissing —her confession led him to believe she'd avoided romantic encounters since the disappearance of her betrothed.

Which had been almost a decade ago.

She broke the kiss and went as though to move out of his arms. "I'm sorry."

Simon held her in place. "For what?"

"You are a servant. I-I'm taking advantage of you."

This woman.

He reclaimed her mouth, taking control so that she was under no delusion as to who was taking advantage of whom.

He explored the flesh behind her teeth now. Along with the tea, he tasted mint from her tooth powder. Her fresh scent fluttered through him, down his throat, into his chest, and of course, the sensation stirred his cock into enthusiastic readiness.

He ignored it.

Because gentle tremors were running through her. She

wasn't afraid, but she was quite overwhelmed. A virgin? More than likely.

But she was not without passion. She'd admitted to having urges. She wanted an affair. An unmarried woman's lot was a sorry one, but it didn't have to be pitiful.

She molded her chest against his, and although the pressure sent a pang through his wrist, he held her more tightly.

If Miss Violet Faraday wished to claim the pleasures denied most spinsters, he was quite willing to step up. He splayed his palm over her backside, massaged, and squeezed. Was she wet for him? A question easily answered by lifting her onto the table, sliding his hand up her leg...

Not tonight, however.

"Prickles," she murmured against his lips. Delicate fingertips danced around his neck, to his face, exploring his jaw. "Your whiskers."

Simon inhaled.

No, not tonight.

He rubbed his jaw along her cheek, and the squeal he evoked was unexpectedly satisfying.

But above that sound, Simon heard the vague rumbling of a carriage out front. "Shhh..."

Her eyes were wide. She had heard it too.

"Stay here," he ordered, stepping toward the small staircase that led back upstairs. "Finish your tea."

"What are you going to do?" she asked. "What have I done? They can't know! No one can ever know!"

"I'm going to get the door," he informed her, "in case you forgot my duties." He was frustrated to be interrupted but also at the horror on her face. She might as well have slapped him. "Once I've locked the doors behind them—" He shook off the unfamiliar stinging sensation. What was it? Rejection? Simon gathered himself. "I'll return so I can escort you back to your chamber. Please, wait here for me."

She pinched her lips together, lips that were plump, red, and glistening, but she didn't argue.

His irritation wasn't only with her, but with himself, rather. Simon turned on his heel, cooling his temper as he climbed the steps.

He didn't dally with unwilling women.

Furthermore, any woman who ever shared his bed knew precisely what she was getting into. The lady was well aware of *who* he was, *what* he was, and precisely what he was willing to offer. Not that he was one of those men who required a constant stream of women, but there had been times when he'd kept a mistress. He'd had a few affairs.

Arriving at the foyer, he stepped forward to take Lady Iris's coat. "How did the cards treat you, my lady?"

"Fickle, Mr. Cockfield. Fickle," Greystone's aunt said. "I imagine yours was a quiet evening with all of us out. Violet, I'm certain, went to bed at sunset. I swear, my niece has always been a country person at heart."

Lady Posy and Greystone followed closely behind.

"Did you enjoy your visit with Lady Isabella?" Simon greeted the younger girl.

"I did. I much prefer an intimate visit than a ball or recital, as you well know." Violet's niece slid her arms out of her coat and allowed him to relieve her of it.

"No fires to put out this evening?" Greys asked, handing Simon his hat and cane.

"No fires." Not in the literal sense, anyhow. "And your meeting with Lord Huntly?" he queried back. "I take it that went well?"

"It did. Preliminary discussions are underway." But his

friend didn't sound all that excited about securing his betrothal. "Clear night. I won't be turning in for a few hours, I think. I'll be in my observatory if you have need of me."

Simon locked up behind them and then returned to the kitchen, where he found Violet pacing and looking as though she was carrying a world of regret on her shoulders. He wasn't surprised to see that she'd cleared away all remnants of their tea.

"Is it safe to go up?" Her gaze didn't quite meet his.

"Violet." Simon shook his head.

"I should go alone." She held the burning tapers out in front of her, and he had the choice of either being burned or stepping back so she could enter the stairwell. "Best that you don't escort me in case anyone was to see us together so late... like this." She waved her free hand down her night rail. "I should have put on a gown. At least then I wouldn't have looked so—what was I thinking?"

Simon clenched his jaw but followed behind her.

She turned back to him. "I'm fine, really. I come down here all the time by myself."

He gestured for her to keep moving. But, quite frankly, as a butler or a duke, he wasn't about to allow a young woman to go traipsing around a large house in the dark alone.

Knight Hall was her family's residence, and the servants were considered trustworthy, but he was a gentleman. He would make sure she was safely ensconced in her chamber before going about his business.

When she didn't move, Simon touched his hand to her elbow, expecting her to argue, her mouth parted as though ready to speak. When she looked at him, though, she must have seen something in his expression, for she exhaled instead and continued up the steps.

Neither of them said a word until arriving at her door. She was ashamed. Simon was reluctant to leave her feeling that way. The woman already carried an abundance of self-doubt.

He opened the door for her, and when she pressed inside, he entered as well.

She didn't stop him or tell him to leave but strode across to her desk and placed the stand of tapers there. And then she spun around to face him. "You don't have to… I don't expect you…" She held her palms to her cheeks.

"I don't expect anything," Simon silenced her. "I merely wish to make sure you're all right. Are you?"

"Of course."

"You're a terrible liar."

"Oh, I know that! But I'm not the sort of woman who… I've never done anything like that." She struggled to regain her composure. "Can we forget this happened?"

She sounded so forlorn, dropping her head forward.

"Is that what you want?" Simon asked.

Lifting her head, she met his gaze. "It is," her voice sounded soft, barely more than a whisper. And yet, he'd wager his dukedom that what she really wanted was for him to take her into his arms again.

The bed was only a few steps behind her, an inviting coverlet pulled back, beckoning…inviting. She licked her lips.

If Simon kissed her now, the night would be pleasurable, indeed.

"Forget the kiss?" he said, not moving. "That's what you want?"

She hesitated, indecision lurking in her eyes.

"I do." She cleared her throat. "Yes." Her answer held more confidence now.

"In that case..." Simon stepped back and bowed. "Goodnight, Miss Faraday."

But as he returned to his own small chamber, her words echoed in his mind.

What the hell was I thinking?

~

VIOLET DIDN'T MOVE for at least a full minute after the door closed behind him. Her body was still, but aching from denial. And her mind was in turmoil.

In less than twelve hours, she'd gone from being thoroughly suspicious of her cousin's butler, wanting him sacked even, to propositioning the man, kissing him, and then taking it all back. She blew out the candles with a sigh.

He must think her a fickle tease.

Violet slipped off her dressing gown and climbed onto her tall bed. He'd told her he would forget what had transpired downstairs, but how was she going to face him again?

She tucked her feet beneath the sheets, which felt cool to the touch. Was that only because her blood raged hot inside?

Her thoughts roared.

"Is that what you want?" His gaze had flicked to the bed. He would have made love to her. Was it considered making love when it was only an affair? Because that was all that it could be.

He is a butler.

Violet closed her eyes and summoned the memory of the only time she'd lain with a man. It had been so very long ago. She'd been so unworldly, so very inexperienced.

She buried her face in her pillow.

She'd gone walking in the garden with Christopher. It had been the night before he was to ship out. They'd been recently engaged, and they'd just finished a large dinner hosted by his uncle, the Duke of Coventry, at his sprawling Mayfair manor. Adelaide and her husband had been there, along with Christopher's two cousins and both their parents. No one had objected when the newly engaged couple slipped outside alone.

There had been no guarantee that he would return.

Christopher had led her off the path to where tall oaks dappled the lawn. It had been dark there, but she'd smiled upon seeing the blanket and picnic basket awaiting them.

"Sit with me?" He'd sent her a pleading look, the one that never failed to charm her into giving him almost anything he wanted.

"Of course." Violet had lowered herself onto the blanket and modestly spread her gown around her. She hadn't been at all worried or concerned. They were *engaged*. Her parents and Adelaide had been pleased, as had his parents. This was to be his last mission and it wasn't really even deemed to be all that dangerous of one.

"Come here." He'd reclined, propping himself on his elbow, pulling her down to lay beside him.

And then he'd begun kissing her. It had been lovely and comforting and so very romantic.

"Violet," he'd groaned and shifted his body to cover hers. "I need you." His touch, which had initially been gentle and coaxing, turned more purposeful. Whereas at first, he'd only brushed his fingers below her breasts, he grew bolder, squeezing and tugging at her bodice.

He'd said he *needed* her, and the sensation had not been entirely unpleasant. And at the tender age of nine and ten, she'd not fully comprehended the act but had instinctively allowed him to settle between her thighs.

"I love you, Violet." He'd paused to stare down at her. "You love me, don't you? Don't send me away without proving your love for me."

She'd nodded. Because, of course, she'd loved him.

And over the weeks that he'd courted her, she'd felt a certain longing as well. She'd wanted to give herself to him.

She'd known the importance of waiting until marriage. But he needed her. And there was no guarantee he'd return alive.

She loved him. Of course she would show him how much she loved him.

And so she'd not resisted when he'd pulled her skirt up or when he'd reached between her legs. She'd not stopped him when his fingers had pressed inside of her, eliciting unexpected fear and pain.

She trusted him. She loved him.

And she'd wanted this.

He'd kissed her like a man who would drown if denied. "I love you," he'd said. "You feel so good, Vi."

She'd wanted to stop, but how could she? He was already touching her. He was going to be her husband.

She'd not cried out when he'd pushed his member inside. No, she'd welcomed him, summoning her own need, feeling some desire despite the pain.

Move in me, she remembered thinking.

And he had.

But rather than the gentle stroking she'd craved, he'd pushed her knees wide and began thrusting jerking motions. He'd slammed into her, his passion unleashed.

Violet had stiffened and clutched his shoulders, gritting

her teeth. She'd expected something different than this... Was this what he needed?

She remembered how her thighs had ached and just when she thought she couldn't endure a second longer, Christopher had thrust deep inside her with a shudder and then withdrawn. He'd gripped his member in his hand and expelled his seed onto the tops of her thighs.

Violet rolled over in her bed, drawing her knees toward her chest. The memory of that night had the ability to shake her, even after all these years. She'd chosen to give herself to him and then felt... violated.

And disappointed.

He'd handed her a handkerchief afterward, and as she discreetly cleaned up the mess, rather than feel closer to him, a cold distance fell between them.

"Always the lady, eh, Vi?" He'd grimaced as he opened the basket and popped a grape between his lips.

"What do you mean?" She'd reminded herself that he loved her. He wouldn't have *made love* to her if he hadn't *loved* her.

"You can't be good at everything." He patted her on the knee. "I forgot for a minute who you were."

Violet remembered being confused. "You will write to me?" she'd reminded him. "I can keep you informed of all the wedding plans."

"Write if you wish, but you know I'm not good with that sort of thing." He had smiled.

He hadn't kissed her again, just gathered up the picnic and walked her back inside to where their families had been playing cards and socializing. When she and her parents took their leave that night, Christopher had bowed over her hand, barely skimming his lips over her gloves.

He'd shipped out the following day, and that was the last

time she'd ever seen him. She'd written him, feeling hopeful, but, of course, he'd not written back.

Three months later, his father had sent over the missive to inform her that Captain Christopher Donovan had gone missing and was presumed dead.

Only days after that, the rumors had started up. Rumors that he was alive.

She'd initially been thrilled, ecstatic to think he might still be alive somewhere. But if he was alive, why hadn't he returned? Either he was being held prisoner or...

And then real tragedy had struck when the ship carrying most of her family capsized in the English Channel, just off the coast of France. Devastated, but numb, Violet escaped to Yorkshire with Posy and Aunt Iris. And in Posy, she'd found some purpose for her life.

Violet squeezed her eyes shut.

Christopher was dead. He had loved her, hadn't he?

She was angry with herself for reliving the memory again.

And why? Why was she thinking about it tonight?

It had been the kiss.

She'd been disappointed after Christopher made love to her, but she'd never gotten over the feeling of need he'd awakened. Did all spinsters suffer these cravings, or just the ones who'd experienced intimacy?

Her hand drifted between her legs, but she knew it would be useless. Even when she was feeling the most on edge, the most... wicked, she'd never managed to reach the place she suspected existed.

SECOND THOUGHTS

*D*espite a restless night, Violet rose early. Tempted to keep to her chamber, she had letters to write, people to see. And, of course, she'd have to see him again eventually. So she donned one of her newer gowns, this one a jade color with conservatively sized sleeves. After tucking in her fichu, removing it, and fussing with it three different times, she chastised herself for being foolish.

Women of the world took lovers all the time. She was a grown woman with no intentions of ever marrying, and Mr. Cockfield would not feel forced to enter an affair or fear losing his job. The mere idea that he'd feel coerced into anything as unseemly as that would be laughable if it weren't so tawdry.

Besides, she and Aunt Iris, and possibly even Posy, would be returning to Blossom Court soon enough. Mr. Cockfield wasn't her servant at all. No, he was employed by Greystone.

Her most respectable and dignified cousin who was also a marquess.

She strolled past the paintings hanging in the corridor—

the Greystone ancestors—which might as well have been placed there with the intent of reminding her that women born into this family were proper ladies.

And proper ladies did not have affairs with servants, did they? If it came right down to it, she doubted she'd even know how.

The meaning behind Christopher's comments afterward had become painfully apparent in the days following his departure.

She hadn't been good at it. What made her think she could satisfy a man like Mr. Cockfield?

As she reached the landing at the top of the steps, she peered over, not sure if she was hoping to see him or not. The foyer was empty, but noises floated up from the dining room —voices and clinking sounds, as though someone was counting the silver.

She could avoid him. She *should* avoid him.

But instead of heading for the morning room, she descended the stairs and then meandered toward the door of the long dining hall.

Where she found the man who'd kept her awake all night hard at work, a box of silverware, a tin of polish, two soft rags, and inventory charts spread out beside him.

But he was not alone.

One of the prettier chambermaids hovered at his side. What on earth was a chambermaid doing in the dining room? Was the poor girl lost, or was she as enamored with Mr. Cockfield as every other female in London?

"What should I do, Mr. Cockfield?" The maid's voice halted Violet before she could make her presence known. "My mother was most gratified when I landed the position here, but Freddie won't take no for an answer."

"I suppose that depends on the question, Suzie," he answered.

Hearing his voice, Violet shivered. The man currently shining the silver—the butler—had kissed her the night before. He had kissed her and then entered her bedchamber! Yet, Violet had done nothing to stop him from doing either. *Because I didn't want to stop him.*

"He says he wants to marry me." This sounded like a private conversation. But rather than leave, Violet remained to hear his response.

"And how will he provide for you?"

"I don't know, Mr. Cockfield. I didn't think to ask."

"A pertinent question if you're considering leaving your post, wouldn't you agree?" He spoke with patience, addressing the young woman's concerns with all the solemnity of a bill in Parliament.

He afforded the same respect to servants that he did to his employer's family. It was as though he was completely removed from the differences imposed by England's class system.

Violet silently shifted her weight from one foot to the other. How many times had she observed Mr. Cockfield in conversation with one person or another and assumed the worst?

What did that say about her?

"I thought all that mattered was how I felt about him. He did mention that he loves me, and I think I might love him back."

"Are you sure he wasn't talking about something improper?"

"Mr. Cockfield!" Suzie's face flushed pink.

"Ask him how he's going to support you and demand the

details. If he has a solid plan for how he will care for you, it was love. If he does not, keep your position here."

Suzie nodded. And then she curtsied. "I will. And many thanks for your advice, Mr. Cockfield. I don't know how things ever got on around here before you came."

He raised his brows and placed a shining spoon back in the velvet-lined box. "I am happy to help. And, Suzie?"

"Yes."

"Don't hesitate to come to me again if you have further questions."

The maid bobbed again, uttering more thanks, but then turned and caught sight of Violet.

"Oh, Miss Faraday! My apologies. I didn't see you there." The girl was obviously mortified, wondering how much Violet had overheard.

It hadn't been fair of Violet to eavesdrop. Mr. Cockfield seemed to bring out all her less-than-ladylike habits.

"I just now came down," Violet reassured her. "I was hoping to have a word with Mr. Cockfield. Beautiful morning, isn't it?"

"It is, my lady," the girl addressed her incorrectly in her nervousness and then hastily escaped, leaving Violet hovering in the doorway, nervous herself now, and questioning her ill-fated decision to seek him out.

The silence in the long hall following the maid's departure was deafening, and rather than invite her inside or ask her why she'd come, Mr. Cockfield replaced the last piece of silver in the box and turned the key to lock it.

Only after it was back in the cabinet was Violet afforded his full attention.

"You wish a word with me?"

"Oh." She had wanted to have a word with him, but the

reality of what she'd come to say struck her with sudden cowardice. "I did. But... I can't seem to remember what it was."

Mr. Cockfield shoved one hand in his pocket and rested his hip on the table. "Perhaps if you take a moment, you'll remember."

A mischievous glint shined in the back of his disconcerting gaze. But, of course, he knew she hadn't really forgotten.

And then she noticed. "You've removed your sling!"

The butler raised his right hand and flexed it before him. "Only for a few minutes. I need to work on getting my strength back."

"But you mustn't overdo it."

"I'll be careful not to."

He appeared more formal than usual this morning, his black coat brushed, his shirt a pristine white, and was that a monocle hanging from his pocket?

But then he said the last thing in the world that she might have expected.

"You left London," he said. "After your fiancé's disappearance."

"Yes. Rather a lot occurred that summer." She strolled closer to him. This was what she'd wanted this morning—to talk to him.

Was that what had drawn her downstairs—the simple fact that she enjoyed the blasted butler's company?

But he wasn't only a butler. He was a person, and she hoped, at the very least... a friend?

"Your parents' passing?" he asked.

"And my sister and her husband. And our grandparents. A ship set for France went down with quite a lot of my family on board."

He swallowed hard. "You were very young."

"I was Posy's age. My mother and grandmother considered themselves great travelers—explorers." It had been the first time Adelaide had ever traveled with them—the only time. "In the end, they failed to consider what might happen to those left behind if their vessel met with trouble on the high seas."

"I remember," he said. "It was in all the papers. You didn't return the next Season—or the one after that."

"Posy needed me, and I was happy to be there for her. She was just ten at the time. And although Greystone was old enough to have a ward, a young man of one and twenty is hardly fit to raise an orphaned girl."

"Greystone could have hired someone."

Violet shook her head. "No, Aunt Iris insisted. And having Posy to care for was... a Godsend." Although she'd never been close to her parents, she had *loved* them. And she'd been devastated to lose Adelaide—especially so soon after Christopher's disappearance. Violet frowned. "Why bring this up?"

"I wondered, that's all, why you've never married." He wasn't the first to question her spinsterhood.

"I had my chance. And raising Posy has been an honor."

"She is a lucky young woman to have had you."

"The feeling is mutual," Violet agreed. "Teaching her kept me..." She shook her head. She would not bring up how dark those days had been. "Aunt Iris was very involved as well."

"I'm glad you had her then," he said. "Both of them."

"Yes. Family is important to me. I don't want Posy to end up alone." And she would do everything in her power to make sure Posy found a good gentleman to care for her—a good and proper husband. It's what Adelaide would have wanted for her.

"Ah…" He nodded. "Did you remember what it was that you wished to speak with me about?"

"Oh. No." Violet wrung her hands together. What had seemed like something that would be perfectly reasonable while she lay abed suddenly sounded vulgar and outlandish in her own mind. "I'm sorry to take up your time. It must have been nothing." She began backing out of the room.

But he continued watching her—watching her and… waiting.

"Is that what you want?" he'd asked when she'd requested he forget her behavior—and that kiss.

"It is," she'd said.

But it wasn't. Violet felt trapped by his gaze—that and the powerful longings inside of her.

As a man of the world, he would forget about their little flirtation. But she would not. She would likely remember that kiss for the rest of her life. And in remembering it, she might very well find herself living in regret—constantly wondering what it would have been like.

Contemplating an affair while lying in her bed the night before, and after she'd awakened, she'd not cared at all that he was a butler or that she was a lady. In fact, she'd reasoned, the differences in their stations meant that afterward, she wouldn't ever have to worry about seeing him in society. She wouldn't have to worry about him gossiping with other gentlemen about her.

And if he found her as disappointing as Christopher had, she could simply leave for the country and never speak to him again.

"Any chance you might make an excuse to get out of the duchess's garden party this afternoon?" His question broke into her thoughts. He'd spoken casually, as though her answer wasn't all that important. He grimaced and then tugged at his cravat.

"Get out of the party…?" Was he asking her…? "Why?"

"If you meet me in the mews at two, you'll find out." He bowed. "Wear the moss-green muslin. It was delivered earlier this morning."

And before she could say a word, with a wink, he disappeared.

ADVICE FROM A MARRIED LADY

*R*ather than risk running into Mr. Cockfield again, and quite in need of fresh air, Violet enlisted Gwen to come along for a brisk stroll through the park.

Away from Knight Hall, she hoped to clear her head. Which, as it turned out, had been wishful thinking indeed. Because having meandered along the water's shore for nearly half an hour, her thoughts were no more clear than when she'd left.

Violet dropped onto an empty bench with a sigh.

"Do you mind, ma'am, if I wait with the other maids?" Gwen asked.

By now, half of the ladies of Mayfair had decided to take advantage of the weather and were mingling in small clusters. They might as well be in one of London's ballrooms.

Violet ducked her head so as not to be recognized. "Not at all."

In fact, having the maid leave her alone might be exactly what Violet required to think clearly. So once Gwen wandered away, Violet removed a pencil and the small book in which she often made notes for herself.

Affair with Mr. Cockfield, she wrote at the top of the page before drawing a line down the center of it.

She titled the left side *Pros*, and the right *Cons*.

I am too old to be considered scandal-worthy.

After a moment's thought, she scribbled *too old for scandal* on the left side.

With a grimace, she added it to the right as well.

Be serious, Violet.

Knowing she didn't have all day, she went to work, emptying her thoughts onto that small page until she'd run out of space on which to write. Staring at it, she grimaced.

The two sides appeared far too even to have made the exercise very helpful.

Pros:

Too old for scandal

Keep Mr. Cockfield away from Posy

Keep the Season from being boring

He's a butler. Once it's over, it's over.

Feel alive

I'll learn the truth about myself

Regrets if I don't

Cons:

Would have to keep the affair hidden

Possible Scandal (even though I'm old)

He's a butler. Society would never forgive me.

Greystone would never forgive me.

I may not like what I learn about myself.

I might be hurt.

I might regret it.
He might reject me.

"RATHER WARM TODAY, don't you think?" Lady Bethany Chaswick's friendly voice had Violet slamming her book closed even though she was pleased with the interruption.

Because she *liked* Lady Chaswick, a young woman who had married one of Greystone's friends very early in the Season. She was a pretty and friendly lady who seemed ridiculously happy with her circumstances even though her wedding had been a somewhat rushed affair.

"You're looking lovely today." Violet went to rise. "I'm afraid I don't have Posy with me this morning."

"Don't get up. I'll join you." The young baroness took the seat beside Violet. "I'm on my own this morning as well. Chaswick and I were... interrupted." An enigmatic smile danced on her lips. "And then he was called away. After that, I was in no mood to just...sit. Since my maid is busy with Diana and Collette, I decided some fresh air might help my disposition. I never imagined so much effort would be involved when I suggested bringing the girls out. I ought to have realized that they hadn't the training my sister and I had growing up."

"They're lovely girls, though." Lady Chaswick was one of the first friends Violet had made since coming to London. She'd been transparent with Violet, discussing the challenges she and her husband faced in introducing two illegitimate ladies into the *ton*.

But as to the first part, Violet was confused. "Interrupted? Were you arguing?"

"Oh, no." Lady Chaswick blushed. "Not arguing."

Violet required a moment to comprehend what the other woman meant.

"Forgive me. I forget that you are an unmarried woman." Lady Chaswick changed the subject. "How are matters progressing with Lady Posy?"

Violet straightened her back. Yes. She was unmarried.

"The same, I suppose," she answered, her mind suddenly filled with so many questions.

In the daytime? "She is still incorrigible..." Violet fumbled to answer before trailing off. She was older than Lady Chaswick but suddenly felt ridiculously naïve and... left out.

Lady Chaswick, waving her fan below her chin, began regaling Violet with a very detailed description of the gowns they'd ordered for her younger sisters-in-law and then shared a few insignificant morsels of gossip.

She was obviously embarrassed by what she considered to have been a *faux pas*.

When her friend fell silent, knowing it was improper, but too curious to stop herself, Violet said, "Would you mind if I ask a personal question?"

Lady Chaswick stilled, but then turned to face her more directly. "Not at all."

"You needn't answer if it's too intrusive, but—"

"You mustn't mind me. I've only been married a short while, though, and... There are days when it's all I can think about. Please, please forgive me."

"But that's just the point... My lady, I..." Violet pressed her fingertips to her cheeks, which had flushed hot. If she was going to ask something like this, she might as well just come right out with it. "Do you find it to be... necessary?"

"For children. Yes, but it isn't only for children." Lady Chaswick grinned. "And you must call me Bethany."

"Please, call me Violet."

Lady Chaswick—*Bethany*—nodded. "Has someone proposed? Are you considering marrying?"

"No. Not that."

"Then why…?" Bethany tilted her head. Violet must have given her thoughts away in her expression because Bethany raised her brows as though she fully comprehended the situation. "But you haven't decided yet, and that is why you are curious as to whether it would be worth the risk. Is that it?"

Violet suddenly wished the bench would open up and swallow her. "Please, forget I said anything."

"No, no. You wouldn't have asked if you didn't think it important. And I am more than happy to offer my input."

"I'll understand if you think less of me for even contemplating it."

"Not at all. You are an adult lady and have every right to take a lover if you—"

"Shhh," Violet hushed her. "I haven't decided anything yet." She covered her face with both hands. "What is wrong with me?"

"I'm fairly certain you aren't the first lady to contemplate an affair."

"A spinster, I am a spinster."

"That's nothing to be ashamed of. In fact, it makes even more sense for a spinster…" Bethany pursed her lips. "But, as I said, I, for one, think about it all the time these days. People simply choose not to discuss it, and I can't help but think we'd be better off if we did." Bethany dropped a hand to Violet's arm and squeezed. "You must remember, half of London witnessed my indiscretion."

"That wasn't your fault, though. It's not as though you chose to—"

"No, but if I could do it over, as embarrassing as it was, I wouldn't hesitate to venture into that garden again."

Bethany's announcement was a startling one. "You must be joking?"

But the baroness was shaking her head emphatically. "Not at all. Before that night, I had resigned myself to spinsterhood. I would never have known anything about it at all, and now... I couldn't bear the thought of living a life without intimacy. I couldn't bear the idea of not knowing my husband the way I do now."

Stinging pricked the back of Violet's eyes. She'd known some of it, but only once, and it had happened so very long ago...

"Had I not gone into that garden, Chaswick wouldn't have ruined me. And if I hadn't been ruined, I can't imagine he would have married me. And if he hadn't married me, we wouldn't have fallen in love. And if we hadn't fallen in love, I would have missed out on some of the most amazing experiences of my life."

"Amazing?"

"Incredible. Life-changing." Bethany stared out at the water and then slid Violet a cautious glance. "Have you ever...?"

Violet knew, of course, exactly what her friend was asking. Yet she hesitated, because the circumstance wasn't called 'ruined' for nothing. And if it became public, a lady's prospects were ruined, her reputation, and possibly her family's.

It wasn't the sort of thing a lady could expose about herself.

"If I had," she whispered, "I could not go on to marry another man."

"Ah..." Bethany didn't sound nearly as shocked as Violet expected. "Your fiancé? Before he went away."

Violet nodded. "Just once. And..." She dropped her gaze to stare at her hands clutching her reticule. "I've always wondered if..."

"If?"

"If there was more to it."

Bethany didn't respond right away, making Violet feel more idiotic than she had before, but then the other woman said, "There is more."

This time, it was Violet who stared across the water. "Thank you. That's far more than my mother ever told me." Even Adelaide hadn't shared that sort of information with Violet. Aunt Iris had certainly never broached the subject.

"Mothers, I've learned, are horribly stingy when it comes to these sorts of things." And then the baroness folded her hands primly in her lap.

Violet vowed she'd have a proper discussion with Posy when the time came. She was going to have to find a book, or perhaps she ought to consult with a midwife.

"I suppose I ought to return now if I'm not to be late for the garden party." Bethany touched Violet's arm. "You are still coming tonight?" She was hosting a cozy dinner party to celebrate her sister's engagement.

"Of course," Violet assured her. "And... thank you."

"Think nothing of it. And, Violet, whatever you decide, it will be the right thing." She gathered her reticule and umbrella. "It will be right because it is what you choose. Never risk going after something that you really want."

"You make it sound so simple."

"It doesn't have to be complicated. But I'd better get back to Byrd House soon or they'll leave without me."

"Go!" Violet waved her friend away, laughing. Of course, they wouldn't leave without her. Not only was Bethany the lady of the household, but she was a *baroness.*

Violet couldn't remember the last time she'd had the benefit of such a friend, someone she could trust with her confidences. Most women she knew at home were either married with children keeping them busy or considerably older than her.

Her mind filled with more questions than when she'd set out earlier, she located Gwen and returned to Knight Hall just as her aunt, Posy, and Greystone were climbing into the carriage parked out front.

She'd not realized how long she'd been gone.

"Wherever have you been all morning?" Aunt Iris, wearing a hat that was sure to rival the duchess's garden itself, turned from the carriage to greet Violet with a frown.

"We were concerned," Greys added but without sounding disapproving as their aunt had.

"I went for a walk and met up with Lady Chaswick. After the two of us began chatting, I forgot all about the time. Go on without me."

"I can have Coachman John return for you," her cousin offered. "Or we could wait."

"No," Violet said. "I believe I'll stay home. I've... a megrim."

Which wasn't at all true and had her wondering who this person was that she'd become. She didn't remember ever lying to her parents when Christopher courted her.

But Greys and Aunt Iris weren't her parents, and there was no possibility that Mr. Cockfield's intentions could even begin to be honorable.

Hers certainly weren't.

"Get some rest then, Violet, so that you're bright and

cheerful for Lady Chaswick's dinner this evening," her aunt advised.

"I will." And remembering herself, Violet turned to Posy. "Do try to find favor with one of the young gentlemen in attendance today. Wouldn't you be thrilled to be rowed around the lake?"

"Only if they'll allow me to do the rowing."

Aunt Iris tutted while Greys assisted them into the carriage. "Have Mr. Cockfield call the doctor if you aren't feeling well, Violet. You have looked a tad flushed these days."

"That won't be necessary. I'm perfectly fine." She stood on the walk and waved. As soon as the carriage disappeared around the corner, she turned to her maid, who had remained standing on the walk beside her. And then Violet touched her bottom lip, having made her decision.

"I'll need a bath and my new gown steamed. I have an appointment at two o'clock."

And feeling as nervous as she ever had, she slipped inside and then wandered downstairs in search of a cup of tea.

She was going to need it.

Because she was going on an outing with Mr. Cockfield that afternoon.

Alone.

And she needed to maintain her composure.

It wasn't every day that a lady began an affair with her cousin's butler.

Simon leaned against the doorframe and lazily watched as his favorite spinster picked her way across the gravel to where he waited for her, just inside the carriage house.

He'd been right. Not only about the color but also the cut of the sleeves. She'd done equally well with the jaunty charcoal hat pinned atop her coiffure.

However, he couldn't help but chuckle at the coiffure itself, which was, if anything, pulled back even tighter than usual. And ironically, he understood her reasoning. It kept her grounded in the person she believed herself to be.

He hadn't expected to like the woman upon first meeting. But the more he'd come to know her, the more he saw aspects of her character that he liked—such as her dedication to her niece, the sense of humor she pretended she didn't have, and that she'd shown him compassion the night before even though she didn't trust him.

And now he was aware that her lips were plump and rosy when she wasn't being disapproving, and something passionate lurked in the back of what he'd thought were plain brown eyes.

He'd been quite mistaken to think anything about her was plain.

So much so that he found himself in something of a predicament.

"Good afternoon, Mr. Cockfield," she greeted him, somewhat breathless as though she'd hurried down the stairs and through the kitchens. But her steps were light, and her smile almost flirtatious.

She smoothed a hand down her dress and cocked her head. "Will this suffice?" The gown complemented her slim figure, pushing up her breasts at the same time it emphasized her trim waist. He imagined long, slim legs, and was immediately ambushed by the image of them wrapped around his waist.

Oh, yes. Seeing her like this was most definitely creating a predicament for him.

Simon's gaze drifted over her shoulders, bare except for the lace shawl she'd wrapped around herself, and then settled on her décolletage. She wasn't as well-endowed as women he'd generally found attractive, and yet, here he was, all but ogling her.

Even as he stared, a rosy flush tinted her pretty skin, and he'd wager that beneath her stays, the tips of those perfect breasts had tightened into enticing buds.

"The gown is perfect for you." He'd suggested it for today's outing because, although made up of a superior fabric and the latest design, it was a subdued color that wouldn't draw too much attention.

Although the destination he had in mind was an established and respectable one, it wasn't the sort of place ladies usually ventured. And that was precisely the reason he'd chosen it.

"Thank you." She appeared only slightly less flustered than she had when she'd found him doling out advice in the morning room earlier.

The kiss they'd shared in the kitchen the night before had been eye-opening. It had evoked feelings he couldn't remember having with any other woman. But also, an excitement he'd never expected to feel again. Much like his first kiss, before it could be complicated by his title and diluted by experience.

Being a duke—a wealthy and not totally unattractive duke —he'd found that almost any woman he desired could eventually be his for the taking.

He didn't blame them. A lady's lot encouraged her to reach for a title, for security and wealth. And he wasn't blind to those women attracted to the power of his position—women who were content to be taken into his bed, to be the object of his attention if only for a few hours.

Simon had always known entitlement reserved for very few. He was grateful for it, and he sought not to exploit it.

And although this stint as Greystone's butler was an enormous inconvenience, he had ironically experienced an unexpected...freedom—temporary though it may be.

Miss Faraday smiled up at him, and Simon felt even lighter.

Something else had occurred when Miss Faraday had stepped into his arms, and he wondered if it had only been an anomaly. He'd felt like himself for the first time in over a decade—himself, Simon, the man—not Blackheart.

Pulling away from the doorframe, he held out a hand. "Shall we?"

"I suppose so. Are we walking or...?"

Simon gestured toward the utility cart he had readied. He was going to enjoy himself.

But for a raising of her finely arched brows, she wasn't at all daunted by the almost primitive mode of transport he'd chosen for their outing.

"I've spent the last ten years living in the country, Mr. Cockfield. Did you imagine I'd demand you take me out in one of Greystone's carriages?"

Had she managed to make him feel sheepish? Simon brushed his hand over his mouth with a grin. "In the future, I'll not presume anything about you, Miss Faraday."

"I thought you were all-knowing." She climbed onto the bench before he could assist her.

"That's what most people think."

She did not edge away from him when he climbed onto

the bench beside her. Instead, she turned and met his gaze. "I find it hard to believe that you are not. All-knowing, that is."

"Believe it," he said, pulling his cap down to better cover his face as he turned the cart onto the road. He hadn't bothered going out of his way to hide his identity while out and about in the past, but for this particular escapade, it was best to appear...insignificant.

"I am quite unsure of you." At the admission, that sensation he'd had the night before swept through him. He couldn't remember the last time he'd felt this way around any woman and hoped to discover if the feeling was evoked by the situation or by Miss Faraday herself.

"Have I stunned you into silence?" He slid her a quick glance.

"I'm afraid I am quite unsure of myself as well." Her proper tones lent a titillating undercurrent to her words. Simon shifted uncomfortably on the bench and then directed the single horse pulling them to walk in the opposite direction of the park.

"Perhaps I can help with that," he said.

"In sorting myself out?" She laughed.

He would not attempt to rush her into an affair with him. She was one of his best friend's cousins, blast it all, and a very respectable lady.

But she was no debutante. She was a woman with a mind of her own. Was she an innocent? She'd been engaged, and he wasn't foolish enough to imagine she'd not allowed her fiancé certain liberties.

She was not seeking to land a husband. If she'd given any indication of that, an affair would be out of the question.

If she had been a widow, an affair would be a given.

Miss Faraday, however, was something quite in-between.

"Where are we going today?" she asked, changing the subject.

"I'll allow you three guesses." Where did she think a butler would take a lady who'd caught his fancy?

"Not the park."

"Was that one of your guesses?" Simon enjoyed teasing her. He enjoyed flirting with her.

"No." One of the wheels dipped into a rut, jolting them and causing her to grasp the bench with one hand and his leg with the other.

Simon landed his weaker hand over hers before she could clasp it primly in her lap again.

"Are we going to visit a museum?"

"You have two guesses left."

"Ah, drat. I was hoping to tour the special exhibit featuring a few of Goya's latest works," she teased him back.

"The Bordeaux or his black period?" he asked.

She stared at him in surprise.

"Do you not think I appreciate art?" Miss Faraday considered his education to have been limited to service. He wasn't sure if the assumption pleased or annoyed him.

"No, but I hoped you would come up with something more extraordinary than that. I am missing the duchess's garden party for this, you know."

Simon liked her answer. Not only was she willing to have an adventure, but she'd thrown off a party hosted by a duchess to do so.

She was not a typical lady of the *ton*.

"Are you taking me to a bookshop?" She made her second guess.

"Not today. Is that something you would enjoy?"

"Always." For the next part of the drive, the two of them

exchanged names of their favorite authors. He'd discovered a new author and, although he kept himself busy most of the time, made a point to allow himself twenty minutes to read each night before bed.

"I wouldn't have imagined you as a man who enjoyed fiction."

"Even a d— Even a butler requires occasional entertainment."

"What else do butlers do for entertainment?" Her voice hitched as though she'd just reminded herself of the night before.

Simon squeezed her hand. "We'll have to think of something."

It wasn't at all what he'd intended to say.

When they arrived at their destination, Miss Faraday stiffened. Simon had pulled the cart to a halt beneath a sign that read *One-Legged Duck*.

"An inn?" Her tone was a startled one. Her eyes were wide, but her lips were parted and her cheeks flushed. Hers was an expression that signified a combination of outrage but also anticipation. Simon held up his hands innocently.

"A pub," he said.

It was also an inn, but that wasn't why he'd brought her there. The timing, at this point in their conversation, had perhaps not been ideal.

She sat silent for a moment and then he felt her relax beside him.

"A pub," she repeated.

"Which," Simon added, "also happens to be an inn."

A REGENCY "DATE"

Simon took advantage of Violet's astonishment to hurry around and assist her off the vehicle. She could have done it herself, but whether he was a duke or a butler, he was first a gentleman.

"Do you like ale?"

"I've only tasted it a few times." She made a face and allowed him to lead her toward the entrance. Sounds of merriment drifted onto the street when he pulled the door open.

Propriety and respectability, and perhaps country living, had kept her on far too short of a leash for far too long.

"I'm happy to give it a second chance, though." She glanced in his direction, and her smile nearly caused him to trip.

"Cockfield." The owner, O'Malley, waved them toward an open table near one of the windows. "Ale for you and the lady?" Although the hour was early, the tavern was nearly half full.

O'Malley kept a loyal clientele by serving liquor that was

never watered down and hearty portions of consistently excellent meals prepared by Mrs. O'Malley.

"Please." Simon pulled a chair out for Violet and then lowered himself onto the one beside her. The One-Legged Duck was one of the rare establishments he could visit in London without being recognized as a duke. Likely, even if any of the patrons did recognize him, it would not have mattered. His position made no difference to them. So, in bringing Violet here, he needn't worry about breaking the terms of the bet.

These people made their livings with their sweat and blood, honestly, dishonestly, and often somewhere in-between.

Sensing Miss Faraday was feeling a little out of place, Simon dropped his arm along the back of her chair and squeezed her shoulder. When she didn't shrug him off, he watched her take it all in until one of the barmaids approached and placed two filled tankards on the table before them.

"Will you be eating?" He recognized the maid, whose bosom threatened to spill out of a bodice that was likely two sizes too small. He'd flirted with her in the past but was glad he had never taken her up on anything other than drinks and a good meal.

"Hungry, Violet?" He turned to his companion, ignoring the server's suggestive smile.

"I—" She blinked and then swallowed hard as though searching for her composure. Was that because he'd addressed her by her given name, or because she was feeling over-whelmed? "I am, actually."

"They have an excellent pot pie here. Unless you prefer something else?"

"Oh, no, that sounds perfect."

After the barmaid moved to another table, Simon lifted his drink in a casual toast. "To second chances."

"For the ale." Violet laughed, lifting hers, and then took a sip. Simon held off drinking his in favor of watching her reaction to the bitter beverage. She made a face but then took a second drink.

"The more of it you have, the more you like it," Simon commented. *Rather like you.*

She gave him a shaky smile. "Do you bring all your lady friends here, Mr. Cockfield, or just me?"

Simon held her gaze and then drawled, "Do you flirt with all the manservants at Knight Hall, or just the butler?"

She winced. "Just the butler… I mean, I don't… I don't flirt with other manservants. I—"

"I'm only joking, Violet."

She gave him an admonishing look but then grinned. "You do that rather a lot. Are you ever serious?" But then she seemed to remember the night before and dropped her gaze to her drink.

"It's important not to be serious all the time," he filled in so she wouldn't feel the need to bring up the night before. "What do you do for fun, way up there in Yorkshire?"

He felt an odd sort of fascination for this woman and wondered if spending an afternoon in her company would put an end to it.

"Aside from church, social gatherings are few and far between near Blossom Court, so nothing exciting, really."

"You attend church?"

"Occasionally—not as much as I used to." She sipped from her ale and then licked the foam off her lips. "Aunt Iris stopped going a few years ago, and Posy's not all that keen. I won't force her. Our local vicar has a tendency to shout." She made a face. "I've always felt closer to God in the quiet, when I'm alone."

Simon nodded. She was spiritual, but not a zealot.

"What else do you do?"

"When I'm not helping my aunt's housekeeper, or doing lessons with Posy, I head up the local ladies' charity for orphans. And I knit, and sometimes paint. I practice my music."

"Isn't Lady Posy a little old for lessons?"

She shook her head. "Not at all. In fact, we do them together. I don't believe there's an age where we should stop learning. Currently, we're making our way through some of Shakespeare's plays—*Macbeth*—which was Posy's choice but we're both finding too depressing." She made a face and swiped a lock of hair behind her ear. "At Greystone's suggestion, we're also reading up on a few recent physics theories. But most of the equations are beyond my abilities."

"I respect that about him—his thirst for knowledge," he admitted.

"It is rather commendable..." She tilted her head with a laugh. "I'll admit I didn't foresee discussing the universe and God this afternoon..." She laughed.

"Serious subjects for a pub," Simon agreed, leaning toward her. "What else do you like to do? In between... let's see: studying literature, astronomy, knitting, painting, and playing the pianoforte, not to mention caring for your aunt and niece?"

"And the orphans," she reminded him with a grin.

"And the orphans."

Simon learned that although this woman was more than capable of navigating the *ton,* Violet Faraday far preferred the country. And she freely admitted to being happier wandering the meadows near her aunt's estate than she'd ever been in a ballroom.

"And I enjoy taking Posy to the fairs that come through." She entertained him with stories of various fortune tellers she'd paid to see at those fairs, laughing but also defending the possibilities of fate and premonitions. "You must think me gullible. But it's nice to imagine there is more to the world than what we see."

"Not gullible," Simon said. "I think you are... charming." And sitting with her, drinking and eating and just... talking, that magnetic pull he'd experienced with her before became even more compelling.

It was as though they were the only two people in the tavern.

"Give me your hand." She stared at him with more confidence than she had before.

Simon did as she asked, and Miss Faraday, spinster, and dedicated chaperone, took his hand and stared at his palm.

"Are you going to tell me my future?" he asked.

She laughed and shook her head, but then drew one finger down the center.

"Does your aunt know you dabble in the dark arts?"

"It's fun, and the proper name is divination," she corrected him. "And of course not."

"Well, go on then, tell me my future," Simon teased but he'd not expected her to be like this. He'd not expected that she would be funny and interesting. He would never have thought she believed in magic.

"Greystone watches the stars; he looks to the outer world to understand it. Reading palms is merely another window... but one looks inward," she explained, sounding almost like one of his governesses. "This is your dominant hand, correct? I notice that you haven't had difficulty writing…"

"No, I'm left-handed," he answered, curious for what she would come up with next.

"The lines on this hand show your life in practice. Your right hand will show your natural tendencies—your essence." She flipped her gaze up to meet his. "May I? Only if it won't hurt you…"

"Of course." Simon slipped his injured hand out of the sling, and she cradled it in both of hers.

"Your head line…" She drew her fingertip along one crease. "Deep and straight. You are very focused. That comes as no surprise. And you are direct—realistic. Oh, but do you see these here? You have had some emotional crisis in your life and will be, or have, made momentous decisions. This," she went on to another crease, "is your life line."

"A long life, I hope?" Simon only half-joked. Because many people depended on him. And then he scoffed at his imagination. This was only a game.

"The life line doesn't usually show the length of a person's life. Yours would have me believe that you are a vital person who requires little rest…" She met his gaze again. Of course, she knew this about him as she'd been watching his comings and goings. "It says that you value family, relationships."

She went on to explain the meaning of the shape of his hands, and then blushed and relinquished them, settling her own primly in her lap. "I do believe I may have had too much ale."

She was fun and creative and… so damned pretty.

How was it Greystone had kept her hidden away all these years? But had she been?

Would he have even noticed her before? She might have

caught his eye a time or two, but she would never have spoken to him with that disdain he'd found so amusing. He wouldn't have shared tea with her in a kitchen by candlelight.

He never would have kissed her.

And kissing her last night had been more than pleasant; it had been outright invigorating.

His gaze caressed the gentle curve of her cheek and an ironic regret struck him. Because, as Blackheart, he never would have known this woman.

She caught him staring and paused. "Do I have gravy on my chin?" She touched her face self-consciously.

"No." He flicked a glance at the mostly empty plates they'd pushed away. "You enjoyed it?"

"The food, the ale, or the company?" she asked. Together they had finished off the pot pie and then shared an apple tart. The ale had flowed freely, and he found himself wishing the afternoon didn't have to end.

"Any of them. All?"

"I am enjoying all three—tremendously." She leaned back, looking quite relaxed, her eyes crinkled from smiling, a hint of ale making her lips shine. "No disrespect to my cousin's cook, but that was quite possibly the best meal I've had in ages."

Simon leaned forward and touched his thumb to the corner of her mouth. "I thought there was a love line, or something to that effect. Aren't you going to read that one?" His voice came out gravelly.

"Not today." She stared back at him, and there was no mistaking her conflicting emotions. He guessed that she associated love with marriage. And as far as Simon knew from Greystone, she had no intentions of ever marrying.

But she was also a woman.

"How long?" He slid the tip of his thumb along her mouth. "Since you've been loved?" It was an improper question, but this entire afternoon was nothing if not improper.

Simon watched her throat move. "Years," she said. "Many years. Nearly a decade."

She was as affected by his nearness as he was by hers. Possibly more. The rapid rise and fall of her bosom and the warmth spreading up her neck gave her feelings away.

"And yet you believe in magic," he accused.

"For others… not necessarily for myself."

This close, Simon noticed tiny freckles dotting the bridge of her nose. "But you want to?"

"Perhaps."

Before, he never—not in a million years—would have considered a fling of this sort with a woman under the protection of one of his closest friends. But the circumstances surrounding Miss Faraday were dangerously tempting.

She had not agreed to come out with him today because he was Blackheart. She was attracted to him even though she believed him a manservant. For that reason, she would expect nothing more than physical pleasure.

And perhaps a little magic.

No one could know—not even those closest to either of them.

Especially not those closest to them. An affair between a lady and a servant was beyond scandalous. If it got out, Grey-stone would be right to demand Simon meet him on the field of honor.

Or marry her.

All of those factors together were daunting, but also powerful, and very, very enticing.

"I'm going to kiss you," he said.

She did not draw back, no, she dipped her chin and then parted her lips.

Simon closed the few inches that remained between them and captured her mouth with his. The night before, her kiss had been minty, clean, and her lips had been cool to the touch.

Presently, they tasted warm and earthy, much like the ale they'd been drinking. Her hands came up to clutch his waist-coat and she tugged him closer.

This woman was starving for intimacy—not so she could land a husband, or even because she expected anything else in the future. But because she wanted to give herself a second chance.

And she wanted to take that chance with him.

VIOLET FELT heavy and light at the same time. And rather than feel guilty over her actions, she felt energized and alive.

How long had it been since she'd thrown caution to the wind? Had she ever?

Because she liked it. She liked throwing caution like this.

He was kissing her. And there could be more between them. *He brought me to an inn!*

He'd not answered her question about bringing other women here. Was she just one of many for him?

She pushed such thoughts aside.

Because right now, he was kissing her—*her*—Violet Fara-day. And this kiss was reminding her of all the reasons she'd come with him today in the first place.

She was enjoying every minute of this outing.

When had she become so infatuated with her cousin's incorrigible and all-too-arrogant butler?

She opened her mouth with a sigh, inviting his tongue to mingle with hers. So exciting but also familiar—like coming home. Inhaling, she fully appreciated how very different he was from her—musky, spicy, very clean but also a hint that reminded her of leather and horses.

"You like this," he whispered against her mouth.

All she could do was nod, and then dip her chin, breaking the kiss. "Perhaps too much," she mumbled.

Because she was sitting in a public taproom, in broad daylight.

She was sitting here kissing Greystone's butler when she ought to be at a garden party chaperoning dear Posy.

"You needn't be sorry for that, you know." His face was so close that she could practically count the tiny blue specks in his eyes, his pupils the color of strong tea. "And I'm not going anywhere for now. We have all spring—the two of us."

She nodded again.

Just a few weeks ago, she'd believed him too sure of himself, too top-lofty and secretive to be a capable butler, for certain. And now… he was all of that, but he was also…

More.

So much more.

"I should take you home," he said. Did he sound reluctant? The idea of returning to reality sent a sinking feeling through her.

"Yes."

That giddy feeling from the ale turned to more of a melancholy. She couldn't help but wonder if she would ever know an afternoon like this one again.

He dropped some coins onto the table, and she straightened. "I cannot allow you to spend your hard-earned money on me," Violet insisted, horrified to allow him to pay out of his wages when she had seemingly limitless funds at her own disposal. She opened her reticule, but his hand stopped her.

The stern glance he shot her halted any further protests.

"A single meal isn't going to send me to the poorhouse."

His pride, it seemed, extended beyond words to actual deeds.

FAILURE TO COOPERATE

"Wherever did you run off to with the butler today?" Aunt Iris found Violet shortly after she and Mr. Cockfield had returned from the pub.

"We, er..." Violet moved her mouth, but no explanation came out. She hadn't realized she'd been seen either leaving or returning with him.

"Never mind that." The older woman waved a hand through the air. "Greystone has finally decided to court Lady Isabella in earnest. And it's about time. Have you met the girl? Lady Chaswick has invited them to her dinner this evening. I told her Greystone would be grateful when I saw her last week. You will be there, won't you? We need to make certain that dear boy doesn't sit around on his laurels too long. She's likely to slip right through his hands."

"He'll manage fine on his own. If Greystone has made any promises to the girl's father, I'm sure he has a plan," Violet said.

"Be that as it may, I don't know a single gentleman who didn't require a nudge when the time came. But, good heavens, he's practically thirty. Not ancient for a man, mind you, but high time he secures the marquessate by setting up his nursery. One cannot take anything for granted these days. All my friends, it seems, are dropping like flies."

"But Greystone is hardly—"

"Speaking of the dead. Did you realize Captain Thompson's family was so well-off? And with both of Coventry's sons gone—typhoid, you know—and now his brother, your former fiancé, would have been next in line to inherit his uncle's title. Such a shame your young man never made it back to London. He had so much to gain if he'd only stayed."

Violet blinked. She'd forgotten about Christopher's cousins. She'd read it in the papers, three? Four years ago. But it hadn't mattered—

"Foolish of your young man not to have considered the possibility."

"I can't imagine the duke would have allowed it," Violet curled in her shoulders. Would all of that have kept him in England when she hadn't been enough? Or was she part of why he'd gone in the first place?

"I'll check in on Posy." Her aunt floated toward the door.

Violet, who was already changed and ready to go out for the evening, was happy to end this particular conversation. She loved her aunt desperately, but the older woman had all the diplomacy of a hammer.

Furthermore, Posy needed nudging as well.

So, once Violet had taken a few deep breaths, putting all thoughts of her dead fiancé's family behind her, she poked her head into Posy's room as well.

And found her niece only half-dressed.

"But I've already attended a garden party today. Why must I go this evening as well? You know I'm not interested in any of these gentlemen here. I do wish someone would listen to me—other than Mr. Cockfield, that is!"

Violet ignored such foolishness. "We only want the best for you."

"But you don't understand! No one does." Posy waved her hands in the air.

Her niece might think she wanted to play coy now, but the bloom of youth didn't last long, and before she realized it, Posy might find herself forgotten and on the shelf. Violet rubbed her forehead. How many times had she explained this?

"But we've promised to be there." Violet would try a different tactic. "Chaswick's sisters, I'm sure, will be rather disappointed if you cry off."

"I do enjoy their company," Posy admitted. "Almost as much as I enjoy going about with Mr. Cockfield. He's a very interesting person. Far more interesting than the dandies in society."

Violet experienced a twinge of guilt that she too, found Greystone's butler more interesting than anyone she'd met amongst the *ton* so far this Season, but that was beside the point.

Posy was an innocent debutante, and Violet... was not.

Dismissing the possibility that she was being hypocritical, Violet asked Gwen to fetch Posy's slippers and wrap, and after extracting Posy's promise to bring herself downstairs without any further delays, walked slowly to the drawing room.

What was Mr. Cockfield doing now? Likely, after spending the afternoon with her, away from Knight Hall, he'd returned to find a good deal of work awaiting him.

Did he regret spending his afternoon with a lonely spinster?

Did he consider her a tease for allowing him to kiss her?

Or worse? He'd told her he'd enjoyed himself immensely. Had he simply been kind?

Her heart had raced when she'd been studying his palm.

Because nothing about his reading would have her believing he was a servant. His hands had been warm, strong, and… the lines had suggested he was a man of great power.

She smiled sadly. Sometimes she imagined reading palms had the potential to offer valuable insight. But then she'd see or perform a reading that proved it was fake—it was only a game.

Especially when her own life line indicated a long and happy marriage.

"There you are, Violet," Greystone greeted her when she stepped through the double doors of the familiar drawing room. As usual, he had dressed spectacularly for the evening and would outshine possibly everyone there. "How was your afternoon?"

"Very nice," she began hesitantly as she took her usual seat and picked up her knitting. Best not to dissemble, as Aunt Iris already knew she'd gone somewhere with the butler.

"Did you stay in?"

"No. Mr. Cockfield… escorted me to… a few shops." The two of them really ought to have come up with some sort of story so that they didn't end up contradicting one another.

"So, you are feeling well?"

"I am."

"Excellent." Her cousin seemed somewhat distracted, which reminded her…

"Are you aware that Lady Isabella and her parents are attending Chaswick's dinner?" she asked. It was quite possible for her aunt to have exaggerated the details of such a significant life decision to her liking.

Greys didn't answer right away, and when he did finally turn away from the window, he asked, "How did you come by this information?"

"Aunt Iris. She told Lady Chaswick last week that you would be grateful for it." Violet explained, partially defending her aunt, who, although bossy and difficult at times, in the end always supported her.

"I wish she hadn't," Greystone muttered.

"I assured our aunt that you did not require her assistance. I told her you were a grown man who would court the lady of your choice when you saw fit. But you know as well as I that she is not going to listen to me."

"It's fine," her cousin assured her.

Violet agreed but then dropped a stitch when the door opened.

She caught his eye as he assisted her aunt to her favorite chair. Violet shouldn't feel embarrassed to see him—she was a grown woman, for heaven's sake. And yet, her nerves stood on end.

Because he was, in fact, *a butler.*

He is my cousin's butler. Proper ladies did not, under any circumstances, cavort with the help. This was impossible!

Should she look at him? If she did, would her expression give her feelings away?

And how long should she look at him?

"Thank you, young man. I can't imagine where I left that blasted cane again." Even her aunt was bowled over by him.

Violet gritted her teeth and focused all her attention on her knitting.

Because he was more than just a butler now. He was a person with siblings, a person who'd lost his parents at a young age. He had worries, he liked to fish… And he hadn't mocked her secret fascination with fortune-telling.

He'd made her feel tremendously special that afternoon—pretty—and uniquely feminine. Did he naturally have that effect on every woman?

"Posy is complaining of a megrim," her aunt informed them. "But I've told her she's coming anyway. She promises to be down in ten minutes. Megrim, my eye!"

Had Posy hoped to remain home alone with Mr. Cockfield tonight?

He would not take advantage of Posy. Would he?

Most definitely not. He'd told her he had sisters to watch out for. Surely that prohibited him from taking advantage of a girl as young and naïve as her niece?

"She told me as much, and I told her the same," Violet answered.

She needed Posy to have a successful Season. She needed Posy to have all the things she never would.

"That girl is going to be the death of me. Perhaps we could hire an etiquette instructor. It's possible that I've missed teaching her something vital…"

"She'll be fine," Greystone offered.

"I hope you're right." But Violet wasn't feeling as confident.

Mr. Cockfield, who'd been moving around the room gathering glasses, sent her a meaningful look.

One that Violet couldn't quite read.

"I'll talk with her," Greystone said, although without much conviction.

"That one is going to require a strong man to take her in hand." At least Aunt Iris realized the seriousness of Posy's situation.

If Violet couldn't launch Posy properly, what good was she, really? Raising her sister's child had been her only responsibility for nearly a decade. She ought not to focus on her own sudden... urges, and instead focus on keeping Posy in check.

"I disagree," Mr. Cockfield broke in, capturing all of their attention. "She needs taken by the hand, not *in hand*—someone to protect her but also allow her to blossom into the woman within."

The words weren't so much shocking as was the fact that a butler would contradict a dowager countess.

"You certainly are opinionated for a butler," was all her aunt said.

"Merely stating the facts, my lady." But his gaze had landed on Violet again, leaving her confused as he slipped out of the room.

"If he weren't so efficient and easy on the eye, I'd advise you to sack him and hire a biddable butler, Greystone," Aunt Iris said.

Violet's maddening cousin pinched his lips together. "Best butler I've ever had."

"There you are, Mr. Cockfield." Lady Posy caught Simon just as he was about to enter the drawing room to announce that the carriage was waiting. "Do you have errands planned for tomorrow?"

"A few. What can I do for you, my lady?" he asked with a slight bow. Although he supported this young woman's endeavor, he didn't want to give Violet more cause for worry.

Even if she was, eventually, going to have to change her way of thinking.

"Well," the young girl clasped her hands behind her back and rolled her lips together. "I'd like to meet with Miss Bruce tomorrow. Her brother can escort her to one of the bookshops or teahouses."

He'd learned that Lady Posy's dear friend Miss Bruce had followed her to London so that the two of them needn't be apart for the entirety of the spring.

Lady Posy, he'd learned quite soon after her visit, was not going to be selecting any of the eligible bachelors Violet had in mind. Her family was going to have to find out eventually. But for now, Simon had conceded to assist Lady Posy, while at the same time ensuring she and her friend didn't make unnecessary trouble for themselves.

"I can escort you if we leave early." He dipped his chin. "But do attempt to enjoy yourself at dinner this evening, for both your aunts' sakes."

The imp grinned. "You're my second favorite person in all of London." She raised onto her toes to kiss him on the cheek just as Violet stepped out of the drawing room.

"You're ready." Violet glanced between the two of them. "Mr. Cockfield. Was that the carriage I heard?" Her voice was as cold as it had been when she first arrived.

"It is, Miss Faraday."

"Excellent, Mr. Cockfield." Greystone followed along with her aunt, who was walking perfectly fine on her own. "We don't want to miss a moment of the social season," he joked as he assisted his aunt into her cloak.

"Of course you don't," Simon agreed.

Perhaps it was better for Violet to despise him. She was Greystone's cousin…

"One would think we were dragging you off to the gallows, Greystone," Violet said, not looking at anyone but sliding her delicate hands into her gloves. "Have a good evening, Mr. Cockfield."

"You as well, Miss Faraday."

CONVINCED

The following day, Violet fully comprehended one of the reasons becoming involved with a servant was forbidden. How was she expected to eject him from her thoughts when he lived in the same house? When every time she left her chamber, she might run into him?

After the afternoon in the pub, she'd fooled herself into believing that he... cared for her.

Not in a marrying way, of course not that. But beyond their flirtations and the two times they'd kissed—in a friendly way.

And if he did possess actual feelings of affection for Violet, he would not have shown so little disregard for her request where Posy was concerned. First, she'd caught Posy kissing the man's cheek, and then the very next morning, while sitting at her window, finishing knitting a tiny hat for one of the orphans, she'd seen the two of them riding away from the manor together for places unknown.

Alone.

It had left her disappointed and miserable. He was all wrong for Posy!

But she refused—she absolutely refused—to feel jealous of her niece.

It was high time she insisted Greystone step in where Mr. Cockfield's association with Posy was concerned.

Not because she wished it had been she who'd slipped away with him that morning but because it was quite unacceptable for her niece to have done so.

Intent on a meeting with her cousin, Violet sent for Gwen and then dressed in one of her newer Kelly-green gowns. For added confidence, she wore her hair in a stern knot at the back of her head.

"Did you assist Lady Posy this morning?" Violet asked the maid vaguely.

"I did, Miss. She wanted to look especially pretty and even allowed me to use the iron in her hair."

Violet's blood ran cold, and Gwen paused. "Is one of the pins poking you?"

"Oh, no. No, I'm fine." But this situation was quickly going from awkward to disastrous. Never would she have imagined that she'd have the same inappropriate feelings for a gentleman as Posy did. It made her feel old, and ridiculous, and guilty that she'd acted in her own self-interest.

It was a shame that the only gentleman to catch Posy's eye was someone so very inappropriate. Violet didn't expect Posy to land a titled gentleman. Any landowner, or solicitor, or even a merchant would have made for a respectable match.

But never a servant!

Besides that, Mr. Cockfield showed signs of inconsistency, and that was the last thing she wanted for someone she cared for.

He quite simply was not husband material. If even a whisper of gossip came out of her going off with him, Posy stood to be ruined.

Determined to enlist Greystone's assistance, Violet marched down the stairs and after finding both the drawing room and the morning room empty, located her cousin in his study.

"Ah, there you are, Violet. Are you going to Lady Chaswick's 'at home' this afternoon? Posy's gone out but ought to be returning shortly." He was dressed for morning visits himself.

"Are you taking Lady Isabella driving today?" Violet was momentarily distracted. Was he prepared to court the girl in earnest?

"I'm taking one of Chaswick's sisters driving—Miss Diana Jones." Greystone cleared his throat. "As a favor."

Violet raised her brows but decided not to question any motives he might have there.

"I saw Posy leave earlier—with Mr. Cockfield." Violet sucked in a deep breath. "Surely, her attachment to your butler concerns you as it does me? It's most inappropriate."

"Not at all."

Expecting him to agree quietly and perhaps announce that he'd speak with his manservant, his words instead summoned her temper, which rarely saw the light of day.

"Greystone." Violet's voice threatened to shake. "He is a butler. If the wrong person sees her cavorting with a manservant, and word got around, not one respectable gentleman will so much as come near her. I really must insist—"

"She is perfectly safe with Mr. Cockfield." He cut her off. Staring at her, he looked torn for a fraction of a second but then tugged at the elaborate lace at his wrist. "You've been away from London too long. If Posy is happy being squired around by my… butler, I've no desire to curtail her activities. You're going to have to trust that I have her best interests at heart."

"But that makes no sense. Have you discussed the situation with Aunt Iris?" Surely, he was joking?

But he didn't appear to be joking. On the contrary, he looked as serious as ever.

He also seemed somewhat distracted.

"She's aware. Please, Violet. Don't make an issue of this."

Rather than protest, she simply stared at him, more confused than she had been before. "You look tired. Star watching again?"

He dipped his chin and shrugged. "A bit more than that, but yes, I spent much of the night in my observatory. A particular equation is giving me fits."

Was it possible her cousin was so caught up with one of his theories that he wasn't thinking clearly where his butler was concerned? Or perhaps he simply regretted speaking with Lady Isabella's father.

Violet was going to have to speak with Mr. Cockfield about Posy again.

And she was going to have to insist he keep his distance. If he didn't agree to do that, Violet would have to do… what?

She searched her mind and then settled on the only remedy available to her.

She and Posy would return to Blossom Court earlier than planned.

Greystone swept his gaze toward the window. "There they are now. See, nothing to worry about. The three of you will wish to travel in the carriage since I'll be driving Miss Jones in my highflyer."

But Violet's gaze remained fixed on the scene outside the window, not really paying much attention to Greystone's words.

Mr. Cockfield appeared perfectly respectable as he clasped Posy's hand to assist her out of the vehicle. Violet was slightly relieved that the two of them weren't gazing into one another's eyes adoringly. But then she stiffened.

Because although Mr. Cockfield appeared almost businesslike in his efficiency, several curls dangled loosely down Posy's back.

Curls that had been pinned up when they'd left.

And Violet remembered how she'd had to adjust her own coiffure upon returning to Knight Hall the day before.

Her blood ran hot first, and then cold as she sat silently, listening to the front doors open. Then, when Violet knew they were inside, she strode toward the door and threw it open.

"Lady Posy." Violet kept her voice even as she stepped into the foyer. "You do remember we have an at-home to attend today?" She clamped her mouth shut at the sight of Posy's disheveled gown. Later, she would demand Posy provide details of this outing. But first, she'd have an accounting from Mr. Cockfield.

"Go upstairs and change your gown. And have Gwen repair your chignon."

Posy was wide-eyed and agreeable, which only worsened matters because her most incorrigible niece was acting... guilty.

"Of course, Aunt." Posy pivoted and escaped up the stairs, leaving Violet alone with Mr. Cockfield.

A man *Violet* had kissed in public the day before.

Fixing her stare on the top button of his white waistcoat, Violet cleared her throat.

"I was rather hoping you would keep your distance from Lady Posy." Violet clutched her hands at her midriff, wringing them together.

"Say there." Greystone appeared from behind her before Mr. Cockfield could provide Violet with an explanation. "I hope Posy wasn't too much of a nuisance."

"Lady Posy is never a nuisance." But the butler didn't move and for a moment, the three of them stood together in an awkward silence; Violet vibrating in anger, Greystone oblivious, and Mr. Cockfield looking as patient as any butler ought to.

"Well then. I'll see you at Byrd House shortly, Violet." Greystone bowed in her direction and, taking his normally long strides, disappeared toward the back of the manor.

Leaving her alone with Mr. Cockfield again.

He exhaled a long sigh. "Lady Posy is in no danger from me."

Oddly enough, she believed him.

"But that is not enough. Frolicking about town, alone, with a manservant is more than enough to ruin her all by itself." Violet refused to meet his gaze. This all sounded so ridiculous in light of what she had done. "Good gracious, she didn't even take a maid along." This last came out as more of a cry of dismay. "She is my only niece. She is a daughter to me. How is it that I've failed so miserably to prepare her for her season? I—"

"Violet." His voice halted her tirade. She glanced up, helpless against his commanding tone. Meeting her gaze, he grasped her hand and pulled her into the small room that was also his office.

Inside, he gripped her shoulders so she had no choice but to face him.

Violet held herself rigid, refusing to be manipulated by his charm. The trouble was, her body wanted nothing more than to melt against him.

"Look at me." His voice demanded, and he kept silent until she relented. "I cannot do as you ask."

"I thought..." She closed her eyes. "I thought we were friends. And now you insist on..." *On what?* What was he up to with her niece?

"Lady Posy's best interests are my priority. You need to trust me."

"Trust you?" She jerked out of his hold. "Trust you? You are Greystone's butler and yet you come and go at will, you have visitors at all hours, and you treat his stable as though you're a guest here. Furthermore, you've got not only the maids, and my niece, but even my aunt and Greystone under your spell." Violet practically choked on a hysterical laugh. "As for myself—mmpf!"

He cut off her words without warning. And she didn't fight him. No, her traitorous body got its way, as she melted into his arms.

She wanted to trust him—to turn her worries over to him.

His lips were firm initially, but then softened. "Violet."

Her name on his lips broke the last of her resistance. She clutched at his lapels even as his hand smoothed down her arm and snaked around her waist.

She was breathless when she jerked back, breaking the kiss but staring up at him.

"Trust you?"

He dipped his chin.

"Will you tell me your given name?"

He didn't answer right away, and she half wondered if he wasn't going to give it up. Was he working for her cousin under an alias, having been a dangerous criminal in a former life? Was it possible that he was running from the law?

Because, aside from the anecdotes he'd shared with her about growing up with his siblings, she knew very few details about his past.

He reached up and trailed his fingers along the side of her face. "Simon. You can call me Simon." He almost looked vulnerable at the admission.

I am going to have an affair with him. The thought jumped into her mind unbidden. And yet she didn't contradict it. It was as though she'd been falling headlong into it from the moment he'd sent her that smirk.

She couldn't have the perfect future with a husband and family, but she could have... this.

Fate had come along to present her with this unexpected opportunity. A chance to... reclaim her womanhood—something she'd lost when Christopher left.

Or had she lost it before that? Had she lost it the night she'd lain with him?

Mr. Cockfield—Simon—dipped his head to kiss her again. And she welcomed it with her entire being.

Now that she'd made her decision, all that was left were the details. When? She didn't want to wait for long. Not that she thought she'd change her mind, but because she wanted to make the most of this before the end of the Season.

Where?

She slid her hands up and over his jacket, his collar, until her fingertips landed on his jaw. Once, a very long time ago, she'd believed herself in love.

She'd believed that she and Christopher would spend their lives together. Most of her wedding had been planned.

With Simon, she was as equally certain that there was no future for them.

And because of this, she would hold nothing back.

A sound beyond his office intruded. Either her aunt or Posy was descending and ready to depart.

He stilled and then broke the kiss with a soft sigh. "You haven't failed to prepare her," he insisted. "But Lady Posy, she..." He cradled Violet's cheek. "You must prepare yourself for the possibility of what she's been telling you all along."

"My niece seems to be constantly telling me things. What do you mean?" Violet squirmed in his arms, not nearly as comfortable with the tone in his voice.

"That she will not marry. But you mustn't think you've failed to prepare her. There are some matters that are simply beyond anyone's control."

"What do you mean? Has she done something?" Visions of all the trouble Posy might have gotten herself into came to mind. "Has she—?"

"Her secret isn't mine to tell," Simon answered. By now, Aunt Iris's voice sounded clearly behind the door, followed by Posy's. But it seemed he wasn't prepared to release her, however, and held Violet's hand to his breast. "She'll tell you when she's ready. But you mustn't keep pressing her to marry. Trust me?"

But Posy must marry. If she didn't, she'd end up just like Violet—a bitter, cynical spinster, contemplating an affair of a most scandalous nature.

But would she, really? And why did the thought of Posy failing to marry send Violet into such a panic?

"I have to go," Violet said, quite unnecessarily. He'd heard the voices as clearly as she had. "But... I would like... a word with you after I've returned, alone, if you don't mind."

His brows raised. "Of course. Now, go discover all the latest gossip."

"Is that what you think we do, at our 'at-homes?'"

"I know it is."

Violet winced. "Would you mind having a look to make sure no one sees me?"

He stared at her, taking the slightest hesitation, and then peered out the door. "Your secret is safe. They're in the drawing room."

Violet scuttled into the foyer and hastily joined her aunt and Posy.

"There you are. You weren't in your chamber." Aunt Iris's eyes lit up and Violet knew Simon had entered behind her. "And my dear Mr. Cockfield."

"The carriage is waiting, my ladies," he said and then turned. "Miss Faraday."

Perfectly composed as usual.

As Simon assisted their party out the front door, Violet realized she'd not really learned anything new about him—nor had she extracted the promise she'd hoped that he'd cease to escort her niece around town.

He'd asked her to trust him.

How was that possible?

Lady Chaswick's drawing room was already overflowing with guests when they arrived. Posy excused herself to join one of the Miss Joneses, and Aunt Iris took a seat with the other dowagers. Glancing around, Violet discreetly joined a few of the ladies who'd been at dinner the evening before: Lady Tabetha Spencer, who happened to be Lady Chaswick's younger sister, along with Lady Hawthorne and Lady Darlington.

The Countess of Hawthorne sent her a welcoming smile at the same time the others burst into giggles at the end of an anecdote Violet missed. She relaxed when Bethany appeared at her side.

"I'm so glad you came today." The baroness smiled fondly, touching Violet's arm.

"Well, this certainly is a crush. Would you prefer I extend my sympathies or congratulations?"

"A little of both if you don't mind?"

Violet appreciated that Bethany didn't feign the ennui many ladies showed. Instead, she was practical, slightly self-deprecating, and possessed a delightful sense of humor.

"Then you have them." Violet laughed. "The room is quite abuzz. Have I missed the latest scandal?"

"Hmm… One can never know for certain," Bethany placed one finger on her lips thoughtfully. "Mr. Somerset's heir lost the family fortune, and from what I've gleaned, if Miss Somerset doesn't land a husband this season, it's going to be her and Miss Delia's last."

Even though Violet wasn't well-acquainted with either of the young women, she experienced a pang of regret for both of them. It bothered her that not every debutante could find that happily ever after. "Poor thing. Do you think she'll be successful?"

"I can't say. She doesn't exactly inspire my sympathy, but for Delia's sake, I hope so."

Miss Delia Somerset was a shorter, rounder, mousier version of her older sister.

"On a more pleasant note, rumor has it that Lady Rockingham is with child." The Marchioness of Rockingham was slightly older than Violet, and she'd lost a child in her first marriage before being widowed.

"How wonderful for her." Violet was happy for the marchioness. Raising Posy was the closest that she herself would come to motherhood, and she'd been lucky to have that.

"And this," Bethany added. "The Duke of Coventry is making inquiries to locate an heir. Lord Percival was the only remaining male, what with losing his sons a few years ago. My understanding is that it isn't only about the title. Before dying, Lord Percival had turned his portion into a small fortune."

The mention of that family jolted Violet. That Christopher's father had been so successful, however, was not all that surprising. "Lord Percival was an astute businessman, as I remember."

"You knew him?" Bethany's brows shot up. "I understand his son was declared dead a few years ago, but no real evidence was ever brought forth. Lady Sheffield said the solicitors intend to have one last look into the matter before contacting some very distant family in Scotland."

Violet felt a little queasy. What if the duke's solicitors discovered new information? And what if that information confirmed those dreadful rumors—rumors that Christopher had not been attacked or captured by the enemy, but that he'd willingly taken up with one of the local women there.

Because he hadn't wanted to return to his obligations in England.

She inhaled. That was impossible.

And yet, even if nothing came of it, an investigation itself would stir up the old gossip.

Shame that she'd believed she'd gotten over threatened to rise up. It was also possible, she reminded herself, that an inquiry could squash those old rumors once and for all.

"I hope the duke finds what he needs," Violet said. But something in her voice must have given away more than a casual knowledge.

"You are acquainted with the family, then?"

Violet sighed. "That fiancé I mentioned... was Lord Percival's son. I was engaged to Captain Thompson—before."

Bethany's brows raised almost to her hairline and then she winced. "Oh, Violet. I didn't realize. I'm so sorry. You must think me utterly insensitive to have brought all of this up."

"But you didn't know. And it was a very long time ago."

Bethany stared at her, looking sad and pitying. "Were you terribly heartbroken?"

"I was. Heartbroken, that was. And no need to apologize." For the first time, Violet had the oddest desire to discuss all of it with another person—someone who'd not been involved.

Was this because of the decision she'd made earlier? Because it all seemed to be happening so fast and she was...

Afraid.

She was afraid to go forward but also afraid not to. And she wasn't about to change her mind now.

Because she liked Mr. Cockfield.

Simon.

"Have you met Lord Greystone's butler?"

Bethany blinked at the abrupt change of subject. "Mr. Cockfield?"

"Yes. He's a most unusual butler. Wouldn't you agree?"

"Um, I'm not sure... How so?"

Violet warmed to this particular subject. "He is not at all humble, as most servants are. There is an edge to him, almost as though he's not the person he portrays himself to be."

"I hadn't noticed." Bethany's gaze strayed around the room. "Whoever would he be, if not a butler?"

"Why, he could be anyone! A highwayman? Or a gang leader, hiding out from the law?"

This suggestion sent Bethany laughing. "You have a very active imagination. Mr. Cockfield? A highwayman?" But when Violet didn't laugh, she leaned forward. "Is there some sort of problem?"

Violet slid her gaze around the room. Such surroundings couldn't ensure their conversation would be private. "I don't know." And then Simon's entreaty that she trust him, along with her own cousin's lack of concerns, made her feel as though she was being disloyal… "He is nothing like any butler I've ever come across."

"Violet." Bethany took her hands. "If you're worrying about Lord Greystone, you are worrying over nothing. I am quite certain your cousin vetted him thoroughly before allowing him into his household. Especially with you, Posy, and your aunt residing there this spring."

"I suppose." Violet stared over Bethany's shoulder where Lord and Lady Chaswick's butler moved about the room, stopping to speak quietly with one of the footmen.

She couldn't help but compare the man to Simon. Simon's presence filled the space he occupied. He was commanding but could also be rather sweet. Just like his kisses, and the way he moved his hands down her arms…

She shivered.

"He hasn't done anything wrong, has he?" Bethany asked.

Inappropriate? Scandalous? Most certainly.

But wrong?

"No." Violet exhaled, suddenly finding it most difficult to describe Simon Cockfield. "He manages the staff well enough and performs his duties as required, but... He is only selectively proper. And he is terribly good-looking. Far too good-looking for a butler! But it is more than that. He is not at all... well, butlerish. One could more easily imagine him a lord than a servant."

"You find Lord Greystone's butler to be good-looking?" Bethany was all smiles again.

This was all Bethany took from Violet's concerns? Even so, it made no sense to dissemble. "Don't you?"

"Well, I suppose he's fine enough..." Lady Chaswick glanced around the room. "But I am far too enamored with Lord Chaswick for my head to be turned by any other man."

"But of course." Although Violet couldn't imagine any lady's head not being turned by Simon.

Whom she'd asked to speak to alone.

"As you wish." Violet hugged the memory of those words. And that kiss...

"Has something happened?" Bethany narrowed her eyes almost suspiciously.

"I... I..." Violet couldn't bring herself to confess that she'd kissed the man working as the butler in her cousin's home. "Do the solicitors sincerely believe they'll discover evidence to prove Captain Thompson's death?"

Bethany blinked but then shook her head, catching up with yet another change of subject. "My husband thinks it's possible. He said tongues tend to loosen when a fortune's involved."

Violet nodded, vaguely noticing that Greystone had

arrived and was deep in conversation with an older gentleman while Miss Diana Jones stood off listening.

"Do you still love him, then?" Bethany leaned forward to voice her question.

"Mr. Cockfield?" Violet started.

"Good heavens, no. Captain Thompson."

She was asking if Violet still loved *Christopher*. Years had passed since she'd been able to summon his countenance. It was a rare moment that she had a memory of the way his blond hair fell forward. Or how his eyes crinkled when he'd smile.

"I don't know."

"Is that why you've never married?" Bethany had lowered her voice, and the two of them were practically whispering now.

"Yes. No." Violet didn't know. "It all happened a very long time ago. I'm a completely different person now." She'd been so terribly naïve back then. "I wish they'd leave it be."

"Of course you do. Will you forgive me for bringing all of this up? I'm here, if you ever wish to speak to someone."

Violet didn't even realize she was upset until Bethany's hand squeezed her wrist.

Duke opening investigation into disappearance.

Simon closed the paper and tossed it onto his desk. He was going to have to look into the matter himself.

He remembered the rumors that surrounded Captain Thompson's death. He'd met the fellow on a few occasions and besides that, news of a duke's nephew going missing had caused quite a stir. It had been common knowledge that the young lord hadn't gotten on well with his family and the gossips hadn't left that detail alone. Was it possible the rumors were true? Could the man have staged his own disappearance?

It hadn't made sense for a captain to go missing like that. The conflict at Maratha had been resolved with nearly all the territory in question under British control. Simon remembered Greys being concerned about his cousin, who'd lost her fiancé, but at the time, both he and Greys had been young and distracted by the management of their own affairs.

Simon stared at the headline again.

There must be some legitimate doubt if Thompson's uncle was investigating. Was it possible that Violet's former fiancé could reappear to claim his inheritance? It was more plausible, Simon thought, that some imposter would attempt to come forward.

Either way, all of this was bound to upset Violet. And he was growing rather fond of her.

One moment, she was all starch and vinegar, and the next, yielding and eager. A cauldron of passion brewed inside her. Which stirred him, to say the least, even as he recognized that she was...

Vulnerable.

He doubted even Greystone, who was distracted by his own romantic affairs, noticed that about her.

Simon rubbed his hand along his chin.

After mourning Thompson, Violet could easily have returned to London for another season. And yet, she'd kept to the country to raise her orphaned niece. Had she returned, Simon had no doubt she would have landed a respectable husband.

Which was what she wanted for Posy now. Violet was

almost desperate for Posy to find the happiness she'd given up on for herself.

And that would be commendable if Posy was of the same mind.

But since Violet had arrived, Simon had noticed a very subtle transformation in her. Something in her eyes had changed. Almost as though she'd begun to see the world in a different light—and then questioned her place in it.

It was something he was not unfamiliar with—acting as a servant—seeing his world from an entirely different perspective.

At first, it had been a novelty, living without the trappings of his title, viewing his world without being a part of it. And now, spending time with a woman, with Violet, merely because he enjoyed her company, and she enjoyed his. It was beyond irresistible.

She had no intention of marrying but wished to push the boundaries she'd lived by all her life.

Their affair would be kept secret. *If we go ahead with it.*

Secrecy suited him just fine. If she'd been looking for anything else, she most certainly wouldn't have looked for it with him—whom she believed to be a butler.

And that was the beauty of it.

Better Simon than anyone else. She would be safe. An affair with him could never be used against her or her family members. He rubbed the place on his finger where he normally wore the ring his father left him. She knew him, he'd realized that when she had read his palm.

She liked the idea of magic, but not for herself.

And she liked the idea of marriage, but not for herself.

It was quite possible that if he wasn't handy, she might become involved with some other man, some man who mightn't have as altruistic of motives as he did.

If he could call them that.

He would also protect Lady Posy—another woman who required protection from herself.

Sounds of footsteps filtered into Simon's office, followed by two sharp knocks—it was Bradley, the first footman. "Mr. Bugsy and Finch are in the mews to see you, sir," the uniformed servant informed him.

"Thank you, Bradley." Simon shook off his musings.

"I'll watch the door, Mr. Cockfield, sir."

Simon nodded and strode to where two of his best men awaited him with their daily reports.

If there was anything to discover regarding Captain Christopher Thompson's suspicious disappearance, Bugsy and Finch were the men who would find it.

NOT A MYTH

*V*iolet set her knitting aside and crossed to where her aunt dozed in her favorite chair. With no festivities scheduled that evening, Posy had retired to her chamber right after dinner, and Greystone had disappeared upstairs. No doubt doing his mathematics and stargazing atop the house in his observatory.

"Aunt, you ought to go upstairs." Violet touched her aunt's arm.

Aunt Iris jerked but quickly recovered. "Just resting my eyes." But she blinked away her sleep. "I suppose you're right, though. Busy day tomorrow."

Violet smiled indulgently. "Indeed." The Duke and Duchess of Cortland were hosting a boat trip along the Thames. Plans were in place to attend the theatre afterward. *Iphigenia in Aulis*, the Greek play by Euripides, was being performed and had received rave reviews so far.

But Violet wasn't interested in retiring for the evening just yet. She felt jumpy in her skin, on edge. After she'd delivered her aunt into Gwen's capable hands, Violet returned downstairs and stepped out the side door.

Most of the flowers in the garden were at the height of their bloom, and she regretted that they hadn't been appreciated well enough. Trailing her fingertips along some ornamental grass, Violet determined to invite Bethany and her young sisters-in-law over for tea within the next few days. She and Greystone hadn't entertained since Posy's ball.

The Season was not going at all as she'd envisioned, and yet it seemed to be passing all too quickly.

A young gentleman at Bethany's at-home, who also happened to be heir to a viscountcy, had offered to take Posy driving. Violet had nearly fainted when her niece refused, making up the thinnest of excuses.

Lord Shortwood had seemed charmed by Posy's bubbly demeanor and bouncing curls. The two of them might have made an excellent match.

But now that he'd been rejected by Posy yet again, Violet doubted any such future invitations would be forthcoming. There were too many willing debutantes for an eligible bachelor to put forth much effort these days.

"I thought you'd retired for the evening."

She needn't turn around to know it was him. Her racing heart was evidence enough.

"It's too lovely of a night to go to bed yet." She kept her gaze focused ahead, where she could just make out the pink and purple lilacs in the moonlight. She'd asked to speak to him alone, and he'd found her.

"Did you enjoy yourself this afternoon?" he asked, having fallen into step beside her.

"I did. And, I'll have you know, I have been thoroughly apprised of the latest gossip." Her smile fell.

"Some of it was unpleasant, then?"

"Is it just you who seems to be capable of reading my mind, or do you think everyone can?" Violet didn't like the notion that she was so transparent. A lady needed to keep a few secrets, after all.

"I'm not sure." At the end of the path, he paused and turned to face her.

Violet licked her lips, keeping her eyes on the top button of his waistcoat. "Those are words I didn't expect to hear from you."

"I'm not sure of all sorts of things."

"You certainly don't show it." Violet lifted her gaze to his. "Tell me. What else are you unsure of?"

"My sisters, for one. I'm not at all sure of their happiness. And since they've become young women, they resist my opinion more with every passing day."

"How old are they?"

"Old enough to think they are grown but too young to be trusted not to make foolish mistakes. I don't know when this happened," he answered.

So, they were in their teens.

Violet smiled sadly. "I believe it's something that happens the minute they begin wearing their hair up. Posy refused an invitation to go driving with a viscount today."

Simon didn't seem surprised. She shouldn't have been either. Violet sighed.

"You need to let her live the life that she wants," he said. "Not the life you want for her."

Violet wanted to be angry with him, but tonight—she was tired of failing.

"Do you think I'm controlling?" she asked.

"You? Surprisingly not. But Posy, Lady Posy, is going to be

very unhappy if she disappoints you. She cares about your opinion."

Violet nodded. But then, exhausted by the subject, she turned to pluck at one of the clusters of lilacs. "Tell me something else you are uncertain of."

Without hesitation, he gestured toward his arm. "This injury has kept me from being as active as I like." A shadow flickered in his eyes. "And I have moments when I worry it won't heal properly."

"It will. You've been careful with it. And, for the record, you accomplish everything required of you," Violet pointed out.

"Yes, well…" And then he grimaced. "No man likes working with one hand tied behind his back, so to speak."

"What else?" If he was prepared to talk, Violet wanted to listen.

He stared into the darkness. "I used to worry about the future all the time—especially in the first few years after my parents died."

"How old were you?"

"Seven and ten."

He was younger than she had been. And he'd had three younger siblings to look after.

"You used to worry about it? But you no longer do?"

"I plan for it instead. Far more productive to analyze outcomes and take preventative measures than allow fate to have its way."

"But you can't control everything."

"I make allowances for that as well." He touched his fingertips to her elbow. "Although, you are correct. But with safeguards in place, I can minimize losses."

"You do my cousin well by taking such care with your duties."

He blinked and then nodded. "His lordship is more than an employer to me."

It was something she'd expect a loyal butler to say, but his loyalty seemed different than that of a servant for a master.

"Was there a relative or someone who could help with your brother and sisters? An aunt or cousin? Anyone? Because raising two girls cannot be easy for a single gentleman. You have witnessed my struggle to raise one." She cleared her throat. "If you'd like, Posy and I could take them along with us... to the museum, or Gunter's one of these days." And then she added again, "*If you'd like.*"

Her offer was an unusual one to make, taking their positions into consideration. But she had been thinking about his sisters since he'd first mentioned them. And now she knew they were younger than Posy.

"I was not without assistance." He finally answered. Had she offended him?

"Of course." He was the sort of person who would have cleared such a hurdle long ago. And he was no longer a boy. "I didn't mean to—"

"But it is kind of you to offer." His voice was low.

They strolled a few minutes in silence—not an awkward one but not entirely comfortable. Because they were knowingly crossing the boundaries that ought to exist between them.

How much of one's life did a person share with a casual lover?

"But something is bothering you," he added.

"Reading my mind again?" she asked.

"Just a feeling." His voice wrapped around her like a gentle breeze. "You can tell me, you know."

And she felt safe with him, she realized—despite the situation with Posy, despite the fact that he was a servant who didn't act like a servant, she somehow...

Trusted him.

"The Duke of Coventry is making inquiries into my late fiancé's death." This was the very last subject she'd thought she'd discuss with Simon. The air was heady with flowers, and the breeze was warm. She ought to be flirting with him, batting her eyelashes and other such nonsense.

Now would be the perfect time for a passionate embrace—or more. And no one would ever know because she'd never have to leave Knight Hall. There were, she supposed, advantages as well as disadvantages to dallying with one's butler.

"I heard." At her surprised glance, he shrugged. "It's my job to know matters that concern this family." The feigned innocence on his face was nearly enough to make her forget what they were talking about.

But only nearly.

"I wish they would leave it alone," she said. And she did. The past belonged where she'd left it.

In the past.

"What are your concerns?" he asked.

"I cannot say." She sighed. But...

One would have had to have stuck his head in the sand at the time of Christopher's death not to have heard the rumors. Because they had never found his body.

"You are afraid he wasn't killed? You are afraid he defected?" Simon guessed correctly.

"It would have been easy enough to identify him by the ring he wore. Not only because it bore the imprint of his family crest but because it had been stuck there for nearly a year. He couldn't take it off if he'd wanted to."

"You'll forgive me for pointing out, Violet, that such a problem would not have deterred a thief."

Violet paused. "I hadn't thought of that."

"I wouldn't wish such thoughts on any proper lady." He reached behind her and plucked a fragrant bundle of lilacs, only to softly tease the tender buds along the side of her face, and the mood between the two of them changed.

"What must you think of me?"

"You don't want him to come back."

"If he is alive, and didn't return by choice…" That would mean she'd meant very little to him. It would mean… She shook her head.

"You are, and always will be, a proper lady, Violet."

She stared up at him. "Even if I am contemplating…?"

"Even if…" He leaned forward, this time to tease her with his lips. "I do want you, Violet. But the decision must be yours."

"It must be both of ours." Her voice wobbled. "Because you, as a servant, are vulnerable too." Never once had he seemed vulnerable in any way, but it was true just the same. "I never want you to feel pressured… and if…"

"Yes?"

"If we both agree to it, we must act with the utmost of discretion."

His mouth moved closer to hers, and his voice was low. "Have you decided, then?"

She swayed toward him as the fragrant flowers mingled with his scent swept away both her morals and her balance.

"I have." She tipped her head so her mouth was only inches from his and became more daring still. "Kiss me, Simon."

She did not need to ask a second time.

The second his lips touched hers, her misgivings vanished.

His good arm wound around her back, drawing her closer. Warmth ebbed from her heart to her limbs. How had she thought she could go the rest of her life without this? Every inch of her skin was alive, begging for his touch. And she met his tongue with hers, dancing and sparring and exploring.

The sounds of his breath matched hers—along with the whispers of their mouths and the leaves in the trees softly rustling.

His scent, mingled with the lilacs behind her, swirled in her brain. She clung to him lest her knees give out beneath her.

And then wanted to cry when he ended it, moving his hand to gently stroke her cheek with the back of his knuckles.

All that warmth turned into embarrassment. He didn't want her like she wanted him. She didn't want to be a duty, a chore.

She dropped her forehead to his chest. "You don't have to. I'm sorry. I never meant to put you in such an awkward position." She spoke into the wool of his jacket, and her voice sounded different than normal...lower, thready.

"Violet." He touched her chin, tipping her head back. "What in the devil are you talking about?"

"You... you stopped."

At this, he raised his brows and then flicked a glance toward the house.

"You may want me, but it might not be worth it to you." She wasn't the sort of woman men took risks for. "I don't want to put you in an awkward position."

"So you've said." Rather than agree and walk her back to the manor, he grasped her hand. "That's what I wish to avoid, for both of us." He drew her across the lawn, into the small gardener's hut, and closed the door behind them.

"What—?"

But before she could ask what he was doing, he'd lifted her onto the worktable that ran the length of the small building, stepped between her legs, and took up their kiss with greater urgency than before.

His hand plucked at her hair, and a luxurious freedom swept through her when her chignon fell loose.

~

"It's beautiful." Simon threaded his fingers through the wavy strands that tumbled to Violet's waist. He hadn't planned this, but there was only so far they could go while standing in the middle of Greystone's garden. "*You* are beautiful."

He'd intended to stop, to allow her more time, but then she'd gone and apologized.

She apologized for kissing me.

The pain he'd heard in her voice had revealed vulnerability —a lack of awareness she had about herself. She didn't comprehend her appeal, and he'd been suddenly desperate that she did—desperate for her to know that someone in this world saw her for who she was—a loving, giving, compassionate—passionate—woman.

She'd offered to befriend his sisters. It wasn't the offer itself that had affected him but the fact that she'd done so believing him to be a butler.

Many women had offered to assist him with his sisters before, but they'd all known he was a duke.

And in addition to all the reasons he liked this woman,

staring at her now, her face flushed and her lips shining from his kiss, she was also sexy as hell.

He would show her exactly how appealing she was. He wouldn't make love to her here, but he would give her a taste of what she hungered for.

"Simon?" His name was a question.

In answer, locking his gaze with hers, Simon slid his hand under her skirts and trailed it up one long, luscious leg until he felt the top of her stocking. "Incredible," he whispered, finding her skin silky and inviting.

At his gentle urging, she spread her legs for him. His cock stiffened almost painfully. "Touch me, Violet." He worked his injured hand free and moved her hand to his trousers. A twinge of pain barely registered through his lust.

"Never be sorry for putting me in a... what did you call it? An awkward position?" Everything about this woman was so damned unique. "Or pressuring me." Simon pushed against her hand.

She was tentative, at first, as she smoothed her palm over the bulge in his trousers. "I didn't know..." Her breaths came in tiny gasps.

Simon edged his hand closer to her center. "What do you like? What do you need?"

She shifted on the table. "I don't know. I..." She rubbed her hand up and down his length now, over the fabric, building an impossible friction. "I'm not sure..."

"What aren't you sure of, sweet?" She spoke like an innocent.

"I don't remember it being like this." She inhaled. "You are... You feel... big."

"Ah..." He slid his hand to her center, brushing his fingers over her intimate folds, flirting with her opening. "No worries. Just feel." He located her clitoris, teasing it. How was it possible that the sensation of touch could be so damned beautiful?

She hummed, tilting her head back.

"You deserve a little pleasure." *She hadn't remembered it being like this…* She'd been with a man before. Her dead fiancé?

He pushed the thought aside. Because in this moment, there was no one but the two of them.

"You like this?" His hand was slick, moving along her opening. "Yes?"

Simon buried his face against her bodice even as he visualized her intimate folds. She was shifting with him now, into him. But she was also holding back.

"Yes," she said. "Please, but I'm not sure… I don't think I…"

"Move with me, love. Just like that."

"I've heard of it," she whispered. "The little death."

Simon paused and lifted his head to meet her gaze. Her hair was soft around her face, her eyes heavy, her lips parted. "But you've never…?"

"It must be a myth." She smiled. "For me, anyway."

Simon moved his hand and slid a finger inside her. It was high time she was disabused of such a notion. "Oh." She closed her eyes, her head falling back.

"Not a myth, Violet."

She inhaled and then met his stare again, this time, her lids heavy.

He withdrew, only to press in again, adding a second finger, his breath catching. "So damned soft."

He pushed deeper.

"Like velvet."

Her lips parted, and her panting encouraged him.

"Not a myth?" Her question was little more than a whisper, and he could see that she was close. "Simon."

He circled his thumb around her clitoris, not breaking the gentle rhythm, moving intimately, in and out.

His injured hand ached to tug at her breasts, to tease her nipples into rigid points. "Your bodice," he ordered. "Pull it down for me."

She blinked but then reached up and did precisely what he'd asked, revealing creamy swells above her stays.

Damned, blasted, blistering stays.

Simon dragged his mouth over the flesh she revealed and then, using his teeth, tugged downward at the restrictive garment.

Limited to one hand in addition to the restrictions of her undergarments, the hindrances nearly had him exploding in frustration.

But then, with her help, her breasts were free, and he took her into his mouth. "Please, Simon." She clutched the back of his head, jerking and pushing her hips. "What—?" she cried, panting, "Yes." She shook beneath him, and Simon pressed his cock into the side of the table, moving against it as he bent his fingers deep inside her.

"Let go, Violet." He bit down softly.

Everything tightened around him. Her arms, her legs, and she'd arched her back, offering herself to him completely. Almost more than he could bear.

Damn. He hadn't expected...

Simon followed her signs, slowing as her completion subsided—stopping when she went limp. When he finally withdrew his hand so he could hold her, he was breathing as raggedly as she was.

She murmured something unintelligible, and when he

glanced up, he inhaled a sharp breath. She possessed all the sensuality of womanhood God could ever have intended.

"Violet?" he asked, reeling from emotions he didn't quite understand. "Are you all right?"

"Not a myth," she enunciated clearly this time.

Simon chuckled. "No, not a myth." Although, he pondered, it was possible she channeled a little Aphrodite.

A BEAUTIFUL MESS

*V*iolet expected the mood to turn awkward between the two of them. Because that night long ago, after...

Before it could even form, she dismissed the old memory.

Because what had just happened between her and Simon Cockfield was incomparable.

When he finally drew himself upright, lifting his weight off her, he moved slowly, reluctantly. He wasn't looking around for the quickest means of escape, nor was he stumbling over uncomfortable explanations and damning praise.

He was just...

Looking.

At me.

"I'm a mess." Violet self-consciously dabbed at where her coiffure ought to be, only to realize her hair was in disarray all around her.

"A beautiful mess," he said. "I feel as though I should come up with a more original word to describe you right now, but it's what I think when I look at you."

She wanted to contradict him. She may be pretty at times, but no one had ever called her beautiful.

"I... feel beautiful," she answered instead.

"Then I must have done something right." He lifted his injured arm slightly. "Even with this."

"It did nothing to detract from... your performance."

At this, he cocked a brow. "Performance?"

"Abilities?" Flustered, Violet hastily... rearranged herself back into her corset.

"A pity." He hadn't moved from where he'd planted his feet earlier, standing between her knees. "Such a pretty, pretty sight. Although, it's probably for the best. I'm not very good at sharing."

"You are incorrigible." She smiled nonetheless as she repositioned her bodice. "But thank you. I imagine they must need you inside to do... whatever it is butlers do this late at night."

"I'm in no hurry."

"I can't be seen looking like this." Violet avoided his gaze as she gathered her hair and began twisting it. "Did you see what happened to my pins?"

Simon covered her hands with his, slowing her, his silence all but insisting she meet his stare. "Violet, are you... all right?"

There was something peaceful and patient in his question.

Was she all right?

She was more than all right. But her mind had also spun into a state of chaos. She had decided to embark on this affair thinking it would be physical, enlightening, and enjoyable.

She had not expected the...

Closeness. She hadn't expected to feel so transparent with him—this... release of emotions.

"I think so. That was lovely. I feel..." She felt changed.

But she couldn't tell him that. He'd think she wanted...
what? A proposal of marriage?

This was an affair.

He was a butler. She was a lady.

"You feel...?" he nudged.

"I feel cleansed." It didn't make sense, but it was true. "You
must think me dicked in the nob."

He laughed softly at that. "Not at all." He gathered her into
his arms.

"And a bit unhinged," she added, still surprised that he
hadn't gone running through the door to get away from her.

"If it makes any difference, you've unhinged me as well," he
answered, still holding her.

"How is that possible? You are..." She pulled away. "Well,
you, a man, of who I've no doubt possesses considerable...
familiarity with ladies—experience. And I am just *me*; a lady
who is practically thirty and not at all familiar..."

"And yet..." He dipped his head to make sure she was
looking into his eyes. "You have slightly unhinged me."

Violet exhaled. "Thank you."

"You are going to have to stop doing that," he said.

"What?"

"Thanking me. You're going to give me a big head—a
complex of sorts."

"Oh," she laughed, feeling more like herself—like a prettier,
more attractive version of herself. "It's too late for that."

"Are you saying I have a big head?" He was twisting her
hair now, even with one hand, and she absently assisted him.

"One would think you were the master rather than the
butler." She twisted around and located two of her pins on the
table. She wound the knot tightly, but he shook his head.

"Not so tight."

She relented. It didn't matter, really. She'd be off to her chamber any moment... and then what? Was this to be the extent of her London fling?

He assisted her off the bench and took her hand. "Walk with me?"

She hesitated, and he added, "Unless you prefer to retire?"

"No." She doubted she'd get much sleep, anyhow. These emotions were not at all conducive to a peaceful night's rest. "I mean, yes. I'd like to walk with you."

He led her out the door, and the slightly cooler temperature in the garden felt magical as the breeze caressed her hair and arms and face.

She had so many questions for him.

"What happens next?" she asked into the silence. She wanted to know. She'd already had too many uncertainties in her life.

He shrugged, his fingers threaded with hers. "What do you want to happen next?"

"Oh, no," Violet laughed. "I asked first. How do two people go about... this. Having an affair?" Her tongue stumbled on the word.

"Ah, so you wish to do this properly, do you?" She had no doubt he was teasing her by saying that word.

"Proper," she repeated the root. "I don't suppose there is any proper manner for a lady to... cavort with her cousin's butler." Because, although society made allowances for affairs under certain circumstances, she doubted anyone would consider anything proper about what she'd done with Simon in that little gardener's hut.

"Is that what this is called, *cavorting*?"

Simon squeezed Violet's hand. She was a lady; it was in her walk, her posture, her speech. But she'd entered this... affair with him, quite deliberately.

He was surprised at the discord he experienced to call this an affair.

Because that meant she—this prim and proper, genteel lady—was his mistress. A shiver of unease slid down his spine.

"Will you meet me in the mews tomorrow afternoon?" There were places he could take her, things he could show her that wouldn't reveal his identity.

She sighed. "I cannot, Lady Chaswick and I have been assigned the task of ordering bathing costumes. Two days ago, Miss Jones fell out of her boat at the duchess's garden party when their boat tipped. It was lucky she and Greystone were in shallow water. So at Lord Chaswick's and my cousin's suggestion, it has been decided that bathing lessons would not be remiss. Did you realize that one of the dukes in town has a swimming bath right here in Mayfair? Inside his manor? He's generously making it available for our purposes later this week."

Simon knew this. Of course he knew this. He also understood Greystone, in particular, had championed such an endeavor for some time now.

"The Duke of Blackheart," she went on. "Have you heard of him?" His name—his title—on her lips sent a sort of buzzing through him.

"I... am well acquainted." And then he surprised himself by asking, "Would you care for a tour of Heart Place before you have those lessons?"

She turned to stare at him, eyes wide. "Oh, but I couldn't impose on him further."

But Simon suddenly wanted nothing more than to show her his home—even if she didn't know it was his.

"It's no trouble, I assure you."

"The duke is not in residence?"

"He is not, presently." Servants gave tours of vacant private homes all the time so it was not all that extraordinary.

"I'll admit I am rather curious as to what sort of manor houses a swimming hole."

Simon smiled at the image of a muddy pond. "Not a swimming hole, a swimming bath."

"Forgive me," she laughed. "But, yes. I would very much like to see it."

"In that case, you must allow me to take you there. I'll arrange it for the day after tomorrow—after you've ordered your bathing costumes."

"I'd like that."

Simon lifted her hand to his mouth, pressing his lips against it, and turned to catch her eye. "As would I."

It wasn't that he needed to impress her by showing her the manor, but he wanted her to have a glimpse into his other life.

The other part of him.

And that made no sense at all. Because this was only temporary. He was a convenient servant and she an unmarried, independent woman with a mind of her own.

It was oddly freeing. But also...

Humbling.

Before they reached the entrance to the house, Simon took advantage of the privacy provided by the darkness and claimed her mouth once more. After kissing her speechless—breathless—he walked her the last few feet to the edge of the garden.

"I'll make my way upstairs alone." She stopped before he

could escort her into the main part of the house. And as though he was returning her to her chaperones after a lively set, she curtsied and blushed. "Thank you for a most pleasant evening."

He bowed and then froze, torn between honoring her request that she return to her room alone and his own instinct to escort her.

"I will be fine," she said, backing away. "Please."

Because now, more than ever, she would fear giving rise to suspicions. And it was right to be cautious.

Simon inhaled. And then... "Very well."

She was correct in that this must remain a secret. Because whether he'd intended to take matters this far or not, Simon had just embarked on an affair with Greystone's cousin—a *secret* affair.

With a woman who believed he was a butler.

Simon scrubbed his hand down his face.

This was beyond reckless, and he felt as though he'd just stepped into a minefield. But it wasn't really. She was a grown woman, he reminded himself.

And he... had no choice but to go on allowing her to know him as Mr. Cockfield. He couldn't reveal the truth, not without welching on the bet and getting himself into further hot water with his friend.

But also, if he was being totally honest with himself, he had no desire to turn back.

Not yet.

THIS BLACKHEART FELLOW

"You are unusually quiet today," Bethany commented as she and Violet watched their younger charges stand for their bathing costume fittings.

"Wool-gathering," Violet answered. But, in truth, her mind had returned to the interlude in the garden hut repeatedly. Not only what they'd done, how he'd touched her, but the intimacy of their conversation afterward.

Rather than feel exposed, she'd felt...

Worshiped. And when it was over, he had been...

Perfect.

Bethany's younger sister, Lady Tabetha, sat on Violet's opposite side. "If I didn't know you were so proper, Miss Faraday, by that smug look on your face, I'd imagine your thoughts to be scandalous ones."

"She does rather look like the cat who got the canary," Bethany added.

Although the two sisters' eyes were similar in color, their similarities ended there. Lady Bethany wasn't plain by any means but possessed a demeanor that lent her an approach-able appeal. Lady Tabetha, on the other hand, was something of a beauty, with golden hair and features to rival any princess. The younger girl had seemed snobbish on first meeting, but Violet had soon realized she was as friendly and kind-hearted as her sister.

Both were recently married and, overall, had little complaints about life.

Bethany sent her sister a disapproving stare and changed the subject.

"Tabetha and I spent many a summer on the beaches at Brighton as children, but I am quite looking forward to diving into Blackheart's pool," Bethany admitted.

"Are you a proficient swimmer, Miss Faraday?" the blonde girl asked.

"Not in the ocean, as I've spent most of my life in the North, but we have a lovely spot that dams up the brook. Posy and I sometimes go there to cool off in the summer months." And then she added, "I've never seen a bathing pool, though."

"Blackheart put it in after the fire," Bethany supplied. "Heart Place is possibly my favorite manor in all of Mayfair. Not only because it is so very grand and fashionable, but because it has been outfitted with all the latest conveniences."

Would Simon be showing her some of those tomorrow? Her heart leapt happily at the prospect of spending more time with him. He'd promised the duke would not be in residence.

"The duke hasn't been at any of the balls I've attended," Violet pondered. "Is he a recluse?"

"Blackheart? Hardly." Lady Tabetha giggled and addressed her sister. "He attended Ladies Lucinda and Lydia's debut ball. Did he leave London after that?" Lady Tabetha had just returned to Mayfair herself and married shortly after.

"He brought two sisters out at once?" Violet asked.

"They are twins," Bethany supplied. "As their mother died years ago, Lady Ravensdale sponsored them. And Lady Lydia will participate in our bathing lessons, so you'll have a chance to meet her later this week."

"But has Blackheart remained in Mayfair?" Lady Tabetha asked her sister. "It's not like him to be so scarce."

"Chaswick has run into him a few times, but Lord Lucas has been acting as escort to the twins." Bethany fidgeted, tapping her fingers to her thumbs in her lap, but turned to Violet to explain. "Lord Major Lucas, er—he is Blackheart's younger brother."

Bethany's demeanor seemed... off, but Violet didn't want to press her.

"It is kind of him to open his bathing pool for us, none-theless." Violet turned back to watch as Posy twirled around for the dressmaker. The bathing costumes provided for adequate modesty, but the material was thin and the pantaloons almost scandalous. "I admit to being relieved that the duke will not be present for our lessons." She laughed. "I'd rather not meet a duke for the first time wearing something that is little more than a shift."

"Oh, but this is going to be fun," Tabetha laughed along with her.

Bethany smiled weakly, not quite meeting either of their eyes. "It'll be different, that is for sure."

BRIGHT AND EARLY THE following morning, a sealed envelope was delivered along with Violet's morning tea.

Miss Faraday was written in an unfamiliar masculine script.

She didn't open it until Gwen disappeared to attend to Posy and her aunt.

Violet,

I'll await you in the mews at one o'clock.

Anxiously.

Yours,

S.

Violet instinctively raised the note to her nostrils and inhaled. The aroma was mostly that everyday parchment but when she concentrated, she caught a hint of leathery spice.

Of him.

My lover. Could she call him that when they hadn't actually *consummated* their relationship?

She poured her tea and then added one sugar.

She'd had a fleeting glimpse of intimacy with Christopher, but it had just as quickly been jerked out of her grasp. And afterward, she did not believe she had imagined the distance between them.

She had not imagined his disappointment.

For months after his disappearance, she'd vacillated between feelings of fear, despair, and guilt. Without a body to bury, his mother and father had hoped it was a horrid mistake, that he was missing due to some clerical mix-up or held prisoner somewhere. Violet had begun to wonder the unthinkable—that he'd gone missing intentionally.

As had some unkind gossips.

Would the Duke of Coventry's investigation dispel the rumors? Or substantiate them? She felt sorry for the duke, she did, but it wasn't fair—that they would drag this up again.

The thought that Christopher might be alive was more possible than she cared to admit.

It would not be the first time he'd jumped into something

he thought would be exciting and then discover he'd bitten off more than he could chew. He'd hated his father's conservative ways and often rebelled against them—with his gambling—his drinking—racing his high-flyer to Brighton. He'd always risked more than everyone else, and she'd ignored the worry that niggled at her happiness. She'd refused to find fault with him. He was fun and exciting and almost heroic.

The day he'd engaged himself to Violet, he'd jokingly admitted that he only wished their parents didn't approve. And in hindsight, Violet could almost believe not returning to London had been an act of rebellion.

"You're awake!" Posy swept into Violet's chamber without knocking. Violet was glad she'd tucked Simon's envelope away when Posy lifted the lid on the pot of tea. "No chocolate? You really ought to take chocolate in the mornings, Aunt."

"Let me ring for some." Violet tugged the bell pull and went back to her own tea even though the contents had cooled. "You look bright and chipper this morning. Did you have a nice time last night?"

They'd attended a poetry reading recital, and the performers had been surprisingly good.

In answer, her niece scrunched up her nose. "I don't think I've ever been so bored in all my life." But then she just as quickly brightened again. "I'm going to go to Cedric's Shop of Tomes with the Miss Joneses this afternoon. Lady Tabetha Spencer has volunteered to chaperone us."

"Lady Tabetha isn't much older than any of you, is she?"

"She is not." Posy raised her brows. "But she is married and has all the freedoms of a married lady now. Which makes our outing perfectly respectable."

Violet would normally have insisted on going along but

quickly remembered she'd made other arrangements for her afternoon.

If nothing else came of all this business with Simon, at least she was keeping Posy from getting herself ruined with him. Violet, of course, no longer imagined anything untoward had ever occurred, but she was relieved not to have to worry about the appearance of such.

And Posy was right. Lady Tabetha's husband was the second son to the eminently respectable Earl of Ravensdale. Her age oughtn't matter.

"I rather enjoyed the performance," Violet mumbled. The two of them used to be so close and suddenly it felt as though Violet was losing her. Gwen appeared in the open door. "Would you bring Lady Posy some chocolate, please?"

"No, never mind," Posy contradicted Violet's request. "I've letters to write before going out this afternoon." She turned to Gwen. "Is my rose frock pressed? Miss Callum said it brought out the green flecks in my eyes. Did you realize I have green flecks?" She peered into the looking glass over Violet's vanity.

"More in your left eye than your right," Violet said. "Who is Miss Callum?"

"One of Madam Chantal's seamstresses." Posy made a face at herself.

"If you keep doing that with your nose, you're going to have wrinkles before you're five and twenty," Violet said automatically, already knowing her advice was going to go unheeded.

Was this what it was like to be a mother? Never having been close to her own mother, Violet didn't know.

And she didn't like it.

She ought to be happy with Posy's independence, and she

was, she just wished matters were progressing in the manner she'd visualized.

"Here you two are." Aunt Iris appeared in the door, already properly dressed with her usual jewels and elaborate coiffure. "Violet, you are coming with me to Lady Rockingham's today, are you not? She's asked me to head up the fundraiser gala for the newest foundling hospital. She's also enlisted the help of the Duke of Blackheart's daughter, Lady Lydia. Have you met her? So thoughtful and serious for such a young lady." She sent a meaningful glance in Posy's direction. "Unlike other young women."

Violet would have loved to take part in the planning—on any other day.

"I'm afraid I cannot," Violet said. "I've other plans."

"Oh?" Her aunt's eyebrows rose. "More important than charity?"

"I'm, er, making final arrangements for the bathing lessons." Best to keep as close to the truth as possible.

At this, her aunt looked even more skeptical, but her skepticism was not because she did not believe Violet's excuse. "Bathing lessons! A waste of time and most improper if you ask me. But nobody cares for my opinion these days." She lifted her nose just enough to show that she knew very well her opinion was heeded more often than not.

"Please though, will you tell the Marchioness that I'm more than happy to volunteer my services to her cause otherwise?" Violet had only visited one foundling hospital to know the importance of proper funding and oversight. Not all orphans were as lucky as Posy had been. Most were not, in fact.

Simon's sisters had been lucky to have such a responsible and loyal brother.

"Very well. I'll expect to see you for dinner this evening, then." The older woman fussed with the lace on her sleeve and then sashayed out the door. Violet couldn't help but smile at the idea of telling Greystone that he possessed some of the same mannerisms as their aged aunt.

Although, he likely already knew. And he wouldn't care. Her cousin was a most original sort of gentleman.

"You are meeting with Lady Chaswick, then? Collette hasn't mentioned it." Posy's voice was only half interested; otherwise, Violet might have felt it necessary to make up a few details to embellish her lie.

Wincing to herself, Violet doubted she'd lied so much in all her life. But this was the only way. It wasn't as though she could be courted publicly by a butler.

Her gaze flicked to her wardrobe, where the evergreen gown she favored hung. It was perfect for her afternoon with Simon.

"It's nothing." Violet smiled to herself. "Just, you know, finalizing details."

THE TOUR

"I wouldn't mind walking," Violet announced when she met Simon in the mews giving directions to a driver she hadn't met before. She had passed Heart Place several times when she'd gone out for a constitutional in the park. It was not quite half a mile distant.

"I prefer to drive you." Simon, quite stunning in his black coat and tan breeches, looked nothing at all like a manservant. "Unless you don't mind being seen walking with me?"

Had he dressed like this for her? Did he think she would be ashamed to be seen out with a butler?

The thought brought her up short. Because she felt many emotions whenever she was with him, but she couldn't imagine being ashamed to have him at her side.

Although, he was right. Suspicions would be raised if she was seen walking with her cousin's butler. And then there might be talk.

Unseemly talk.

Violet stared across the mews at the very plain carriage

awaiting them. It was black, scuffed, and except for the gorgeous team pulling it, inconspicuous.

"Is this one of Greystone's?" she asked.

"I've hired it for the day." Simon handed her through the door and climbed in behind her.

"Because we must be discreet."

"Yes," he confirmed, and then he winked. "But also, because it might rain."

Violet glanced out the window, and sure enough, dark clouds were moving across the horizon. But Simon was seated beside her now, and rain was the last thing on her mind.

"It would be a shame for you to ruin that gown. It's perfect on you."

She sighed dramatically. "As much as I resented your opinions at Madam Chantal's, I must admit I've grown rather fond of my new wardrobe."

"I'm glad you are coming to realize it." He sounded sincere despite the teasing look he sent her.

"Realize what?"

"That I am always right."

She'd thought she would feel uncomfortable with him—embarrassed. She'd also half expected him to cancel their outing.

The coach lurched as it turned onto the graveled road, and Violet jostled into Simon's side before she could catch herself.

"My apologies, Mr. Cockfield," she murmured instinctively as she moved to slide back to her side of the bench.

"Mr. Cockfield?" He assisted her upright but with a flirtatious light dancing in the back of his eyes.

"Simon," she corrected herself, smoothing her skirts around her legs. What did a lady say on such occasions? No suggested conversation had ever been taught in any of her manuals on mannerly behavior.

And he wasn't helping manners by staring at her, looking all-knowing. And he knew her well enough. Heat flushed up her neck and into her cheeks.

"You are certain the duke will not be in residence?" She suddenly remembered what she'd learned about the man from Bethany and Tabetha. "Lady Chaswick said he was in town."

"Rest assured you are not about to surprise *His Grace* with your visit. You have nothing to worry about on that score."

"Well, that is a relief, anyway. You are well-acquainted with his butler, then?"

"Very." Already, they were pulling through the iron gates that surrounded Heart Place.

Violet clasped her hands around her reticule. "You are not being very forthcoming today."

He smiled at her scold, drawing her gaze to the almost unnoticeable dimple on his chin. "I half expected you to change your mind."

The carriage jerked to a halt, but Violet sat frozen, stunned, really.

"You? Were nervous?"

"Does that seem so very impossible?"

She went to shake her head but only blinked instead. This man, this charming, charismatic, gorgeous gentleman, was nervous over...

Her?

"I keep my promises." Her voice came out breathy while he stared into her eyes. When he leaned forward, she parted her lips but was utterly disappointed when the door to the carriage was swung open by a liveried footman.

"Pardon me, Your—Mr. Cockfield." The manservant

appeared flustered but then just as quickly closed the door again.

Violet blinked at the interruption. "I suppose we ought to go in." Still breathy, still quite overcome by what he'd just told her.

"I suppose we ought to." But he waited a few seconds before turning to push the door open himself. "Shall we?" He assisted her to the step and onto the paved stones that made up the walkway.

"I am so sorry now that we didn't arrive in London in time to attend the duke's sister's come out," she said as they climbed the steps to the entrance. "Do you ever wish you could take part in society? Do you ever resent it, being a butler, I mean?" Perhaps if she reminded herself often enough who he was, she could keep herself from becoming thoroughly besotted.

Because she liked him. She liked him very much, and yet nothing could ever come of it.

This was merely an affair with another consenting adult.

"Servants don't miss out, really." Before the two of them reached the landing, the door swung open, and the duke's butler bowed and then gestured for the two of them to enter.

"Mr. Sterling," Simon greeted the man, somewhat tightlipped. "This is my very special guest, Miss Faraday, cousin to Lord Greystone. She is visiting from Yorkshire for the Season."

"Welcome to Heart Place, Miss Faraday, Mr. Cockfield," the man responded. "I've been instructed by the duke himself to honor any requests you might have." Mr. Sterling stood very stiffly and spoke in dignified tones.

"But that won't be necessary," Violet protested.

"If His Grace says so, then it is quite necessary," Mr. Sterling corrected her.

"*M*y thanks." Simon turned to Violet. "Would you care for tea before our tour? Or biscuits? Or any refreshment?"

"No." Had the world flipped on its axis? "But thank you."

"Very well, we'll ring then," Simon addressed Mr. Sterling, "if we have need of anything." With that, he dismissed the duke's butler with a nod and then offered Violet his arm. "Shall we, Miss Faraday?"

She acquiesced without answer, silenced by such an unexpected reception. Only after they were some feet down the long foyer did she dare speak up.

"Now that, Simon, is how I expect a butler to act. You could learn a thing or two from Mr. Sterling."

He chuckled. "Would you have preferred someone like that, then, to butler for your cousin?"

"Initially, I would have answered yes." Violet halted to tilt her head back and examine the elaborately painted ceiling. "But upon closer acquaintance, absolutely not. I'll take you just as you are."

She slid a glance in his direction. Had that made him uncomfortable?

"These are original from before the fire," he told her. "The entire ancestorial gallery was destroyed but... the duke was lucky that this particular ceiling could be restored."

"Oh, how very tragic. When was the fire?"

"1816," he answered. "Both the duke and the duchess died, but the servants saved their young daughters. They were only four at the time."

"Where was the current duke?"

"Away at school, having his jollies without a care in the world while Heart Place burned to the ground."

"He was very young then?"

"Not very. Seventeen. His father had suggested he finish out his schooling at home, with a tutor—to train him specifically to take over the dukedom when the time came. But Blackheart was enjoying himself too much at school to agree to it. There was too much fun to be had sporting around with the other chaps there."

"That's a little harsh, don't you think?" Violet asked, feeling tentative, almost as though she was reopening some wound on Simon's part. "I understand he also has a younger brother?"

"Yes."

And then she realized.

Simon, too, had been orphaned and left to care for two sisters and a brother. He must feel an intrinsic connection with the Duke of Blackheart.

She clutched his arm beneath her hand. The last thing she wished to do today was unearth sad memories.

"But Blackheart rebuilt everything."

"Yes."

Simon showed her to the two main drawing rooms, one

more classically decorated than the other but both in pristine condition and smelling of lemon oil.

"You said servants don't really miss out. What do you mean by that?" She was a little sheepish to be so ignorant about the life he led.

"Servants live with their employers. They are privy to some of their most intimate moments." Violet's heart skipped a beat at the word, but she ignored it.

"My cousin trusts you implicitly," she commented. "Some would say that a butler is more in control of a household than the master."

"So long as he has the respect of the staff."

"And how does one garner that?" Simon would know. She'd very nearly caught a few housemaids curtseying to him.

"It's not all that different from managing an estate," he said. "I imagine."

Violet did not doubt that Simon could manage a dukedom if he were called upon to do so. Perhaps someday he'd be promoted to a position of great power. She shivered, recalling the length and placement of the lifeline on his right palm.

"Respect isn't inevitably given," Simon explained. "And it shouldn't be. It's gained through consistency, kindness, and honor."

Warmth spread in her chest. For her affair, she had chosen a very good man.

"And here is the ballroom." They'd entered a tall-ceilinged room, and he drew her onto the landing that provided a magnificent view of the gleaming parquet floors below.

"It's… incredible—so very grand and stylish." The other parts of the house were more modest, but the duke, it seemed, had spared nothing while rebuilding this part of the house.

"It is only half the size of the original ballroom."

She took one more glance around before descending the staircase at his side.

"The bathing pool is just beyond those doors."

Violet was distracted by the tall windows that lined the room on one side, reaching from the distant ceiling to the floor. "It all makes one feel rather insignificant, I think." And yet...

"But that's the opposite of what he intended. It's designed to make the room's inhabitants feel as royal as any king." He pointed out the gilded molding.

"Even a marquess's cousin? And a butler?" She smiled up at him. Because he was right, she did feel rather royal walking across the floor on his arm. "I could almost imagine you and me dancing here." Amongst all of the *ton*, like any other couple. Tears stung the backs of her eyes.

"Shall I call for an orchestra?"

Violet laughed at his earnest expression. "Foolish man."

But he took her hand in his, and she remembered how he'd danced so effortlessly with Posy. "My dance, I believe."

She would never have an opportunity to dance with Simon at a ball—not even a small country affair.

Violet took a step away from him and dropped into her best curtsey. "I am honored."

He shrugged off the sling and placed his hand on the small of her back. When he grasped her hand with the other, she paused.

"Does it hurt?"

"It's improved considerably." He leaned forward, humming a low note before the solid length of his thighs pressed against her legs. She responded from memory, lifting onto her toes.

The tune he hummed was familiar, and she added her voice to his as the two of them danced across the floor.

Violet hadn't ever particularly enjoyed waltzing, but…

Simon's steps were long and sure, and his pressure on her back made following his lead feel effortless.

They danced close enough that she felt the rumbling of his voice in her chest. Oh, but the ladies of Mayfair were missing out by not having this man as a guest at their balls.

SIMON CLOSED his eyes for a moment, inhaling Violet's scent. It wasn't overly fussy but warm and clean and held only a hint of something floral. When she'd called him Mr. Cockfield, in that proper voice of hers, he'd been tempted to close the curtain and have her straddling his lap. He'd very nearly directed the carriage to drive randomly around London rather than come here.

What had kept him from doing that? He pondered his self-restraint as he danced her across the room that he had personally assisted in drawing up the design.

Her voice blended softly with his, and he drew her closer.

"What if someone comes?" Their music ceased with her question, but Simon kept right on moving.

"We tell them to go away."

"Oh, Simon," she laughed.

"What?"

"Just that: 'Oh, Simon.' It is all I can say when I am over-whelmed by your audacity."

He stilled his feet but wasn't prepared to release her just yet. "Would you care to see the bathing pool now?"

She stood in his arms, her hand moving from his shoulder to his neck, and tipped her head back with parted lips, offering an invitation he wasn't about to refuse.

Odd that a simple kiss could ignite him most inconveniently at the same time it made him feel as though he'd come home.

Her lips were tender, caught between his teeth. He inhaled, breathing the same air she did.

"Oh, Simon." She lifted onto her toes so she could deepen the kiss.

He should tell her. If he gave up the bet, he could court her publicly. But if he gave up the bet, he'd be at Greystone's mercy.

And he'd never been one to shirk a bet, so he wasn't exactly eager for his friend to make special allowances. Only a few weeks remained in the Season.

Simon slowly released her.

"I don't know what I'm thinking." Violet touched her hand to her hair.

"The same thing I am," he said.

When he moved to slide his wrist back into his sling, Violet took over and adjusted it for him. "Did the doctor tell you when you could return to your normal activities?"

"One more week." He cleared his throat. "But it's much better now."

"It still pains you."

Simon grimaced. "I don't mind pain."

"But there is something. What is it?"

The injury had served as a constant reminder that he'd failed to help one of his friends, and in the end, Mantis had nearly been killed for it. Would matters have come about differently if Simon hadn't been trying to be two people at the same time?

"Nothing." Simon straightened his shoulders.

"Hm… I wish I could read your mind."

"I just…" Simon began. "I wasn't the only person injured. It shouldn't have happened." He turned her in the direction opposite the stairs. "The bathing pool is this way."

He left the subject behind by telling Violet a few general anecdotes from his youth that wouldn't give himself away. After he'd shown her all the interesting chambers downstairs, he led her up the grand stairwell. He'd known Violet to be a good listener from the times they'd spent together already, but he was learning that she was also clever and intuitively sensitive.

Running her hand along the banister, she sighed. "The wood has burn scars. It must be original from before the fire as well. Do you think it's difficult for him to live here? With constant reminders of the tragedy that killed his parents?"

Simon swallowed hard, taken aback by her question. "He… I think he made enough changes so that there weren't constant reminders."

"But not so many that he would never forget."

"Yes," he agreed.

"Do you know how many bedchambers there are?" she asked. "And, yes, I mentioned the word *bed*." She rolled her eyes at him.

She made him laugh when a moment ago he'd been damn near tears.

"Thirteen," Simon answered. "The original home boasted twenty, but when… Blackheart had the pipes installed, he decided on quality over quantity. As a result, the pipes extend upstairs into the attic so the servants have modern conveniences as well."

"Thoughtful of him. I like that. But with only thirteen chambers, I suppose he does his serious entertaining in the country." She smiled over at him as they arrived on the upper landing.

"If he entertained much, I imagine you would be right. Crescent Park is near Sussex and boasts nearly forty chambers. Although most have been closed up for decades."

"You have been?"

"I have." Simon opened a door and gestured for her to enter.

"This is the master chamber?" Her eyes were wide, and her voice an awed whisper. "We shouldn't come in here. I'm quite certain he cannot have meant his private chamber to be part of our tour."

Simon wasn't certain of anything except the fact that he experienced far too much satisfaction seeing her standing at the foot of his bed.

He closed the door behind him. "It's fine."

He watched as she smoothed her hand over the coverlet. Damned ironic that he had her in his bedchamber and...

"Go ahead. Sit on it."

"It's a duke's bed." She shook her head.

"Go on. It's only a bed," he urged.

She surprised him by smiling mischievously and then climbing the three steps, where she turned and dropped to sit at the edge of the mattress. "Just for a minute. And we'll have to make sure I don't leave any wrinkles on the counterpane."

But Simon had other ideas—all of which would leave the bedding more than a little wrinkled.

Standing at the bed beside her, he reached up to exert a gentle pressure. She had no choice but to lay back.

"Simon," she warned.

But her gaze held his, almost as though she knew precisely where he was going with this.

"Comfortable?" He cocked a brow.

"We shouldn't. We can't."

"That, Miss Faraday, sounds like a challenge."

Her head rested on his pillow, her face slightly flushed, her hands at her sides. A sense of rightness spread through him.

"Someone will come," she whispered.

"We won't be interrupted." He stroked his fingertips down her arm and she shivered. "Before I begin cursing my wrist again, pull down your bodice for me." Simon felt suspended in this moment. "I want to see you."

He half expected her to refuse—to go running out of the room as a proper lady ought to do.

Instead, she reached up, shrugged her shoulders, and tugged the fabric downward. Without baring herself completely, however, she crossed her hands over her chest.

"We can't do this here." She clung to her last vestige of caution... of modesty.

"We can do whatever we damn well please." He pulled one hand down and with a sigh she moved the other, revealing plump, pert breasts, the tips tight and rigid.

"Do you know how irresistible you look right now?"

"Do I?"

"Oh, yes." Simon cradled one breast with his palm. "You like me to touch you."

"I do. More than I should." Her voice caught.

He squeezed, watching her pupils dilate. And then he rolled the tight bud between his fingers.

"Simon." She arched her back, offering more of herself to him.

On his own bed, by God. He'd make love to her, but he didn't want to be rushed their first time. Because as much as he'd prefer lolling around with her for what remained of the day, he was going to have to return to Knight Hall before the dinner gong.

Blasted, stupid bet.

"The pain of my wrist." Simon felt compelled to share more of himself with her. "It reminds me of my foolishness. It reminds me that I make mistakes. And that my mistakes have consequences." He'd agreed to this damnable wager without contemplating the repercussions—the deceit that would be involved. And then he'd been counting silver when he ought to have delved deeper into the threats to his friend.

He hadn't considered that he'd have to neglect some of his responsibilities, because even with the most successful delegating, he had to leave his sisters to navigate their season with only Lucas and Lady Ravensdale. He ought to have been the one taking them about, and it was due to his own stupidity that he wasn't.

"And you hate that." She stared back at him.

"I do."

"But no one is expected to be perfect all of the time. You're only human, after all."

Simon nodded and leaned forward to kiss her. "You have no idea how beautiful you are, do you?"

She simply shook her head.

He moved his hand down to her skirts. "Open your knees for me."

She didn't even hesitate.

Simon dragged his jaw along her chin, her slender neck, and then clasped his mouth onto one nipple, drawing her in, sucking, scraping his teeth over the sensitive skin. There was a very fine line between pleasure and pain and the closer one got to it, the greater the pleasure.

He rubbed his palm over her center.

"Touch me," she ordered, thrusting her hips up. He rubbed harder, giving her the friction she demanded, and both her hands clasped onto his head.

"I'm going to taste you," he warned her.

"All of me."

Impatient, he lifted his head and shifted her legs around. Her eyes widened when he slid a pillow beneath her hips. "Slide over here."

He would inhale her, taste her, touch her, and he'd see her.

And with her knees draped over his shoulders, Simon gazed on the banquet of her sex.

"What are you doing?" She lifted onto her elbows with a frown.

"I'm looking at you."

"Must you?" she groaned, and he chuckled.

"All great artists study their subjects before painting them." Ridiculous comment, and yet... appropriate.

"You are an artist?" she teased, her voice weak.

"Consider me inspired." He met her eyes.

Simon stroked glistening flesh with the tip of his thumb. He was going to make love to her, and soon. "The next time you doubt your beauty, remember this very moment, and remember that I am so in awe of you, that I can hardly breathe."

She wasn't embarrassed now. She held his gaze solemnly. "I will remember everything."

And intent on ensuring those memories were unforgettable, Simon buried his head between her legs.

∽

THIS HAD TO BE A DREAM.

An incredible, earth-shattering dream that had all the potential to turn into a horrific nightmare.

But Violet didn't care. Not when this enchanting man pleasured her in ways she'd only dared imagined in her most wicked thoughts.

The warmth of his mouth on her, the texture of his tongue and of his hand and fingers, fondling, entering...

His supremely orchestrated onslaught was a glorious one; it was unreal. And with each new stanza, she gave in to one wave of pleasure after another, each increasing in intensity. How had she surrendered her body so thoroughly?

She didn't know. She didn't care.

She wanted him everywhere. She wanted his cock inside of her.

Cock.

The combination of simply thinking the word and increased pressure from his mouth sent her crashing over another wave. She cried out, shaking, swirling into a vortex of hedonism.

And as that wave finally subsided, he slowed his caresses until they both lay spent, breathing heavily but not quite in unison. After a few minutes, him half lying on her, her, a twisted wreck of a woman on the bed of a duke that she'd never met, Violet exhaled.

"Simon?"

"Yes?" He kissed his way up her belly and she giggled, stilling him.

"That's ticklish," she gasped.

"I'll remember that. What were you going to say?" He removed some of his weight and stared up at her.

"I did not think of... any of this when I contemplated an... affair," she admitted. Her anticipation had been limited to the slightest hope that she wouldn't walk away feeling empty, and that she'd know she wasn't broken.

Simon moved his hand slightly, his fingertips still inside of her, and she gulped.

"You mean, this?" he asked. "Have I disappointed you?"

She smiled. "You know that you have not. It's just that, this... it's terribly... fun. And I don't think I've had fun in a very long time. Not the sort that makes you feel excited to wake up in the morning. And, even if this is all we ever have, I wanted to be sure to thank you."

"You never have to thank me."

"I know. But I want to."

He pinned her with a stern gaze. "Likewise, then."

"But I've not done anything for you." She pushed herself up, suddenly conscious once again of where they were and how catastrophic it would be if somebody decided to come seeking the impertinent couple touring Heart Place.

"Violet." He stilled her with a frown. "It's not your responsibility to please me. I've found a great pleasure simply knowing you. That, in and of itself, has been a gift. The extraordinary fact that you allow me to touch you... And that you would touch me." He took her hand in his and settled it over the rigid bulge beneath his trousers. "It's more than any man could hope for."

"You are not at all what I expected." She kept thinking she needed to labor in order to maintain his affection. It was how she'd felt before...

"What did you expect?" He assisted her off the bed, and as she contemplated her answer, she smoothed the counterpane.

Which was dreadfully wrinkled and slightly damp. "The maid is going to know," she conceded in dismay. "She's going to know."

But he pulled her away. "Don't worry about that. Now tell me…" He drew her up against him. "What did you expect?"

Was there just a hint of vulnerability in his question?

"I expected you to be slightly… heartless." And then she winced at how that sounded.

His brows shot up. "But I am not?"

"No, you are not heartless." Violet reached onto her toes to press a kiss against his mouth. Kissing him impulsively was quite liberating. "Am I what you expected?"

"Considering that for weeks, all I got out of you were disapproving frowns." One corner of his mouth twitched, and his eyes twinkled.

She loved it when his eyes twinkled like that.

"No?" she guessed.

"No," he confirmed.

"I'm not so sure I approve of you still." But she was smiling when she said so. "However, considering how much I've come to like you, I'm going to forgive the fact that you're a terrible butler." She stepped into her slippers, which she hadn't even realized she'd kicked off, and then glanced around the room. "We ought to be leaving before someone comes looking for us."

Simon was staring at a burnished gold timepiece that had been left sitting atop one of the dressers. "You'd be surprised how long historians take touring old houses," he murmured.

Violet gave the coverlet a last hopeful brush and then took his arm. "That will have to be our story then, that we are historians, adding to our stores of knowledge we will one day pass on to future generations."

"I'll have you know, Miss Faraday, that your cousin insists I am the best butler he's ever had." He held the door wide.

"Of course you are, Simon." She patted his hand. "Of course you are."

~

EVEN BEFORE HIS PARENTS' death, Simon had realized that being a duke attracted a specific type of woman. And if his parents hadn't perished as they did, they likely would have assisted him in navigating the pool of debutantes, all vying to be a duchess.

As it turned out, by the time he was one and twenty, he'd already grown weary of that particular aspect of his title. He'd actively participated in several seasons and even courted a few debutantes, but ultimately, he'd question if the lady's affection was for himself, or the prospect of becoming the Duchess of Blackheart—not to mention his property and wealth.

And although he'd come close, he'd never felt compelled to commit to any of them. Not only because he hadn't been confident in their affection, but because he, fool perhaps that he was, had been holding out for something more.

He wanted to love his wife.

Westerley, Greystone, Mantis, and Chaswick, with titles of their own, had admitted to experiencing similar issues. But they'd argued that it was unavoidable. As human beings, they could not separate their actual person from their titles. So, one must concede to the fact that any interested lady would be attracted to both.

Greystone had argued it was better that way. Because the woman would become a part of that title as well. Better that it was something she wanted.

As Greystone's butler, Simon had been able to separate

himself from Blackheart—not forever, and not completely, but enough.

And Violet was attracted to him as Mr. Cockfield, believing him to be a manservant.

Violet, he realized, was wholly attracted to *him*, and that was surprisingly... eye-opening.

Being with her allowed him to see himself through a different lens, one that wasn't warped by the treatment he received as a duke.

It sounded trite, but it was... meaningful.

"...no one is expected to be perfect all of the time. You're only human, after all."

He stood beside her as they waited for the carriage Mr. Sterling had summoned at Simon's request.

And yet, that perspective could not continue indefinitely. In the familiarity of his foyer, Simon found himself missing his own home. He was Mr. Cockfield, he was Simon, but he was also Blackheart.

And he wanted Violet to know all of him. Was that why he'd brought her here?

Less than five weeks and he could tell her the truth. She'd shared herself with him thinking he was someone else. Were his lies forgivable?

He could, of course, forfeit the bet and then refuse to honor the consequences for doing so. He adjusted the sling around his neck at the strangling sensation.

He could never do either. Although the bet itself was frivolous, failing to honor his word would haunt him for a lifetime. Honor was the foundation of his existence. He'd not only lose the respect of his closest friends, but he wasn't sure his own self-respect could suffer such a blow.

Five weeks.

Mr. Sterling opened the door wide at the precise moment his carriage pulled up.

"I hope you enjoyed your visit, *Mr. Cockfield*, and please, Miss Faraday, feel free to return any time you wish."

Simon nodded and Violet thanked him graciously before the two of them stepped outside.

Inside the carriage, he drew her close and glanced down at his timepiece—quarter 'til six. He'd be back just in time to ring the dinner gong.

"Did you enjoy your tour?" He drew her up against him. The distance between Heart Place and Knight Hall was negligible, so they only had a few more moments alone.

"I did, Mr. Cockfield." She smiled up at him. "When can we do it again?"

MUSIC AND MAGIC

*V*iolet winced at the dissonant sounds coming from the small stage. Still, Viscountess Fitzgerald sat proudly off to the side as her three daughters performed—a recital featuring two violins and one cello.

"I'm not sure my ears are going to survive this," Bethany whispered from beside her where the two of them, in addition to her sisters-in-law, sat, fortunate to be in one of the more distant rows.

One of the violins squeaked, and Violet resisted the urge to cover her ears.

"They should be nearly finished. And the next performers must be better than this—a professional quintet, I believe," Violet said.

"I hope that's soon; otherwise, I'm going to require an exorcism," Miss Collette Jones leaned forward to whisper loudly.

"Shhh…" Lady Whipple turned around and held her finger to her lips to shush them. It was known to most that the countess was selectively deaf. Her admonishment merely cemented the fact.

The recital ended to polite applause.

Unfortunately, however, the performance that followed began most inauspiciously when one of the musician's strings broke. And although they stopped so it could be replaced, the replacement hadn't been tuned properly.

The enthusiastic applause at the end was more likely inspired by relief than appreciation.

"Greystone could not have chosen a better night to abandon us in favor of dining with his intended's family." Violet smiled at the ladies seated around her.

"Let's locate the refreshments." Posy shot to her feet. "After enduring that, we can only hope Lady Fitzgerald hasn't skimped on the pastries." The two Miss Joneses joined her as well, giggling as they walked away together, leaving Bethany and Violet to wait as the rows of straight-backed chairs emptied.

"That was... interesting," Violet commented.

Bethany glanced around and then leaned toward her. "I've heard something, and I'm not sure whether or not I ought to tell you."

Violet's heart stopped, her first thought being that she and Simon had somehow been discovered. But surely, she would have been given the cut direct by now if they had. Likely, she wouldn't have even been admitted this evening.

Which was a rather sobering thought.

"You cannot toss out a herring like that and then not tell me," Violet said.

"Chaswick has heard something. It is about your Captain Thompson."

A week ago, Violet wouldn't have expected to feel relief

upon such a statement. But seeing as she had an affair to hide now, her panic subsided.

"Have they discovered something conclusive?" she asked.

"Rather the opposite." Bethany was watching her closely.

"What do you mean?"

"A witness has come forward, one of the soldiers who has been living in Rajasthan…" Bethany touched Violet's hand. "He's reported that he may have observed Captain Thompson living there."

Rajasthan—it was the Indian state he'd disappeared from. Violet had hoped never to hear the name again.

"How long ago?" She had dreaded such news for years. But now, finally knowing her fears could be realized, she didn't fall to pieces as she'd once imagined she would. That he'd not been captured, though, that he'd defected, was becoming more of a likelihood than a suspicion.

He hadn't wanted to return to England. He hadn't wanted to return to her. She blinked, feeling… numb.

"The next time you question your own beauty, remember how I am looking at you now." Simon's words from two days ago came to mind. His eyes had been filled with desire, appreciation, and awe.

And quite unexpectedly, the possibility of Christopher's betrayal didn't hurt quite as much.

She was not undesirable. She was not unworthy. Perhaps once and for all, she could put the past to rest.

"The young man, a lieutenant, said he saw him last spring, just after Easter," Bethany said.

The words didn't penetrate right away. But then Violet jerked her head back to stare at her friend. "As in the spring of 1828? But why wouldn't he report it sooner?"

"He didn't realize the significance until he saw the duke's notice."

"It cannot have been him. He cannot—" Violet shook her head. Christopher was dead. He had been dead for years.

Bethany squeezed Violet's wrist. "Likely, you are right. But I wanted you to know that Coventry's solicitors are looking into it. It would mean a great deal to the duke since he is the last of the line."

"Because he's lost his own sons."

"Yes," Bethany said. "Finding him alive would mean a great deal to the duke."

"It's wishful thinking, then," Violet said. Yes. That was all it was.

Christopher was gone. Dead.

"Perhaps," Bethany said. "But I thought you would want to know."

"Yes." Violet nodded, feeling as though a fog had fallen around her. "I appreciate that."

"And you mustn't get your hopes up."

"No, I mustn't get my hopes up." What if he was alive? He couldn't be.

The younger women returned, laden with napkins of scones and very small cups of what appeared to be tepid lemonade. "We brought these for you."

"Thank you, Posy." Perhaps the sugar and drink would help. Violet hadn't eaten much over dinner since her stomach flipped each time Simon entered the dining room. Inevitably, their gazes would lock and without fail, excitement lurched, robbing her of her appetite.

The two of them hadn't been alone together since the tour of Heart Place. If not for those secret knowing glances, she might have wondered if she'd imagined it.

Violet bit into the scone. It was dry but it was sweet. She followed it with a sip of her drink.

Christopher was gone. He was dead.

But Simon was here. And his affection, his desire for her was real—even if it was only temporary.

For the first time in nearly a decade, she believed in a little magic for herself.

"Simon?" Violet's voice cut through the darkness at the same time Simon silently closed the door behind him.

"It's me," he reassured her right away. The hour was late, very, very late, but it was the first he'd been able to get away. And he had missed her.

But he'd also noticed the tight and distracted demeanor she'd had after returning from the recital. She had to have heard the same news he'd gotten wind of, and it had to have come as a shock.

She turned to the night table, and after a moment's fumbling, lit a single taper.

Her eyes looked on him warmly in the soft glow of the flame. "You are... here?"

Simon swung a wooden chair from across the room, pulled it up to the bed, and sat down beside her. "I've been thinking about you," he admitted.

Her lips tilted up. "And were those thoughts proper ones?"

She was flirting with him.

"Most definitely not," he said. Which was no less than the truth. But then he reached out to take her hand. "You heard."

"About... Captain Thompson?" She nodded. "I did. But how did you?"

"You forget, servants hear everything first." And he had his own sources, much more accurate sources. "It upset you."

"Hearing the news that my dead fiancé has been alive these past ten years?" The sound she made wasn't quite a laugh. "Not at all. Happens all the time." But then she covered her mouth, her eyes large. "I don't know what to think, Simon. I don't know what I should feel. It's not really possible, is it?"

He didn't want to give her false hope. Was that what it would be? Because she had loved the man once, enough to give him her innocence.

But the return of a duke's only heir was prone to be complicated—especially one who might have defected from his unit.

But what did the news mean for her? "Is that something that would make you happy?" he asked.

"Of course it is. Shouldn't it be? What kind of a woman would I be to wish otherwise?" She stared down at the coverlet on the bed.

The last thing he'd wanted to do was upset her. "Slide over."

"What?"

"I'm joining you. Two days is too long for me to go without holding you." Not even hesitating, she pulled back her cover so Simon could slip in beside her. "Other than the upsetting news about Thompson, did you enjoy yourself?"

"The company was lovely, but the music could not have been worse. Greystone was smart to have absented himself. It seems he's going forward with this courtship and..."

Simon stroked his hand down her arm. "You don't approve of it?"

"Greystone spent the evening with Lord and Lady Huntly —and Lady Isabella, so my approval is a moot point. And she's positively lovely, but I'm not sure she's the right person for him to marry. He's been acting odd ever since he announced his intentions to court her."

Simon kept silent for a moment. Because, as a butler, he couldn't disclose private matters pertaining to his employer. Nonetheless, the woman already worried too much.

"Hold off on your worry." He stared at the shadows dancing on the ceiling as she twisted in his arms.

"What do you know?" But then she settled against his side, placing one hand flat on his chest. "No, don't tell me. That isn't a fair question to ask of you."

Simon exhaled. Because not ten minutes ago, he'd escorted a young woman who most definitely was not Lady Isabella upstairs to Greystone's observatory. And the visit had not had the appearances of a platonic one.

"Where marriage is concerned," Violet said, burrowing closer to Simon. "My cousin insists love not be a part of the equation. And I understand his reasoning. But I think that perhaps there must be some sort of affection between husband and wife. Did your parents love one another?"

Simon swallowed hard. She was asking questions about his family—about love.

"They did." It had been an arranged marriage, but his mother and father had grown to love one another.

"It is more common for the middle class, is it not? For marriages to be entered into for affection rather than convenience?"

"Yes."

"But you never married," she sighed.

"You didn't marry either. Did you love him?" Simon turned so he could face her.

She was quiet, and he almost began to think she wasn't

going to answer. "I'm not sure. I thought I did, but it was so long ago."

"It's possible he could return." Simon refused to keep more from her than he needed to. "The witness is... credible."

"Just as I'm not going to worry about Lady Isabella and Greystone, I'm not going to worry about Captain Thompson." She swirled her finger over his chest, his nipples tightening at her touch. "I'd rather we spend our time... discussing more pleasant topics."

"Such as?" Simon inhaled the scent of her hair.

"Did you always want to go into service, then?"

"It just sort of... fell into my lap." But his voice caught.

Because her hand was trailing an exploratory line across his chest and then...

Lower.

"It fell here?" she teased.

This sort of intimacy with a gently-raised young lady was more than enough to demand that he marry her. But the two of them had agreed upon an affair.

"Violet," his voice came out sounding strangled.

"Here?" She was stroking him over his trousers.

Simon loved that she was feeling more confident.

"Mmm..." He didn't answer but instead captured her mouth with his, his cock throbbing and hard.

They had hours. With Greystone preoccupied in his observatory, Simon could take his time with her.

But when he went to slide his arm out of the sling, she stopped him.

"Lie back." She rose onto her haunches and her braid draped over her shoulder. And then, she licked her lips.

A slow, wicked smile stretched across his mouth when his

debauched mind summoned the the image of her straddling his face. "What do you intend, my sweet Violet?"

"You have been working very hard lately, my dear Mr. Cockfield. So tonight, I am ordering you to lay back and do nothing. It's my turn to take care of you."

He raised his brows—a little curious, a little excited, but also a little concerned.

"Trust me." She leaned over him, trailing kisses from one shoulder to the other. When she'd accomplished that, she dragged her mouth down his immobilized arm to his wrist.

Simon inhaled sharply, loving the feel of her tongue sliding over his hand—his palm.

"Tracing my love line?"

"You are a man of great passion." She took one finger inside her mouth—which felt soft and velvety just like—

Wet suction pulled his finger inside farther, causing Simon to lose his train of thought.

Too much time had passed since he'd known a woman's touch. Her hands were at his trousers now, brushing his length—rubbing along the straining fabric.

Violet.

He slumped into the pillow, allowing her free rein. He'd stop her before she went too far. Or perhaps she'd grow shy and stop herself.

But for now, he allowed her to unfasten his falls, his heart racing. Simon reached down to assist her and then closed his eyes, anticipating her touch.

Wet heat had him nearly shooting off the bed.

"Violet, you mustn't." He choked.

She pushed him back into the pillow. "Why not?"

Overwhelmed and stunned in the best way possible,

Simon required a moment to summon a convincing answer—for himself, as well as for her.

Why not, she'd asked.

Why not?

"Because this isn't something a lady does. When a woman has her mouth on him like that, he thinks of her…"

"How does he think of her?" Her features were soft and feminine in the light of the single taper. And her lips… Her lips were plump and glistening.

When he didn't answer, she added, "What are you thinking now?"

"I'm not thinking much of anything at all, to be quite honest. All the blood seems to have left my brain."

"Simon, you've given me… enormous pleasure and received little in return. I want to do this. I want to… know you."

"But you're wrong. I've loved everything we've done. I fall asleep dreaming of your taste."

Her eyes widened and then she lowered her lashes. "I want to fall asleep dreaming of yours."

She wanted him in her mouth? "You might not like it, he warned."

"I'll stop if that's the case." She looked so very earnest.

"Pinch my leg," he said. "When you want me to stop. And pinch hard otherwise I may not notice.

She licked her lips. "Very well, then." She pressed her hand against his chest. "Hush now, then, and lay back and let me love you."

VIOLET TOUCHED her tongue to the velvety soft skin. This was something she had been thinking about ever since he'd pleasured her in the Duke of Blackheart's bedchamber.

And the idea had grown.

The day before, she'd located an illustrated book in Greystone's library—on the very top shelf located in a difficult spot near the hearth. Having caught her cousin hastily returning it to that spot when she'd been in London as a debutante, she'd ignored its existence all this time but suspected it might be helpful for when the time came to speak with Posy.

So she'd recently sought it out and gone through it quite thoroughly—in the spirit of education.

One of the drawings had portrayed a woman being pleasured orally by a man. Looking at it had made her heart race... Because the actual act had been nothing less than spectacular.

There had also been a drawing of a man being pleasured this way. He'd had his hand on the woman's hair and more than half his cock disappeared into the woman's mouth.

She once would have considered such an act demeaning —vulgar.

But it had only sent her heart racing more quickly. And she'd wondered...

With that image in mind, Violet took the entire head of his cock into her mouth. Simon tensed beneath her, and she took more of him.

He groaned. "You really don't have to."

He'd told her to pinch his leg if she wanted him to stop. It was an odd sort of direction. Surely, she could simply stop.

She rolled her tongue around his girth, which was a

considerable feat. Not only was he tall and broad-shouldered, but her precious butler was well-endowed otherwise.

She explored his length, cupping his bollocks, growing bolder with her mouth.

Simon had grown quiet, his muscles tensed.

She turned her head, releasing him with a soft *plopping* sound. "Don't you like it?"

In fact, he appeared rather pained. He stared down at her with hooded eyes. "I like it too much."

"What are you thinking, then?"

"That I cannot allow myself to get carried away. I don't want to make you uncomfortable."

"What would you be thinking if you weren't worried about that?"

His jaw ticked. "Words not fit for a lady's ears."

This dear man's honor knew no bounds. She'd have to breach them if her endeavor was going to be successful.

"Stop thinking of me as a lady and tell me."

His pupils grew, and he stared down at her with eyes as black as the sea at night.

"Tell me," she insisted.

His throat moved. He exhaled. And then he said, "I want to fuck your mouth."

His words, she believed, had quite the opposite effect than he'd intended. Because rather than frighten her or dissuade her in any way, heated longing pooled between her legs.

She lifted her knee and straddled one of his thighs. "Very well. You have my permission to do just that."

This time, when she opened her mouth to take him in, his hand landed on her head.

His muscles remained tense, but she no longer felt as though he was a reluctant participant. He'd taken hold of her braid, wound it around his hand, and used it to guide her.

Gentle at first, and then with greater purpose, he helped her move on him. And he was talking to her, telling her what he liked, instructing her.

Violet rolled her hips over his thigh between her legs, her own desire growing with his.

Simon's motions increased in vigor, striking her with a bite of fear. Rather than cool her ardor, however, that tension, the possibility of something unknown, only heightened her own excitement. He was large and insistent, his hand working her up and down his shaft, slick from her mouth but also beads of his seed. He tasted salty. She inhaled through her nostrils, taking him deeper and grinding down on him.

Carnality rolled through her like white lightning. *"Fuck your mouth,"* he'd said.

The words rang in her ears until she heard her own voice chanting the words in her mind.

Fuck my mouth.

Fuck my mouth.

He felt harder, hotter, and the pulsing more insistent.

"Violet." It seemed he was pushing her off him, but she instinctively knew his release was near. Focusing on the breaths through her nostrils, she took him one last time, deeper, and then he was throbbing and pulsing at the back of her throat.

He pushed his hand between her leg, and not a second later, as though being tossed by a violent wave, she found her own release.

Spiraling, her nerves took in every sensation—his scent, the springy texture of his hair, the sounds of his satisfaction, and the taste of his seed.

And when it was over, she collapsed into a boneless heap. Tonight, she wouldn't have to dream of his taste in her mouth. Because he was right here, in her bed.

A HAPPY ANNOUNCEMENT

*T*ypically, Simon wasn't the sort of person to be disturbed by everyday annoyances, but whether it was the fact that he was both figuratively and literally working with one hand tied behind his back or the nature of pressing issues themselves, the last few days had set him on edge.

The doctor was insisting he wear the sling another week, Greystone had gotten himself into a tangle between Lady Isabella and Miss Diana Jones, Posy was becoming increasingly impossible to rein in. Furthermore, Violet's former fiancé was, indeed, reportedly alive and on a ship sailing for England.

The only times he wasn't bothered by any of it were the moments he was able to spend with Violet. She made him happy. He wanted more of those.

He *needed* more of those.

The one night he'd spent with her in his chambers—the night she'd pleasured him—Simon had nearly been caught exiting her room. When he'd told Violet about it later that day, she'd been horrified. For herself, but mostly for him. If he were to be sacked by Greystone, she'd pointed out, he'd have no way to provide for himself and his sisters. And she'd told him that she couldn't allow that to happen.

And so, for now anyhow, her chamber was off-limits.

Meeting in secret was necessary, and both had agreed to it. But the constraints of doing so were wearing thin.

Because the more he cared about her, the worse he felt about lying.

Simon tapped the end of his quill on the wooden surface.

He was going to have to tell her about Thompson tonight. If he didn't, she might hear it in public, and she deserved better than that. He only wished he didn't have to waste precious moments alone with her discussing her former fiancé. He much preferred making her smile.

Thompson's return wasn't fair to her—the events of the past had been cruel enough; she shouldn't have to face them all over again.

Only this time, she wasn't going to have to face them alone.

The bet was beginning to seem less important with each passing day, and his resolve to carry it through till the end was slipping.

Was it worth it?

He glanced at his timepiece—nearly half-past five. Greystone had gone off hours ago on some urgent errand, but Violet, Posy, and their aunt ought to be returning from Lady Merkle's garden party soon.

And right on time, the sounds of a carriage outside filtered into his small office. Simon shoved the file into his desk, ran a hand through his hair, and then took his place at the door.

What had been something of a novelty, in the beginning, was becoming rather tedious.

One of the first things he was going to do when this was all over, he decided, was give all his servants raises.

Excited chatter grew louder from outside the door just as Simon pushed it open.

Violet must have been watching for him and when he caught her gaze, she flashed a smile that damn near made him forget everything.

In fact, all of them were unusually jovial—even Greystone —who, with Miss Diana Jones on his arm, looked to be over the moon.

While Posy squealed with delight and their elderly aunt touched a hand to her forehead, Violet laughed. "Isn't it wonderful, Mr. Cockfield? My cousin and Miss Jones are engaged!"

"It is." Simon grinned back at her and then dipped his chin in agreement. Greys, it seemed, had finally listened to his heart.

Simon extended a hand to one of his most valued friends. "My congratulations." Later, no doubt, Westerley, Spencer, Chaswick, and himself would taunt Greystone for such a hasty engagement—in the most benevolent fashion, of course.

Because not one of those gentlemen stood on solid ground as far as unanticipated engagements were concerned.

"I am a lucky man, indeed." Greys shook his hand with an abundance of enthusiasm. He met and held Simon's stare meaningfully, and Simon nodded. "Would you send a missive off to Byrd House? Invite the baron and baroness to dinner?"

"Chaswick knows, then?"

"I have his heartfelt blessing." Greys shook his head. "Never realized what a know-it-all he could be, though."

This was why his friend had been distracted as of late.

"I'll send a message right over. Anything else?"

"Tell Cook to spare no expense. And bring up a few bottles of *Clicquot*—the 1814. Nothing but the best to toast my future bride." Greys stared down at the woman at his side, looking utterly besotted, and then glanced back up at Simon. "And a scotch, as well."

The scotch, of course, was for later—after the ladies retired.

And as the excited group stood in the foyer discussing all sorts of arrangements, Simon conceded he'd have to deliver less-happy news to Violet another time. But, for now, Simon was going to have to tell the kitchen there was a slight change in plans for this evening's meal, and he apparently also had missives to send out.

VIOLET LAY in bed later that night following a very happy evening of celebration. But as thrilled as she was for Greys and Diana, she couldn't help but wish that Simon would come. She knew he could not. He'd nearly been caught before, and she'd convinced him they needed to exercise greater caution.

But too many nights had passed since they'd last been together, and as she lay there alone, she ached for him.

Yes, *she ached*.

In ways that she had never ached for another human being.

Physical, sleep-depriving desire, but that wasn't all. Her heart ached for the moments when she could simply look at him—watch his smile, listen to his voice. But having spent the evening watching Greystone with Diana, touching her elbow, holding her stare, and not caring who witnessed it, Violet wished for more. Greystone's love for Diana was real. Neither ever need deny it.

She could never know those displays of affection from Simon, and thinking like that would only rob her of the magic she could have with him now.

He'd wanted to come to her chamber again, but she'd been afraid for him. But laying here alone, her resolve weakened. They would simply have to be careful.

It wasn't as though they had time to waste.

Violet climbed out of bed and wedged her feet into a pair of slippers. She would go to him. And if anyone caught her entering or leaving his small chamber, she would simply tell them that she needed… tapers.

With a plan in mind, Violet donned a modest dressing gown, slipped out of her chamber, and made her way downstairs.

She wasn't surprised to hear masculine laughter and general merriment floating out of Greystone's study. As the door was partially open, she crept over to take a peek. If they'd opened the scotch as she suspected, she didn't doubt they'd already be deep in their cups. And so long as that was the case, they wouldn't be requiring the butler for anything.

But when she glanced inside, her anticipation faltered and then vanished.

Several of Greystone's school chums were indeed celebrating, but there was one person she hadn't expected.

Simon.

Cigar hanging out of the side of his mouth and a tumbler of scotch in one hand, he lounged in one of the larger chairs near the hearth. He looked perfectly at ease amongst the room full of lords. Violet froze, perplexed but also disappointed for herself. However, she wasn't angry, and oughtn't be surprised, really.

She stared at him from her hidden vantage point, slightly in awe that she, Violet Faraday, had been singled out by such a man.

Besides the fact that he was more handsome than anyone she'd ever known, with his mesmerizing eyes, silky hair, strong features, and mouth-watering physique, he was so much more: charming, funny, loyal, and determined to protect those around him. The list went on and on.

What would it be like, she wondered, if he was one of them? If he truly could exist in her world?

She shook her head to dispel such wishful thinking. And then sighed, terribly disappointed to have to abandon her plans to seduce him tonight.

Terribly, terribly, disappointed.

She returned to her chamber and, as she'd insisted two days ago, Simon did not steal into her chamber later that night. Or the next night. And it wasn't at all fair to blame him for her frustration.

Because the entire household had gone to work arranging a grand engagement ball for the happy couple. Simon was busy with the additional staff, and Violet had been enlisted by Bethany to assist in sending out wedding invitations and then later, coordinating the production of fashionable table pieces for the up-and-coming engagement ball. And in addition to those projects, the Season went on with festivities and balls to attend daily.

The wedding date loomed less than four weeks away, and with surprising enthusiasm from most of the *ton*, both the engagement ball and the wedding promised to be pinnacles of this year's Season.

Miss Diana, whom Violet had liked very much even before she'd become betrothed to Greystone, was turning out to be one of the most delightful persons she'd ever known. She was a little bit like Posy, free-spirited, but she was also well-grounded. And despite having been born into highly questionable circumstances, Violet believed the young woman was going to make for an excellent marchioness.

Even Aunt Iris had come around to liking her.

It wasn't until the morning of the engagement ball when Violet took tea and went over her checklist in the morning room, that Simon found her alone.

Greystone had risen early and gone riding with Lord Chaswick, and her aunt and Posy were having a lie-in because the evening promised to be a late one.

Meeting her eyes, a light in his, Simon closed the door behind him.

"Hello, I'm Simon Cockfield. Have we met?"

The sunlight slanting through the room seemed a little brighter.

Violet resisted the urge to dash across the room and throw herself into his arms.

Because in marking the time to the wedding, she was also marking time until she was going to have to return to the country with Aunt Iris.

From the very beginning, the two of them had known this affair was temporary. If they were going to take it any further than they already had, the two of them were going to have to take a few risks.

And so, although she didn't run to him, she did walk purposefully into his arms. And after relishing in his kiss, savoring every second of it, Violet tipped her head back and answered, "I'm not sure if we have, Mr. Cockfield. You may need to refresh my memory."

He did, leaving both of them breathless and wanting… more. But, unfortunately, one of Greystone's footmen could enter at any moment.

"Can you join me for a cup?" Violet stepped back, clasping the back of a chair in case her knees, now the consistency of pudding, gave out on her completely.

"Come sit down," he took her elbow and led her back to her chair. "I've been wanting a word with you."

"That sounds ominous." She attempted to sound breezy but couldn't prevent the wobble in her voice. His demeanor was that of a man about to say something she didn't want to hear.

Was he going to end their affair already? He must fear losing his job if they were found out. Or he hadn't found their time together as satisfying as she had.

In other words, she wasn't worth the trouble.

She dropped into her chair, and he took the seat beside her.

"It is somewhat troubling, but I wanted you to hear it from me."

Her breath caught. "It's all right. I quite understand."

"You know?"

The door flew open again. "There you are, Violet." She jerked her hand out of Simon's as her cousin entered. "Cockfield."

Greystone's gaze narrowed as he glanced between the two of them, but rather than attempt to provide an explanation, Violet scowled at being interrupted.

If he was allowed to drink scotch whisky with the butler, then she darn well could take tea with him.

"Going over details for this evening?" he asked.

"As a matter of fact, no. But how was your ride this morning?" she asked.

"Brisk. Invigorating." Greystone didn't move to sit. "But I've heard something… disturbing, and I needed a word with you."

Violet stiffened. Had Greystone discovered what had been going on between the two of them beneath his very own roof?

"You are aware that the Duke of Coventry has made inquiries after Captain Thompson?"

The question took her by surprise, although Simon made no move to leave but remained seated beside her. She did not push his hand away when it clasped hers beneath the table.

Greystone was quite unaware.

"What I'm about to tell you, Violet," her cousin continued softly, "is going to come as quite a shock."

"Please, just tell me." She felt almost dizzy. How long had she been holding her breath?

"I ran into Coventry while riding this morning."

Violet just stared at him. "The duke? Is he…? Is he well?"

Greys nodded. "Old as time but looking fit as a fiddle, but that is not the point. The point is that Captain Thompson has been located."

"His… body?"

Simon squeezed her hand.

"No. The man. And he is very much alive. At least according to the investigator's reports."

"But that is not possible." Violet shook her head, grateful for the strength of Simon's hand in hers.

"But… How?" Cold swept through her limbs. "Where?"

"Details are unclear for now. But the duke's story is that his nephew was taken prisoner and then suffered an injury to his head. When Thompson saw an image of his likeness in one of the papers, an ad Coventry's solicitors were running, he replied, and he is already aboard a ship bound for England. The packet is scheduled to arrive any day."

"So he didn't defect? He was captured?"

Greys didn't answer right away.

"That is the official account." It was Simon who answered. "His timing is rather convenient."

Could it be him? The image of the man she'd once agreed to marry flashed in her mind—medium build, blond hair, laughing eyes, and an easy smile.

She'd thought she'd forgotten.

"He is coming home," Violet murmured. "He lost his memory?"

Not that she loved him, and not that it ought to have mattered, but she couldn't help but experience a small amount of relief to believe he hadn't intentionally abandoned her.

She turned to Simon with a shaky smile. "He is not an imposter?"

A shadow crossed his face. "No one will know that for sure until he can show himself. But, if the story is true, if he was held captive, he'll be a very different man than the man you knew before."

Violet nodded.

Simon removed his timepiece from his pocket and frowned. "I've some deliveries to inspect. If you'll excuse me, I'll leave the two of you to discuss this alone." As he rose, Violet only barely kept herself from begging him to stay.

Greys addressed him instead. "My thanks, Cockfield. I've

some new cheroots—Chaswick sent them over. Join me later in my study, won't you?"

Violet would have rolled her eyes if she wasn't so shocked at the startling news about Christopher. By now it had become obvious to her that Simon was as much friend as he was butler to her maddening cousin.

She stared at the door after Simon disappeared, feeling far more bereft than was good for her. Had he been going to break things off? He had known that Christopher had been found.

Was that what he'd needed to discuss with her?

She hoped so. Oh dear, she most certainly hoped so. She wasn't ready to let him go yet.

Not even close.

"Violet?" Greystone's voice captured her attention. "You must be terribly distraught over all this. What can I do to help you?"

She forced a smile in her cousin's direction. "I don't suppose anyone can do much of anything until we know this man isn't some imposter. There's a great deal at stake, after all. I'm surprised no one's come forward before this."

And with her words, she very nearly convinced herself that the man sailing toward England could not be Christopher.

"True," Greystone agreed. "I should have realized you would handle the news rationally."

"And besides, we have an engagement ball to prepare for." This time, her smile felt more natural. "I don't want anything to take away from your special night. Especially not this. I do like Diana so very much, and I couldn't be happier for the both of you. You know this, don't you?"

"I do. I only wish the same for you." Greystone smiled.

Violet didn't protest as she usually did. But neither did she agree.

"Lord Huntly is not at all happy with me, but—" Her cousin met her stare and shrugged, unable to hide his contentment.

"Was Lady Isabella disappointed?" Violet felt sorry for the girl and had been thinking about her.

"Her heart wasn't broken," he answered, looking serious. "And although I wouldn't change things for the world, I was sorry to have gotten her hopes up."

"She'll find someone else," Violet assured him. "What matters most is that you are happy." That made Violet happy.

Despite the stinging in her chest. What would it be like to love someone like that, knowing they loved you as well?

"Disgustingly so." He grinned and leaned back in his chair, looking more relaxed than he had since arriving. "Speaking of happy, how is Posy managing?"

Not a happy subject.

"I feel as though I've failed her." Greys held up a hand to contradict her opinion, but Violet continued, "Not in any of the learning she's had, but… I cannot help but wonder if I didn't unintentionally convey my own disdain for the notion of love, for marriage—from my experiences. Because, unfortunately, she's chased away the few young men who were brave enough to approach her."

"There is always another year," he said.

"But we won't worry about that today." The last thing she wanted to do was set a pall over Greys and Diana's engagement celebration. "Are you going to see Diana before the ball today?"

Greys smiled. "I'm taking her for a drive." He glanced at his timepiece. "And as she's expecting me early, I suppose I ought to wash the smell of horse off me."

"No horse would dare leave his scent on you," Violet teased, because even though he'd just gone riding, Greystone, of course, looked impeccable as usual.

"Normally, I'd agree with such an expectation," he replied. "But today, I am unwilling to test your theory."

THE BETROTHAL BALL

*V*iolet touched her fingers to her hair and took a last look in her vanity mirror. Her hair had been curled and pinned up loosely, and the gown she'd chosen for that night was an emerald silk, embellished with darker green embroidery around the bodice and forest velvet trim.

Not at all an ensemble she'd imagined for herself when she'd planned for the Season. She stilled at a realization that she had changed. She felt very different than the person who'd stepped off that carriage little more than a month ago.

And it wasn't only because of the affair, but because of what she'd learned about herself having entered it. She…liked herself more. She wasn't afraid to pursue something important to her. She didn't need to go through life hiding. And even though Simon couldn't dance with her at the ball tonight, she wasn't going to sit by the wall with the chaperones. She would mingle and she would be happy. She was going to enjoy herself.

And—if the opportunity presented itself, she was going to invite Simon to her chamber that evening.

Her heart raced at the thought that time was running out for the two of them. With each day that passed, she'd become less concerned about being discovered and more anxious about their attachment coming to an end.

A knock sounded at the door and Posy peeked inside. "I thought I'd go down with you."

"Is it time already?"

Although the engaged couple hadn't decided to forgo a formal dinner, Lord Chaswick and Bethany, along with the elder Miss Jones and Diana, were scheduled to arrive early for drinks and lighter fare. That would allow all of them plenty of time to settle in before taking their places in line to greet what promised to be a long line of guests.

"Close enough. Oh, Aunt Violet, that color is beautiful on you."

"Not too much for a spinster?"

"Not at all." Posy stepped around her to examine the gown from all angles. "And why shouldn't a spinster dress to dazzle if she is so inclined?"

At this, Violet was reminded of the concern that had been pressing into her.

She took Posy's hands. "I feel as though my own reluctance to marry has somehow put you off the idea of finding a husband." Her niece began shaking her head, but Violet persisted. "There are so many aspects to recommend it. And you will want children and a home. Not to mention companionship."

"Aunt Iris doesn't have children, and she is content. I rather respect her independence, really—and yours."

"But look at Greystone and how happy he is with Miss Diana. Don't you want the chance to know such... joy?"

Her own feelings for Simon nudged into her thoughts,

squeezing her heart at the same time. He may be the only person who could ever have brought her the unique happiness Greystone looked forward to.

Even if he was the sort of gentleman who was inclined to marry, the situation was impossible. She'd bring disgrace on the people who loved her. She would be shunned from the life she'd been born to.

Violet shook her head. She could *not* allow her thoughts to flirt with such an idea.

Foolish. Impossible.

"I think," Posy squeezed Violet's hands back, looking more serious than she had all spring, "that rather than hunt for a husband, I'd prefer to wait for that perfect person to come into my life willingly."

"But..." Violet paused. "But you are not against the idea of marrying?"

"I wouldn't be." Posy smiled. "But only to a person who loved me for myself and only if I loved that person more than anyone else in the world. And if I could marry that person, I would."

Violet nodded. So, not all hope was lost. "But to allow that person to find you, you need to give him a chance. Will you at least consider that? Allow yourself a chance to get to know a few of the gentlemen who have come forward?"

"Oh, Aunt," Posy sighed. But then there was another knock. This time it was Gwen.

"Lady Iris asked me to remind you that Lord and Lady Chaswick will be arriving any minute."

Violet nodded but felt some hope for her niece, whereas before she'd been prepared to give up. But she did so want Posy to find happiness.

"We'd best be going down now." Violet tucked Posy's hand into her arm. "We've an engagement to celebrate!"

Violet and Posy reached the doors to the formal drawing room just as Simon was exiting.

"Have they arrived yet?" Violet asked, meeting his gaze and doing her best not to show that she was buzzing inside.

"Not yet." He turned to Posy, his hand brushing Violet's— not unintentionally, because he stilled, and the backs of their hands remained touching.

"Did you accomplish your errand this afternoon…?" he asked Posy.

"I did, thank you, Mr. Cockfield," Posy answered, and Violet glanced between the two of them, wanting to inquire as to what her niece was up to—but if she did that, she might not get the opportunity again to speak privately with him this evening.

As Greystone's butler, he was going to be overseeing a good deal once guests began arriving.

"You go in, Posy." Violet stepped away from Simon and gestured toward the door. "I wish to, er, finalize a few last-minute details with Mr. Cockfield."

"You needn't worry, Aunt. I'm fairly certain he has every-thing well in hand."

"Yes, well." Violet frowned. "One can never be too certain."

"All right, then. But you aren't fooling anyone. You merely wish to be alone with our handsome butler." Violet thought her heart was going to drop into her slippers, but then Posy burst into laughter.

"Posy!"

"I'm only joking."

"Posy…" Violet stiffened. "You mustn't joke about such matters."

"I wish you a most pleasant evening, my lady." Simon bowed in her niece's direction, and, of course, Posy responded to his dismissal without question.

Violet remained silent until the drawing room door had closed behind her, leaving the two of them alone. She couldn't count on that for long, however, as servants were rushing throughout the house in preparation for the evening.

She closed the distance between them and touched her hand to his sleeve. And staring into eyes, which were becoming far too lovable, she said, "I simply wanted to—I wanted to make sure—was there some other reason you needed to speak with me this morning?"

Simon tilted his head and then, glancing around the foyer, pulled her around the corner. "Other than Captain Thompson's...?"

"Yes, I wondered if..."

"If?" he pressed, and Violet exhaled a breath she hadn't even realized she'd been holding.

A breath, it felt, that she'd been holding all day.

"So, you did not wish to... end things with... me?"

He stilled and then touched the side of her face. "No. Most definitely not. Rather the opposite. I wished to ask... Tonight. After the ball. If I come to your chamber, will you receive me?"

Would she receive him? She couldn't help but grin. Because now she wasn't going to have to summon the courage to ask him to come.

"Yes."

The blue flecks glowed in his eyes at her answer.

"Please," she added.

The door to the drawing room swung open, and Violet

jerked out of Simon's arms. Aunt Iris glanced between the two of them suspiciously. "Are you ever coming in, Violet?"

"Of course." Violet turned back to Simon. "And thank you. I'm quite sure you'll manage this evening without any troubles."

"With that vote of confidence, how could I not?"

SIMON RUBBED his chin after Violet disappeared with her aunt. Was she going to be angry when she discovered he'd made himself scarce for the evening? Because he couldn't possibly stay—not if he wished to finish out the wager. Simon was well-known amongst the guests who would be arriving shortly. He'd be recognized the first time he opened the door. Furthermore, the servants must go on knowing him only as Mr. Cockfield.

Footsteps sounded as a familiar gentleman approached. His own butler, no doubt, was going to manage the evening better than he himself would have. He'd met with the staff earlier, all of whom knew that Mr. Sterling was to be in charge in Simon's absence.

It was disappointing not to be present for the evening and somehow take part in Greystone's celebration. Simon wouldn't be able to keep watch over Violet, or be there to assist her if she needed him… for anything. He'd miss out on her laughter as she encouraged the other young ladies. She had no idea how much she lit up a room.

Although, he conceded, consoling himself slightly, it would have been frustrating not to have been able to lead her onto the floor or walk her in the garden.

She would not be without dance partners. She somehow

looked more beautiful every day, and no doubt other gentlemen of the *ton* would be noticing. So long as none of them asked her into the garden.

She was wearing one of the gowns he'd chosen for her, without a fichu tucked into the bodice, revealing a generous view of decolletage, of which Simon had grown rather fond.

"You can be reached at Heart Place, then, Your Grace?" Mr. Sterling confirmed.

"Yes, send Bugsy if you have any trouble." Simon glanced at his timepiece. He needed to leave before the guests began arriving. "But I believe everything's covered. What sort of calamity could occur at an engagement ball? Besides a dropped tray of desserts or perhaps a few flat bottles of champagne?"

*V*iolet stood in line beside the ladies and gentlemen dancing the Roger de Coverley, smiling across at her partner, Lord Burke, as they awaited their turn to go round. She'd danced far more than she'd expected, considering she'd not bothered with a dance card.

Nonetheless, her feet ached in her slippers, and she was quite looking forward to sitting down for supper.

It had been an emotional night. Greystone was going to marry and, of course, everything would change.

She had teared up only once when Greystone and Diana had taken to the floor. Never in her life had she watched two people who seemed more in tune with one another. Diana was lovely and poised, but best of all, she seemed to adore Greystone with all her heart.

Which was a very good thing. Violet could already see that the young woman was going to face more than the usual challenges as the Marchioness of Greystone. And not just amongst the *ton*, but from servants and possibly merchants. Because, as the illegitimate daughter of the late Lord

Chaswick, she was going to be viewed by many as an imposter.

A few of Greystone's servants appeared none too fond of her. Greystone would speak with them, of course, but Diana would have to gain their respect on her own.

Lord Burke grasped her arm to swing her around, and she set aside her wool-gathering.

Many guests would remain until the early morning hours, but Violet intended to make her escape shortly after the supper dance. She wished she could have a bath after, but the servants had too much to do already.

Her heart fluttered.

Simon was not ready to end things between them. He was coming to her chamber later. And by the look in his eyes, Violet guessed he was as eager to resume this affair as was she.

"This way, Miss Faraday." Her partner drew her toward him when she missed a step.

She laughed. "I don't know what's the matter with me." But she knew the precise source of her inability to concentrate. She was eagerly anticipating a night that she would never forget. It was the closest, she realized, that she would ever come to feeling like a bride.

And she was happy.

Tremendously happy.

When the dance finished, Violet moved along the wall until she found Diana's older sister, Miss Collette Jones, seated partially behind one of the potted plants that had been brought indoors for the event.

"Are you hiding?" Violet asked as she collapsed onto the empty chair beside her.

Miss Jones smiled slyly. "As my sister insisted I dance all of five sets already, I feel I've earned the right."

Violet laughed. "I quite understand. But you are enjoying yourself?"

Violet truly was curious. Neither of Chaswick's sisters had had an easy time of it. Although many socialites were willing to look beyond the girls' circumstances in deference to Chaswick's position, a number of sticklers were not.

"I've only been given the cut once this evening. And although it was satisfying when your cousin asked them to leave, I hate that there was any ugliness at all tonight."

"I'm afraid he's going to have to get used to that. At least until word spreads that such behavior will not be tolerated."

"I hope she doesn't have too difficult of a time." Miss Jones stared across the dance floor where her sister was making conversation with the Duchess of Corbridge.

"It isn't going to be easy for her," Violet conceded. "But she is a force in her own right, and with Greystone's support, she'll find her way." She met the other girl's stare. "I understand you have chosen another sort of life…"

"I have." Miss Jones smiled. "This is all fine, but it isn't… me. Chase, Lord Chaswick—he's made arrangements for me to begin teaching next autumn at Miss Primm's Private Seminary for the Education of Ladies."

"And that is what you want?"

"It is." The girl seemed quite sure of herself, giving Violet pause to stare out at the world she'd belonged to all her life.

"They can, indeed, present a formidable challenge at times," Violet acknowledged.

"Yes. But it is more than that, I think. No one is who they seem. Present company excepted." She touched Violet's arm.

"But growing up in Mayfair, I remember watching all the lords and ladies driving in their fancy chariots." Miss Jones smiled. "Believing that their lives were perfect. It made me feel as though I must be flawed. But I've since realized that there is no such thing as a perfect life. I would rather focus my energies on teaching, improving the lives of students, and also my own, rather than pretending to be something I'm not. If that makes any sense at all." She laughed and then reached into the folds of her gown before offering a small tin. "Would you care for a comfit?"

Violet accepted and popped one of the mints into her mouth. "Thank you." But she was mulling over Miss Jones's words.

With Simon, Violet never felt the need to be anyone but herself. She'd told him things she'd never told anyone—and he'd never once balked.

She'd felt no need to impress him, and she'd never feared that he would betray her confidences. That sort of freedom was new to her.

And thinking about him sent her gaze searching the ballroom for the man who stood out to her more than any other.

She hadn't seen him since before the guests had arrived. For him to have neglected his duties upstairs, the kitchen must be experiencing some sort of difficulties that required his presence.

If he didn't appear when supper was served, she'd have to go down to check with the cook herself.

But then her concerns jumped to her more immediate responsibilities. Although Aunt Iris had promised to keep a close eye on Posy, Violet barely caught sight of her niece exiting onto the terrace alone, looking quite purposeful.

The back of Violet's neck tingled.

She'd encouraged Posy to be friendlier to any suitors, but

she'd not intended that she have an assignation with one of them.

"Would you mind terribly, excusing me for a moment?" Violet rose, anxious that she catch up to Posy.

"Of course not." Miss Jones stood as well. "But I hope I haven't offended you."

Violet shook her head. "Not at all. Because you are correct. It can be exhausting. But putting on a brave face for the world is very English, is it not? And quite appropriate most of the time." Violet smoothed her skirts, restless to take her leave but also wanting to make a point. "So long as we have people in our lives with whom it's not necessary to pretend, I think we can strike a favorable balance. I think your sister and my cousin have found that together."

"I hope so, Miss Faraday." Miss Jones sounded a little forlorn, and Violet realized that with her sister's marriage, this young woman faced significant changes as well.

"Don't abandon the idea of marrying altogether, Miss Jones," Violet said. "Just remember, even the loftiest duke puts his pants on one leg at a time."

"But with the help of a valet," Miss Jones pointed out.

"I suppose there is that." Violet laughed.

And on that note, she smiled and left the young woman to her place in the shadows. Then, after glancing around one last time in hopes of finding Simon, Violet ventured toward the terrace to locate Posy.

Outside, Violet's eyes required a moment to adjust to the darkness despite the orange glow of a few lanterns. The air was warmer than it had been the night she'd gone walking with Simon, and that memory gave Violet an idea as to where to check first.

It was possible she was wrong in thinking Posy would do

anything scandalous, especially after she'd shown so little interest in any of the gentlemen she'd met all spring.

But Violet had seen a certain look on Posy's face when she'd stepped through the door. One that had felt oddly familiar.

Familiar, because she'd felt that sort of anticipation every time she thought of Simon's promised visit later that night.

Or… Violet laughed to herself. Perhaps she was simply imposing her own feelings on others around her.

She slowed her steps as she neared the gardener's hut, relieved.

She was relieved because, although she heard giggles inside the small building, they were girlish ones. Posy, Violet surmised, had taken Miss Jones's idea to hide one step further.

Violet twisted her mouth into an admonishing expression. The supper dance wasn't far off, and she knew for a fact that her niece had promised it to a very eager and brave Lord Shortwood.

Violet grasped the handle of the door and pulled it open.

And nearly stumbled backward. Was her mind playing tricks on her?

She shook her head and blinked, and when Posy glanced over, catching her eyes, Violet grasped the doorframe for support.

Because Posy had not been hiding away from the festivities.

She was in a passionate embrace.

With a… woman.

BREATHE

"*A*unt Violet." Posy did not push the other lady away—a lady Violet vaguely recognized but couldn't quite place. "I was going to tell you."

Violet inhaled a deep breath and let it out silently. And the awareness struck her that this moment, perhaps, was to be her most difficult test of all. As an aunt—but also as the person Posy depended on for support, advice, and to love her unconditionally.

A myriad of memories she'd dismissed as insignificant suddenly fell into place. Memories of little things that Violet had chalked up to nothing more than… quirkiness.

Violet wasn't angry; she was *not* angry. And although this was something she'd heard of but never quite understood, she was not disgusted.

How could she be disgusted? *This is Posy.*

Violet tore her gaze from Posy's tortured look to the blonde girl standing beside her. "Do I know you?"

The young woman dropped her lashes. "Yes, Miss Faraday.

I'm Susan Mallard. My parents own the mercantile back home."

"But of course," Violet answered through lips that felt numb. And then she glanced back at Posy, who was staring at Miss Mallard looking concerned and, but also caring... and completely besotted.

Violet didn't want Posy to feel her panic, so she kept her voice level. "Do Mr. and Mrs. Mallard know you are here?"

"They do. Not that I'm here tonight. My older brother and his wife live just off Oxford Street. He is a solicitor, and his wife gave birth to twin boys recently. My parents allowed me to come to London this spring to assist her with them."

Violet nodded slowly. All of Posy's secretiveness was taking on new meaning.

"Is your family aware of... the two of you?"

"No, Miss Faraday, and I can never tell them." At her admission, Miss Mallard looked quite hopeless.

"But we love one another." Posy lifted her chin. "Mr. Cockfield has been urging me to tell you. He promised you would understand. But I couldn't find the nerve. I've been terrified that you would be disgusted and hate me and I... I hate to be such a disappointment. I love you, Aunt Violet, but—"

"Mr. Cockfield knows?" But of course, Simon knew. And it irritated her to no end that he hadn't thought to share any of this with her. But he'd been urging Posy to tell her.

He'd told Posy that she would understand.

"Yes, he's... helped me." Of course he had. Posy went on to defend him. "But please, don't be angry with him. And I beg of you not to tell Greystone. I imagine he'll find out eventually, but I don't wish to take anything away from his wedding."

Violet scrubbed a hand down her face. Posy was her niece,

for heaven's sake! This dear, sweet, firebrand of a girl was a daughter to her!

"I won't say a word. Oh, Posy, I could never hate you. You are not a disappointment—never a disappointment. You are... absolutely perfect, just as you are." *She is Posy!* And the only disappointment Violet had was in herself. She'd been so busy planning Posy's life that she hadn't truly listened to her. And she was also scared and a little sad. Because such a love changed everything. Posy and Miss Mallard could never marry, or have children, or...

They would have to hide their love.

But Posy could have love. And that was more than Violet hoped for herself. Because at the end of the Season, Violet was going to return to Blossom Court with Aunt Iris, and Simon would remain in London, butlering and all the other things he did that she didn't really understand.

Orchestra music floated from the house, across the lawn, reminding her that privacy was not completely assured.

They did not have time for a lengthy discussion. When Violet had come outside, she'd noticed other couples lingering in the garden. Any of them could get the idea to seek out the privacy of the small hut at any moment.

But before going inside, she needed to make herself clear.

"I am not disgusted. I will always love you, Posy, no matter who you love." She blinked back unexpected tears and then shook her head. "But for now, I think it's best we return to the house. We will talk tomorrow?"

"I did promise Lord Shortwood the supper dance." Posy grimaced, making Violet chuckle.

And, ironically enough, the two young women could return to the ballroom together. So there was nothing untoward about two ladies walking in the garden with one another. And because ladies partnered other ladies all the time, the girls could even dance together if they wished to.

"I'll follow shortly," Violet said. Because despite her acceptance of this, she needed a moment to compose herself, nonetheless. She was not disgusted or disappointed in Posy, but there was a part of her that was… devastated.

Posy stepped forward and into Violet's arms. "Thank you, Aunt Violet. Thank you for not hating me." Posy's voice broke.

Dear God, how long had Posy known this about herself? How long had she been hiding this secret? Violet couldn't even begin to imagine the torment Posy had felt, or she might fall apart completely. "I could never hate you," she said again, her voice thick.

Posy didn't release her right away, and so Violet squeezed her dear, sweet girl even tighter.

"I could never hate you," she repeated. Posy would face many challenges in her life, which made it even more important that Violet not add to them.

"I'm sorry, Miss Faraday," Miss Mallard said, sounding more than a little tentative. "But thank you…"

Violet shook her head. "It's fine. And… You needn't be sorry." She would do what she could to support them both. They were certainly going to need it. "We'll all talk another time."

Once the door closed behind the two girls, Violet closed her eyes, trapping sobs in her chest. This wasn't the end of the world.

And Simon knew. Violet could share her concerns with him.

But for now, she needed to return to the ball. She needed to put on that brave face she'd told Miss Jones about and pretend her heart wasn't aching.

Only aching, not broken.

With a brush of her skirts, Violet touched her hand to her hair and stepped outside. The moon still hung in the sky, the stars still twinkled, and the fragrance from the flowers was sweet and refreshing.

Posy was in love, and the object of her love seemed to love her back.

It would not be unexceptional for Posy and her friend to live together as spinsters. Ladies traveled together. They helped one another dress. Why, it was likely far easier for two ladies to have an affair than it was for a single woman to dally with…

A butler.

Violet exhaled. She needed to find Simon. He would send her one of his looks, maybe even offer a reassuring word, and she'd be fortified to endure the remainder of the evening.

Because it was a celebration!

But just as her calm returned, when she turned the corner that led back to the terrace doors, for the second time that night, she was shaken to the core.

"Violet." His voice was unmistakable.

And at this shock, for the first time in her life, Violet fainted.

Violet was asleep. But she was not sleeping. Because if that was the case, then the cool damp of the ground wouldn't be seeping through her gown.

She opened her eyes to see Miss Collette Jones's face hovering over her.

"Miss Faraday?"

Violet glanced to one side and then to the other, and then

pushed herself up. "Was there a man here? How long have I been laying here?"

Miss Jones pressed a hand to Violet's shoulder, stilling her. "Barely a minute. I knew you'd come outside, and seeing as they were beginning to serve supper, I came to find you. I'm so glad I did."

"Did you see a man? A gentleman?"

"Yes, as a matter of fact, but when I arrived, he insisted on leaving. He said you would prefer that a lady assist you."

Violet blinked. He had looked so very much like Christopher—only not. But he could not have been a ghost.

Perhaps he was simply one of the guests—a gentleman who'd come outside for a smoke. But when Violet closed her eyes, his image appeared behind her lids.

His hair was different then she'd remembered, and she hadn't seen his face properly, but there had been something familiar in the way he'd reached for her, and his voice had been unmistakable.

Violet lifted her hand to her mouth. Was it possible she'd conjured him out of her imagination?

"Miss Faraday, you're white as a ghost. Should I send for your cousin, or your maid?"

But this was Greystone's betrothal ball. Violet wouldn't ruin it for him and Diana. "No. No, I'll be fine. Please don't mention this to anyone. I…I haven't eaten today. Silly of me, really."

Violet gathered her gown clear of her feet and then rose on shaky legs. Greystone would know something was amiss if she wasn't inside when supper was served. And Posy might think Violet was upset over what she'd learned, which she was, but she didn't want Posy to worry.

"Is my hair mussed?"

Miss Jones fussed with it a moment. "A few loose strands, but it's rather lovely, actually."

Violet nodded. "You won't tell anyone…?"

"Of course not. It's no wonder ladies aren't dropping constantly. If I had my druthers, all corsets would be cast into Hades. Pardon my frankness, Miss Faraday."

"Not at all, and please, call me Violet."

"And I am Collette." Violet swayed, and the young woman reached out to steady her. "You are certain you are well?"

"I'll be fine." Violet inhaled what she hoped would be a fortifying breath. *I'm perfectly fine.*

No matter that the ghost of her long-dead fiancé had appeared to her out of the darkness.

"I'm fine." But her lips felt numb, and she didn't quite feel the ground beneath her feet.

Collette grasped Violet's arm, and Violet leaned on the other woman more than she'd have liked. After they reached the doors, however, Violet stepped away and smoothed her skirts. "I'm going to take a moment…"

"Of course, and you know where to find me if you need anything at all." Collette grimaced.

"Behind the plant?"

"Shh… And not until after I've eaten." Collette grinned. "Don't tell my brother or Bethany."

Violet smiled weakly, thanked her again, and then excused herself. She wouldn't bother Greystone or Posy or even Lady Bethany. There was only one person she wanted to see. She simply needed to find him.

Upon entering the supper room and not seeing Simon there, Violet approached the servants' entrance just as one of the kitchen maids appeared.

"Excuse me." Violet stopped her. "Do you know where I might find Mr. Cockfield?"

The harried-looking young woman shook her head. "He isn't here tonight. Mr. Sterling is filling in for Mr. Cockfield this evening. I believe he's assisting the footmen with the champagne downstairs."

"Mr. Sterling? The Duke of Blackheart's butler?"

"Is he? I didn't realize." The maid flicked her gaze to the tray in her hands, laden with carefully arranged meats and cheeses. "Can I help you with anything else?"

"Oh, no. I'm sorry. Thank you." But in the wake of the maid's hasty rush to get on with her duties, Violet stood frozen in the center of the empty ballroom, confused, but also worried.

He isn't here?

Where would Simon go on the evening of Greystone's engagement ball?

Something must have happened to one of his sisters, or his brother. That would be the only reason he'd not perform his duties on such an important evening.

Because he hadn't mentioned anything to her earlier. Did that mean he wasn't going to come to her chamber later?

And then her heart stopped. What if he'd taken ill? Or he'd been in some sort of accident?

The maid came rushing back through, a stack of empty trays on her arms. And this time, she approached Violet without being asked. "Are you unwell, Miss Faraday? You're as pale as a ghost."

A ghost.

Violet licked her lips. "No, I'm fine. Er. Did Mr. Cockfield say why he was leaving?"

"Just that he had pressing matters. He promised to return once it was all over. I thought you would know."

Violet straightened her shoulders. So he was safe at least, and apparently well. "Of course, he—I—Lord Greystone failed to mention it to me. I suppose."

She then dipped her chin in thanks, and with a deep breath strode into the supper room where she joined her brother and Diana just in time for the toast.

And somehow, she made it through the remainder of the evening without giving any indication of what she was feeling.

She was English, after all. And that's what the English did.

DOUBTING

*V*iolet closed the door of her chamber behind her and glanced at the clock on the mantle.

It was nearly half-past three in the morning. Once supper had finished, Violet had danced, made small talk, and even managed to laugh a few times. There had even been brief instances when she had forgotten everything that happened in the garden.

She would have thought that once alone again in the privacy of her chamber, she would shatter into a thousand pieces. But she did not. All she felt was… nothing. She was, in fact, numb, perfectly, soothingly, numb.

Violet had realized that feigning enjoyment was a particular skill of hers. She did it so well, in fact, that she could almost fool herself.

Incredible that she could make herself believe something simply because she wanted it to be true.

With Posy, Christopher's death…

And Simon?

A knock sounded and Violet's heart, which had leapt, just

as quickly fell when it was Gwen who appeared. "Let's get you out of this gown."

Violet nodded. Only a few hours ago, she'd donned this beautiful dress, excited and filled with anticipation for the evening—for Greystone and Diana but also at the prospect of Simon seeing her in it.

And she'd had romantic thoughts that later, it would be Simon who helped her out of it.

Gwen loosened the fastenings, helped Violet step out of it, and then draped the gown over the tall back of a chair. As the maid bustled about, Violet stood unmoving and stared at the dress, thinking the material looked tired and sad. She had chosen it to impress Simon, and he would not have even seen it had she not caught him in the foyer.

The vibrant fabric mocked her disillusionment—her disillusionment with Simon, but also herself—for being so dreadfully naïve about…

Everything. She'd been a fool to go searching for him—thinking he would be…there—thinking he would be watching over her. Thinking he would have wanted to be near her.

On one of the most important events of Greystone's life, Simon, who was not only her cousin's butler but some sort of friend as well, had simply… disappeared.

Holding up her arms for Gwen to drop the night rail over her head, Violet shivered. Something dreadful must have happened for him to abandon the ball as he had.

But how had he convinced Mr. Sterling to fill in for him? And why would a duke's butler agree to do it?

What power did Simon have over the man?

She hated that she doubted him. There must be a reasonable explanation. There had to be.

Violet lowered herself onto the stool at her vanity and

stared into the glass. The maid drew the brush through Violet's hair while her own hands shook in her lap.

The hour had grown very late. Was he still going to come?

She'd entered this affair impulsively—because for the first time since Christopher's death, she'd met someone who had been worth the risk of sharing herself. But it was only an affair.

She'd made a mistake by building it into something more.

He wasn't coming, surely. Not after having been called away for some mysterious emergency.

Gwen touched her shoulder. "You're freezing. Shall I have tea sent up?"

Violet hadn't even realized she was shivering.

"Yes, thank you." Tea was always an excellent idea. The hot liquid would bring her back to life—and then she would sleep.

She would try, anyway.

"I'll have one of the kitchen maids bring some up and then attend to Lady Posy."

"Of course." And then, before the door closed behind her, Violet added, "Thank you, Gwen. What would I do without you?" She was feeling unusually grateful to her maid that night for being as utterly dependable as she'd always been.

Alone at last, Violet collapsed on the tall-backed chair beside the hearth, thinking how lovely a fire would be.

But that would be silly; it was practically summer. The room would be stifling in moments.

The tea would take away her chill.

But could it fill this emptiness inside her?

SIMON GLANCED up and down the corridor outside of Violet's chamber. It would be morning soon. The ball had dragged out considerably later than expected, but he'd told her he would come. She'd know by now that he'd neglected his duties for the evening, and of course, she would want to know why. Although Simon had a vague excuse readied, he already hated the thought of lying to her. This charade was almost over. A few more weeks and he could tell her everything.

But for now, tonight, he wanted to see her. He wanted to touch her, kiss her, hold her for the short time he had before the household came to life again.

He pushed her door open easily. But she wasn't in her bed. Instead, she had fallen asleep in a chair by the hearth. He closed the door and locked it behind him.

Had she been waiting for him?

He should have come up earlier, but there had been trouble lowering the chandeliers, and then, of course, he'd needed to settle a skirmish between two of the footmen who'd taken it upon themselves to dispose of the leftover champagne.

Simon knelt beside the oversized wing-backed chair she'd fallen asleep in and then cursed his injured wrist.

He'd need both of his arms to carry her to the bed.

Dash it all. Sliding it out of the sling, he lifted her out of the chair.

"Simon?" She stirred, only half awake, allowing him to cradle her as he crossed the room to the bed.

"Our night didn't exactly go as planned, did it?" Her maid had already pulled the coverlet back, making it easy to lower her onto the sheets. "Go back to sleep, sweetheart." He crouched down to remove his boots. "I just want to lie with you a while."

Ignoring him, she squirmed and sat up instead. "Where were you tonight?"

Simon put off answering until he was climbing onto the bed beside her. "My brother had need of me." The lie tasted sour on his tongue.

Violet slid over, making more room for him. "Is he all right? Did something happen with that woman who broke his heart?"

"She's taken off and eloped with another man." Ironically enough, it was the truth. But Lucas had insisted he was over her.

"I can only stay a little while." Simon gathered her into his arms.

"He must be devastated." Violet was looking up at him, her eyes filled with concern and fully awake now.

He only nodded. Simon didn't want to discuss his brother. Or make up more lies. He simply wanted… her.

This woman. Right now.

Tonight.

He should tell her the truth now, to hell with the bet. Only…

He swallowed hard. She accepted him for… himself. She wanted him for himself. She would forgive him eventually, wouldn't she? But even as he contemplated how he would eventually tell her the truth, she crumpled before him.

"I needed you." She buried her face in his shoulder and the anguish in her voice pierced his heart. "But you weren't here. I understand, though. You're a good brother, Simon Cockfield."

Berating himself as a cad of the worst kind—a liar, a fraud —he tightened his arms around her. "Don't cry, sweetheart. Please, don't cry." *She had needed him?* "I'm here now."

What had happened tonight? Worry slithered down his

spine. A ship had arrived at the docks earlier that afternoon. Was it possible Thompson had come ashore unnoticed and then made an appearance at the ball?

But that cannot be what upset her. Sterling would have informed him if there had been any trouble.

"I found Posy with Miss Mallard." Her eyes filled with tears again. "And I wasn't angry. But you knew, didn't you? How have I been so blind?"

"But no one else saw them?" Simon's heart stopped.

"No," Violet was shaking her head. "I was alone. I saw her go outside, so I went looking for her. They were in the gardener's hut. I never imagined…" she smiled weakly. "I had no idea…"

Simon touched his forehead to hers. "I wanted to say something, but your very stubborn niece swore me to secrecy. I've been trying to convince her to tell you for weeks now." Another secret he'd kept from her. Once this was all over, it would be a wonder if she ever trusted him again. But she had to.

Because this woman *mattered* to him. More than he'd imagined was possible.

"I'm not disappointed in her." Violet gulped. "But I'm terrified for her, and so very, very sad." Another muffled sob shook her. "But she couldn't tell me. And I never allowed myself even to consider it. I've been a horrible aunt, haven't I?"

"No. You've been a perfect aunt. You've been a mother to her." Simon rubbed one hand down her back, annoyed with himself for his total awareness of her breasts pressing against him. She needed comfort, not him pawing at her. She'd been sleeping. The timing was all wrong—even though the two of them were safe from interruptions for at least an hour. "You cannot have known."

"I should have. There were signs, I simply chose to ignore them."

Which was to have been expected by any mother.

"What did you tell her?"

"I told her I loved her and that, of course, I could never be disgusted by her." At these words, a shudder ran through her, followed by shivering.

Simon pulled the coverlet over her shoulders. "Of course you wouldn't be. And neither will Greystone when she chooses to tell him."

"Oh, Simon, that isn't all! I saw Christopher. At least I think I saw him. Outside, in the garden. I thought I was seeing things—or that he might be a guest who resembled him. But he said my name."

"He came here?"

"I fainted. Simon? I've never fainted. Not the day they told me he'd gone missing, or when I heard my parents' ship capsized, not even when I learned they'd all died. But seeing him…"

"Are you injured?" Simon touched her head, cursing himself for not being there to catch her—to protect her. Did she need protection from Thompson? Until Simon knew, he was going to have to keep better watch over her.

"No, I fell on the grass."

"Were you alone?"

"Only for a moment. Collette, Diana's sister, saw me fall." Violet stared down at her hands. "I thought he was a ghost, but she told me a gentleman had been there."

Simon tightened his arms around her as she talked.

He should have known. And he ought to have been here. He reconsidered conceding the bet all over again. Was his honor worth risking Violet's safety? He knew the answer before even asking the question.

"He said my name. If he's real, if he isn't a ghost, then I assure you he isn't an imposter. So many things don't make sense anymore..." Violet's voice came out weak. "What's the matter with me?"

"Nothing is the matter with you, sweetheart. He isn't a ghost." He went on to tell her all he knew about Captain Thompson—that the man had told Coventry's men details only he could know, that he still had his family ring, and that a ship had docked that afternoon. Simon clenched his fist. She deserved the truth about everything. He needed to talk with Greystone first thing the next morning. They needed to resolve the bet as soon as possible. It wasn't a game anymore. People stood to get hurt.

Violet stood to get hurt.

Pox on it all. If he hadn't been so busy finalizing details for a ball, he would have realized the man had arrived in London already. Damn Coventry was going to be ecstatic at the prospect of finding his heir. But how was this going to affect Violet?

Is she'd loved the bastard once...

"You've had two shocks in one night," Simon soothed.

Enough moonlight shone through the window that he could see her face, tear-streaked and so very dear to him.

"All I wanted to do was find you. And..." Her lips trembled.

"I wasn't there."

Her smile was a sad one. "Am I losing my mind, Simon?" The bereft look in her eyes undid him. "How did you convince Blackheart's butler to come and perform your duties tonight? Are you holding something over him? Are you... some sort of crime boss?"

He would have laughed at that if she wasn't being so serious. "God, no. I swear."

"Then who are you?" Violet squeezed her eyes together as though she was terrified of what he might tell her.

"*I am not a criminal.* I promise you that. And you are not losing your mind. Trust me? Please? For just a little longer? I promise you that I'm not being underhanded." But was he? He'd been lying to her all along about his position in life. And yet, he'd been himself with her.

More than he'd been with anyone in years.

"Then what is it?" She all but pleaded.

He shook his head. He needed to speak with Greystone. "It's... a tangle that I can't explain yet."

She dipped her chin in a most unconvincing nod. What a mess. What a hellish mess.

This thing between the two of them was separate from everything happening around them. It was separate from the bet, from the return of a dead fiancé, and all the responsibilities awaiting him at Heart Place.

Because when her world had turned upside down tonight, she'd needed *him*. Simon Cockfield—not the butler, not the duke—just him.

And truth be told, he needed her. Only her.

Simon did the one thing he'd wanted to do since he'd caught sight of her on the stairs earlier that evening. He kissed her.

SPEECHLESS

$\mathcal{V}$iolet had promised herself she would not allow matters to proceed until she had some real answers from him, and yet...

She kissed him back anyway.

He tasted of something spicy, and port, with a hint of mint and just...Simon. And when his hands smoothed over her gown, and then her skin, she had no will to stop him.

None.

He had come. And when he'd climbed into bed and simply held her, she had known.

Butler or highwayman or crime boss, or whatever this man was, she loved him. And despite all the contrary evidence that ought to send her running, she trusted him.

Because...

She loved him!

Fiery bursts of warmth filled her at the realization.

"Simon." She grabbed his jacket to slide it down his arms and realized the sling he'd been wearing hung loose around his neck. "Your wrist. We need to be careful."

"It's fine," he breathed, shucking his jacket behind him, and then claiming her mouth again. "I just need you."

She'd once believed it would be foolish to fall for him. But now... she knew she'd be a bigger fool to live a life without knowing him like this.

He whipped her night rail over her head, and the cool night air kissed her bare skin.

"You're the one." He hovered over her and then slowly lowered himself, pressing her into the mattress so their bodies touched everywhere. "You're the one." Her breasts muffled his voice. "I need you, Violet. You're everything."

His words rendered her speechless.

"Simon." She cradled him between her thighs, her knees wide. *Take all of me.* Not only her body, but her heart, her soul, her past, her future.

How had this happened? How had she found someone that she'd sacrifice everything for?

He filled her emptiness—in more than a physical sense.

The intimacy between the two of them had been daring and exciting, but it had grown into something more. This. Tonight. It was more than physical pleasure. She would make love with him.

Their breaths mingled in staccato bursts and hers hitched when he settled his cock at her entrance.

They'd waited long enough for this. She'd waited a lifetime to find him. "Yes," she breathed.

He thrust inside and the world shifted into place. He was home. This was right. This had been meant to be all along.

"God, Violet," Simon breathed, his forehead resting on hers. He withdrew and thrust again.

There was a flash of stretching and the most exquisite,

beautiful pain as her body accommodated his girth, softening —welcoming all of him.

And again.

Deeper.

She had been walking through life only half alive. Violet tensed her arms around him and thrust up with her hips. She never wanted to let go.

Because she knew now.

She finally knew.

All her life, she'd been living with half a heart—his was the silent beat she hadn't realized was missing.

SIMON BURIED his face in Violet's neck, his mouth open against her skin, tasting the sweet perfume of this woman.

The evening had gone long and failing to return at a decent hour, Simon been certain their plans would be post-poned. He'd known she would not enter their affair lightly, and he'd wanted everything to be perfect.

He'd intended to take his time, explore every inch of her and ensure their first time together went beyond her wildest dreams.

But this... this was beyond his.

And all because she was simply Violet—and she was magic without even knowing it.

He stilled, except for his arms, which shook as he held himself above her. "We didn't wait."

"I'm glad," she whispered. "We've waited long enough already."

A delicate curve lifted the corners of her mouth, and in an instant, Simon's life made perfect sense. He'd thought he'd been content, guiding Luke, Lydia, and Lucinda, managing his estates, deliberating in parliament, and taking care of the responsibilities that came with being Blackheart. But something had always been missing.

And through it all, he had been waiting, hoping.

That missing piece had been love.

To be more precise, it was Violet.

Surrounded by her scent, her warmth, her voice, he was whole.

How could he not be, when her essence filled him in every way? Simon buried his face in her neck. He had everything he could ever need in life, and it had happened without him even realizing it.

He hadn't expected the chaos of this overwhelming emotion to sneak up on him. He hadn't expected that one small woman would erode his defenses without even trying. Nor had he expected it to feel so perfectly natural and... right.

And, if he was not mistaken, Violet felt the same.

She had somehow become...

Everything. She was *the one*.

Simon claimed her mouth again, and then drew back so he could lose himself in her gaze. Or was she lost in his?

And then she was moving with him, holding him deeper, clenching around him. They worked their bodies in perfect harmony, nearing the pinnacle as one.

"It was you," she whispered. "All along."

"All along," Simon spoke against her mouth, starving for her, driving the intimate rhythm of this carnal song.

She arched her back. "More, Simon. Now."

An all-encompassing ache swelled. It replaced need with promise. It flooded desire with a painful pleasure. He was beyond speech, knowing only… feelings. His cock conquered, his heart raced, and he surrendered all.

"I love you, Simon," she gasped. "Love you."

Simon thrust twice and then once more as deep as she would take him, joining, claiming. Lost to all reason, white and black and red exploded behind his eyes.

"God, Violet." Shaking, he jerked back just in time for his seed to spill between them.

When he was spent, she dragged him back down beside her.

"Mmm…" she hummed by his ear.

Simon gathered her into his arms. Now that he understood what this was, he needed to tread carefully. Because amidst all that was right, he had waded into this all wrong.

Unexpectedly panicked by what he'd done, he sent up a silent prayer that when he told her the truth, she would forgive him.

She would, wouldn't she? He'd spend the rest of his life earning back her trust, if that's what she wanted.

But to do that she'd have to be at his side.

And that was exactly where he wanted her.

"I have to get downstairs."

Violet stirred and opened her eyes. Simon was already out of bed and shoving his arms into his jacket.

"You're going to be exhausted today." He'd come to her very late, and she doubted he'd slept more than half an hour. "I think the butler needs a day off," she teased.

"Didn't you say that my life line showed that I didn't

require much sleep?" Simon reminded her, holding up his hand for proof.

She couldn't help but smile at that. "But not that you didn't need any at all."

Violet stretched and pushed herself to sit up, feeling twinges in places she'd forgotten existed. She needed to hold him one last time before he left. She needed to touch him, fully awake, and assure herself that it had not been a dream.

"Stay in bed, love," he whispered, holding her gaze.

A light shined in the back of his dark eyes—a light that sent hope blossoming around her heart. She slid off the bed and moved into his arms.

After a leisurely kiss, she pulled away, straightening the collar around his neck and smoothing his hair. He'd come to her after all. He'd given her reassurances about Posy, listened to her complaints about Christopher, and then...

They had made love.

She'd told him *she loved him*, and he wasn't running. He'd stayed to hold her afterward.

He hadn't said the words back. Nor had he answered the questions about who he really was.

He stilled her hands and lifted her chin so he could stare into her eyes. "You're going to have all your answers soon enough." He was all seriousness now.

"Promise?"

"Trust me. You'll understand soon, very soon. Can you trust me for now?"

She nodded. She loved him. What choice did she have?

He raised his timepiece for a quick glance. "I'd better go now, though, before Gwen comes knocking on the door with your tea."

The sight of the gold in his hand shifted something inside her. "It's a lovely watch. Where did you get it?"

A shadow seemed to cross his eyes. "My grandfather left it to my father. And my father left it to me."

Violet stepped back, hugging her arms in front of her.

"Now go back to bed." He leaned in, and she savored the taste of his kiss, not moving even after he closed the door behind him.

Because…

He had just lied to her.

The watch was the same one that had been sitting on the dressing table in the Duke of Blackheart's chamber.

Her butler, she realized, was a thief.

She was in love with a thief!

NOT A GHOST

"I'm here to see Miss Violet Faraday." The gentleman standing on the step straightened his shoulders as he stared up at Simon.

"Who may I say is calling?" Simon knew. Even if he hadn't seen the renderings used for the ads, he vaguely remembered the man.

He would have known.

"Advise her that *Lord* Captain Thompson is here to see her."

"Ah yes, Captain. Reports of your death have, indeed, been somewhat overstated." But Simon didn't step aside, nor did he invite the caller in.

"That's *Lord* Captain, sir."

So, this was the blighter who'd hurt Violet. This was the man who'd not only taken her innocence but shattered her confidence when he'd abandoned her—betraying his country as well.

There wasn't anything extraordinary about him. Thompson's blond hair was tied behind his head. He was of medium height, sturdy build, and had large, wide-set brown eyes. And for having been imprisoned and then alone in a foreign country, the gentleman looked surprisingly healthy and hale.

Simon was tempted to send him away, but that wasn't his choice to make.

"Do you have an appointment?" he asked instead.

"No, but the lady will be more than happy to meet with me, if you'll please tell her I am here."

Would she be happy to meet with him?

"Follow me." He gestured for Thompson to enter, and then led him into the front drawing room. Violet's former fiancé stepped inside and then paused for a moment to take in the surroundings.

"Nothing ever changes in England. I can always count on that," he said, looking more at ease now that he'd been allowed inside. "Same old furnishings. Same streets, same balls…"

Did he think Violet was the same as well?

Simon refrained from commenting.

"I imagine the future marchioness will make some changes, though. I understand she is not at all traditional." Thompson had been lurking around the ball, so of course, he knew about Greystone's engagement.

"Wait here. I'll see if Miss Faraday is in."

After closing the door behind him, Simon took the stairs two and three at a time. He didn't turn in the direction of Violet's chamber, however, but went in the opposite direction.

And, as luck would have it, found Greys exiting his chamber looking far too chipper, considering the copious amounts of champagne that had flowed the night before. The marquess halted with a start when he caught sight of Simon.

"Simpson tells me we have a visitor. Is it him?" Greys asked.

"If, by him, you mean *Lord* Captain Christopher Thompson, then yes. He's asked to speak with Vi—Miss Faraday." Simon frowned. He was none too enthusiastic about her former betrothed's return. Not today—not before matters were resolved between the two of them.

"And after he's gone, Greys, you and I need to talk," Simon said. "About Vi—about your cousin."

Greystone, who had been plucking at the lace at his wrist, glanced up with a cocked brow. "I thought the two of you were getting on better these past few weeks. Has Violet threatened that I would sack you again?"

"Not at all." One of the maids rushed along the corridor. He'd have this conversation in private, with no distractions.

"I met him before he left. He hasn't changed much." Simon extracted some folded papers from inside his jacket and handed it over. "I received this report earlier this morning."

True, Lord Captain Christopher Thompson was the Marquess of Coventry's next in line, but he'd spent the past decade pursuing a dubious lifestyle, at best. And although his newfound fortune and title ensured most of the *ton* would turn a blind eye to questions surrounding his disappearance, as a suspected defector, he'd always have that black mark on his character.

Violet would see right through him. Of course, she would.

She'd told Simon she *loved* him.

"Violet was heartbroken when he went missing," Greys said. "So much so that she determined never to marry. I wonder if he's of a mind to take up with her again."

Simon stiffened at the suggestion.

Greys went on. "As Coventry's heir, even if he is a defector, most would consider him a decent prospect for someone like my cousin."

"I doubt that," Simon said.

"She's been on the shelf for ages. The two of them cared for one another once; they very well could get on again." Greystone shrugged, and Simon was filled with a flash of rage at his friend for suggesting that Violet take up with anyone but him.

"He's wrong for her," Simon ground through his teeth.

"I suppose anything is possible." Was Greystone being deliberately obtuse?

"Not this," Simon muttered. "But you will want to meet with him first. Before he's allowed to speak to her."

Greys glanced over at him. "She'll speak with him. But I doubt she's dressed for the day. Either way, it won't hurt him to cool his heels for an hour or two."

Simon clenched his fists. "What are you going to tell him?"

"Oh, I don't intend to do much talking—other than a few questions, that is." Greystone held up the report. "He's a good deal to answer for."

Simon swallowed hard. Violet would not send him away. She would want answers too.

The marquess straightened his lapels. "Allow me a moment, and then send him into my study."

VIOLET TOOK comfort from Simon's hand, which rested at the small of her back.

"Greystone is with him now. You don't have to do this today." He spoke softly near her ear.

Christopher was here. The man she'd seen in the garden

last night had not been a ghost, rather he had, quite literally, returned from the dead. It was as though, deep down, all this time, she'd been expecting this. A part of her had never truly believed that he'd been killed—the part of her that remembered the last moments they'd spent together.

"I need to speak with him alone." She smiled weakly up at Simon.

Simon—the man she loved with all her heart—despite his flaws and secrets. Because apparently, one couldn't choose who to love.

He hadn't told her he loved her back, but he'd asked her to trust him. And she intended to do just that.

Violet stared at the door to her cousin's study where inside, once and for all, she would face her past—and then put it to rest.

"I'll be right here." Simon's hand made a smooth circle where it rested, and she turned to stare up at him.

"Thank you." Her voice nearly broke. She loved him.

She *loved* Simon Cockfield, whoever he was.

His eyes burned down at her—with love?

"You can do this." He was not going to try to prevent this meeting.

A few hours before, the two of them had joined in the most intimate way two people could be together. He had *made love* to her.

With her.

Anxious to put Christopher behind her once and for all, she turned for the door. This time, when she laid eyes on the man she'd loved long ago, she was prepared.

The two men in the room rose—Greystone, looking concerned and supportive, and Christopher, with a pleading adoration showing in his eyes.

"Violet." He reached as though to take her hand, but she kept both clasped behind her back.

"Lord Captain Thompson," she acknowledged him with a nod.

Greystone crossed the room and kissed her cheek. "I'll be in the foyer if you need me," he said and then exited, leaving the door slightly ajar behind him.

"Please sit." Violet gestured toward a settee near the hearth and then lowered herself into one of the high-backed chairs. She'd experienced her hysterics over him the night before, but this time she was prepared. She was a lady, after all. "It was you, then, in the garden last night."

"Oh, my dear." He leaned forward, resting his arms on his thighs. "I couldn't bring myself to stay. Seeing you... I feared I would sacrifice what little dignity I have remaining. Memories of our time together overwhelmed me."

"I was lucky to have Miss Jones, then." Violet had once loved this man.

He looked sturdier now—more manly. Creases etched around his eyes, and his hair was much longer, which suited him. Rather than appearing ravaged by his hardship, he was more handsome than before.

This was the man who had pledged to marry her. She'd imagined spending her life with him. *She'd lain with him.*

And yet, sitting here, she felt oddly disconnected. As though all of that had happened to another person.

After leaving England, he'd not written her once. And then he'd never returned.

The night before, she hadn't had a chance to feel much of anything. She'd already been reeling over the revelation about Posy, and then there had been that fainting business, but...

But without those distractions, she'd thought she would

feel something at the sight of him. Something other than disappointment, melancholy, and...

Regret.

Not regret for giving herself to him—she'd done that in good faith. But regret that he'd never been the person she'd wanted him to be, and also that she'd wasted so much time dreading this moment.

But she'd met Simon. The past was over and done. She was going to make the most of every day because she had no idea what the future might hold.

"I've missed you." Christopher filled the silence. When she didn't answer, he added, "Did you miss me, Violet?"

"Of course." She sat staring at him. He really was a very handsome man—no wonder she'd fallen in love with him.

His satisfied grin brought with it a rush of memories, but that... was all.

"Your uncle must be pleased that you have been found." The entire business indeed was tricky. His return ought to have been cause for celebration and yet... "I am sorry for the loss of your father. I spoke with your mother a few times after we received the news that you were missing. I know you didn't get on all that well with them, but one can never truly be prepared for the loss of their parents."

She certainly hadn't been prepared to lose hers.

"I won't pretend to mourn my father, but my mother loved me more than anyone, and I will miss her dearly."

And yet, he'd abandoned her as well.

Christopher seemed lost in thought for a moment and then shrugged. "I was equally shocked to have learned that my cousins had passed," he said, speaking of the two other men who'd stood between him and the Duke of Coventry's title.

"Indeed, your uncle has suffered many losses over the past

decade." But she'd had enough. "Tell me what happened, Christopher. Were they cruel to you? Was it horrible?"

"They…?" He seemed confused for a moment. "Ah, my captors. To be frank, Violet, it's hard to say." He touched his head. "Since I lost my memory for a while. Amnesia. It was lucky I saw the advertisement in the paper. Brought it all back to me."

Violet wanted to give him the benefit of the doubt. It was how she had always been with him. Because she'd loved him. At the time, she'd stood to lose too much otherwise.

But she was older now, wiser. Wasn't she? Or had she simply fallen into old habits?

No. It was different with Simon.

And yet, a cold chill swept through her.

"You don't know what happened, then? Nothing?" she asked.

"Ambushed, ruffians of some sort. When I came to, I was a stranger to myself in a strange land. I could never have stayed away if I'd remembered you."

"When was that?" Because he'd gone on to make a life for himself there.

"You don't want to hear the unseemly details, now do you? We have a good deal to make up for though, you and I."

"You did not marry?"

He had the decency to look chagrined. "I was not always alone, but no, I did not marry. I believe that somewhere deep inside, I knew you would be waiting here for me."

Violet simply stared at him. It was a very romantic idea. Christopher had always been able to make things sound exciting and romantic.

But she had *not* been waiting for him. Not really. She'd been waiting for… herself.

And when she'd finally arrived, she'd found Simon.

"But I have returned," he continued. "And you have not married. So we can come to know one another again. Violet? You once loved me, but all is not lost. I was a good prospect for you before, but as Coventry's heir, I'm an even better one now, am I not?"

Violet was shaking her head. Surely he didn't expect her to pick up where they'd left off? Surely he didn't still consider her his betrothed?

"I am back, Violet. And I've kept you waiting long enough," he continued, undaunted by her silence. "Be my wife, and soon after, my duchess." And then it struck her. Coventry was as conservative as Christopher's father had been. Christopher must need her very much—more than when he'd left.

She watched him closely. There was a calculating look in his eyes that she wished she'd comprehended when she'd been younger.

His father had been the force behind their engagement before. Was it possible that he'd put some marriage stipulation in his inheritance? And as a suspected defector, he might not find a suitably proper lady of noble birth so easily this time.

She had always been that to him.

Suitable. Proper.

She only hoped that in the end, she wasn't too suitably proper for Simon.

"I—"

"Don't answer yet. All of this must have come as quite a shock to you." He rose, and Violet followed suit. "Take some time. Come driving with me this afternoon."

"I don't need time, Christopher." She moved across the rug to walk him to the door.

"I'll speak with my uncle. He'll be so pleased to know that

you've waited for me. I'm all he has left, and he's anxious I secure the line."

It dawned on her that perhaps Coventry was insisting he honor their previous arrangement. But it didn't matter. It was over. It had been over for a very long time.

"Oh, Christopher," she sighed. Christopher had always gotten his way. It was what he was used to. And hearing him today revealed that he hadn't changed all that much.

But she wasn't going to fall for it.

Not this time.

As they exited the study, Violet wasn't surprised to see Posy and Iris waiting in the foyer.

At the same time, Greystone stepped out of Simon's butler chamber, followed by Simon, who then leaned against the wall looking none-too-pleased and not at all butlerish.

Always one to make the most of an audience, Christopher took Violet's hand and bowed over it. Taking his time, he pressed his mouth against the back of her wrist, leaving her squirming.

"I shall anxiously await your answer," he said with all the passion of a true Shakespearean.

At this, Posy giggled and her aunt pinned a curious gaze on Violet.

"It has been nice to see you again," Violet responded in the most polite way she knew how without giving him reason to hope for more. "We are happy to have you back in England."

Only after he'd exited onto the street did she exhale a sigh of relief.

Silence hovered once the door closed, and Violet turned to her family. At their curious stares, she barely kept from squirming to be the object of so much attention. "What?"

"He has renewed his offer for you?" Aunt Iris demanded.

"Do you still love him?" Posy asked.

"It is him, then." Greystone looked concerned.

But Violet's gaze drifted to Simon, who looked very serious as he stared at the floor. Perhaps if she gave them all some sort of answer, they'd leave her alone.

"He is not an imposter, he has renewed his offer, and as to the other, that isn't the sort of thing a lady discusses in public."

"But we are not in public; this is Greystone's foyer," Posy pointed out.

Aunt Iris scowled at their niece. "This isn't a proper discussion for you. And if we don't leave now, we're going to be late for our appointment."

"Madam Chantal will wait." Posy waved a hand.

"Madam Chantal waits for no one." Aunt Iris donned her gloves. "Besides, Diana is meeting us there."

Her aunt sent Violet a look that somehow conveyed that the reprieve was only a temporary one. Violet appreciated it nonetheless. Now that her meeting with Christopher was over, she felt as though a giant weight had lifted off her shoulders, but she was also tired. She wasn't all that surprised, when she went to smooth the skirt of her gown, to realize that her hands were shaking.

Christopher was alive. She'd seen him. And she didn't love him anymore.

But she loved Simon—who had not met her eyes once since she'd emerged from the drawing room.

"Take your time, Violet. We'll support you regardless of what you decide." Greystone said and then turned to Simon. "You wanted a word?" He gestured toward his study. "No time like the present."

Seconds later, Violet found herself standing alone in the

foyer. She glanced around and then, confident he wouldn't mind, slipped into Simon's tiny office to await him.

As she closed the door behind her, she found some of the comfort she needed. Because the scent reminded her of him— spicy and leathery and... familiar.

Desiring more of it, she lowered herself into his seat behind the desk. A place where he spent many, many hours.

It felt rather intimate, really.

She glanced down at an envelope that had been opened, addressed to... Blackheart?

"He's a con man." Followed by a muffled thumping sound.

Violet jumped. That had been Simon's voice, and it had come from...

A vent near the floor.

MY CHOICE

"*H*e's a con man." Simon slammed his fist onto Greystone's enormous mahogany desk.

That blighter had asked Violet to renew their engagement —and Violet had not dismissed him.

She had not said no.

Was she seriously considering accepting him? Simon would not have believed she valued status above affection. She wouldn't. She had told *Simon* that she loved him.

But this morning, Captain Thompson had offered her the position of Marchioness, and someday, a duchess. She knew Simon only as a butler.

A *butler*, for God's sake!

Which, of course, was something any rational lady of the *ton* ought to take into consideration.

But Simon didn't like it.

He didn't like it at all.

"She ought to at least consider his offer, don't you think?"

"In the manner you considered Lady Isabella?" Simon barely kept himself from growling.

"Let's not be testy." Greystone lowered himself into one of the chairs near the hearth and laconically crossed one leg over the other. As a man who'd all but secured his bride, Greys, of course, could be casual about this.

Simon huffed.

"What's got you in such a foul mood this morning? Surely Captain Thompson's visit cannot have set you off like this?"

Not the man's return so much as Violet's unwillingness to send the coward packing.

Simon exhaled and then ran a hand through his hair. "I can't continue on like this. You're going to have to find yourself another butler."

Greystone leaned forward with narrowed eyes. "You're going to forfeit?"

"In all good conscience, I can't keep lying to her."

"Her?"

"Violet."

Greystone jerked his head back, brows raised.

"I've... not acted honorably toward her, and it isn't fair." Simon felt a pain at the back of his throat. "She deserves to know the truth."

"And by what degree, might I ask, have you dishonored my cousin?"

Simon shook his head. Greys need not hear all of the details. "Enough."

"Then I must demand you offer for her."

"Trouble is..." Simon laughed somewhat cynically, staring at the bookshelves behind his friend and astonished at the predicament he now found himself in. "That's the last thing I want."

"I'm not giving you a choice." It wasn't often Greystone invited confrontation, but of course, on this subject, he would.

"That's the crux of it." Simon lowered himself to sit adjacent to his old friend. "I want it to be my choice." *It has to be my choice.*

Greys simply stared back at him, studying him, weighing Simon's meaning. "You should have thought of that when you agreed to the wager."

This time Simon's fist hit a small table. He was as surprised when it shattered beside him as Greystone. This wasn't like him. Simon didn't lose his temper like this.

But in forfeiting the bet, Simon was conceding the choice for his bride to Greystone. And he couldn't go on lying to Violet.

She is not going to marry Lord Captain Christopher Thompson, damnit!

But... "The woman I marry needs to know that it was my choice."

Greys leaned forward in his chair, arms resting on his thighs, hands clasped loosely together. "In that case, we'd best call a meeting."

"For what, another wager?" Simon asked.

Greystone laughed. "Perhaps."

∾

VIOLET BURST out of the chair, not wanting to believe what she'd overheard.

Of course, she should have known that one never learned anything good while eavesdropping. But... Simon didn't want to marry her! He was resigning from his position because he'd said he couldn't do this any longer.

Do what, exactly?

And Greystone was willing to wager for her honor? She was tempted to keep listening but too stunned to do so. And disappointed.

By Simon, her cousin, and... herself for being gullible.

She backed away from the vent.

London had been a mistake. For Posy and for her. What had she expected to come out of her decision to have an affair with a butler?

She certainly hadn't expected to fall in love.

That was the biggest mistake of all.

Violet pressed her hand to her chest, feeling suddenly like something very large and heavy was sitting on it.

She needed air.

She needed out of this tiny room. She fumbled at the door and stepped into the foyer.

"You're going to have to make her an offer..."

"That's the last thing I want."

She hadn't misheard.

"That's the last thing I want..."

Tears stung the backs of her eyes. Simon didn't want to marry her, but the salt on her wound was that Greystone seemed to think it was some sort of joke. Perhaps Posy and Susan had the right idea. If this was the way gentlemen handled their affairs, then good riddance to them.

Simon had asked her to *trust him*. He'd promised everything was going to work out, hadn't he? But was his promise the same sort of promise that Christopher had made long ago? Was he only stringing her along for his amusement?

No. No.

She shook her head. It wasn't fair to compare Simon to Christopher.

Only a few hours before, she had declared her love to him. He hadn't said the words back, but she hadn't thought she needed to hear them. What *had* he said? She tried remembering, but at the time, she'd been overwhelmed with... feeling.

She stood frozen, contemplating calling for one of Greystone's carriages or perhaps hailing a hackney and buying a ticket on a mail coach. She could run home to Blossom Court and never return to London again.

Or she could march into the study and demand the two of them explain themselves. She imagined that scenario, one that had her acknowledging her indiscretions to Greystone and then being rejected by Simon.

"That's the last thing I want."

A shudder swept through her. She wasn't ready to face either of them yet. Would she ever be? Her throat thickened but she stifled her sob.

Yesterday at this time, she'd been well in control of her life and those she was responsible for—at least she'd thought she had. And now...

The last twenty-four hours had exposed that her perception of reality was suspect. Clutching her hands at her waist, she paced across the foyer.

She almost wished Posy hadn't left with Aunt Iris so she had someone to discuss all of this with. But Posy had troubles of her own. Violet couldn't add to Posy's burden.

But she couldn't remain standing here. Fearful that Simon or Greystone might appear, Violet scurried upstairs to fetch her reticule and wrap. Only when she was outside on the walk did she stop to think.

Where could she go?

And then she realized she wasn't completely alone. Setting

off in the direction of Byrd House, Violet knew exactly who she could talk to about this.

Even if Bethany didn't have any solutions to offer, Violet instinctively trusted her and at the very least, she could offer Violet some sympathy.

And sometimes, that was all a lady required.

"Wait." Bethany's eyes widened. "You mean to tell me you are involved with Greystone's butler?"

Diana glanced between Violet and Bethany, looking confused. "But I thought that he was—"

"Mr. Cockfield." Bethany supplied.

In searching out one friend, Violet instead found herself in the company of four sympathetic ladies: Bethany, Collette, Diana, and Bethany's younger sister, Lady Tabetha Spencer.

Upon Violet's arrival, Bethany took one look at her, invited Violet into her private drawing room, and immediately ordered an early tea.

Violet had not divulged all the details of her involvement with Simon, and before they pursued that line of questioning, she added, "Lord Captain Thompson presented himself this morning."

"Your dead fiancé?" Tabetha asked.

"But no wonder you are a wreck!" Collette patted Violet's back.

"And then to hear that you'd been lied to by not only a man

you have feelings for, but your cousin as well?" Bethany asked. "You poor thing!"

Violet covered her face with both hands. When she'd listened in on that dreadful conversation, the numb feeling from the night before had returned. She'd not allowed herself to give in to self-pity.

But now, experiencing the support and agreement of these ladies broke something. Holding back tears was no longer possible. Kindness and compassion, it seemed, were going to be her undoing.

"If a gentleman is pronounced dead but then is discovered to be alive, is he even still her fiancé?" Collette asked the room in general.

"I don't think so," Diana answered. "Perhaps there is something written in *Debrette's* or in *Burke's Dictionary* that applies to that sort of thing."

"I think it must be up to the two people involved," Bethany settled the matter.

"I very much understand how tempting it must be to accept Lord Captain Thompson's offer. You would eventually become a *duchess*." Tabetha took one of Violet's hands. "But trust me on this, in the end, it is love that truly matters. Right, Beth?" She turned to her sister, who nodded and then turned back to Violet.

"Do you love the captain, Violet?" she asked.

Violet shook her head almost violently. "No! I'm not in love with Christopher at all." And then she squeezed her eyes closed and cried, "It's so much worse than that."

"I don't understand."

"I've fallen in love with Greystone's butler!" *Simon*. She loved Simon but he didn't want her. "I'm in love with a butler!"

"Oh my." Lady Tabetha's brows shot up to her hairline.

"Mr. Cockfield?" Diana whipped her head around, grinning.

"What's wrong with falling in love with a butler?" Collette asked.

"I need a moment." Bethany silenced them all and then burst out of her seat, her fingers frantically tapping against her thumbs on both hands.

"But when Greystone demanded that Simon offer for me, he refused!" Violet added, lest anyone think this was romantic.

"Mr. Cockfield refused? Are you quite certain of that?" Bethany halted, looking considerably more distraught than Violet would have expected.

"He said it was the last thing he wanted." Saying the words summoned more tears. Such an admission was more than a little humiliating. But she'd come this far...

"What else, exactly?" Bethany asked.

"I would have stayed to hear all of it." Collette was shaking her head. "In for a penny, in for a pound, and all that."

"Simon—Mr. Cockfield told Greystone that he was going to have to find a new butler... He couldn't continue living this lie... He was going to forfeit something or other... and that when he married, he wanted it to be his choice..." Violet shook her head. "And then my cousin suggested they call some sort of meeting... to take up another wager to resolve the matter."

But the only thing that had mattered to Violet was that Simon had not wished to marry her. And that he would resign from his position because he couldn't bear... seeing her? No, he'd said he couldn't continue living this lie.

What was the lie?

Their affair?

"I cannot think that Greystone would not take all of this seriously. It simply isn't like him," Diana defended her future husband.

"I agree with Diana," Bethany said, but then returned to where she'd been sitting beside Violet, placing her hands on Violet's knees and squeezing. "Did Mr. Cockfield say he did not wish to actually *marry* you, or did he say that he didn't wish to be *compelled* to marrying you? Because those are two very different scenarios."

Violet rubbed her forehead. Greys had said... "*I'm going to demand that you make her an offer,*" and Simon responded by saying... "*That's the last thing I want.*"

"I suppose it could have been either—marrying me or being forced into doing so," Violet admitted. "But what about this meeting, and *a wager,* of all things? What's the meaning of that?"

"It means not all is lost." Bethany straightened.

"But how?" Almost in answer to her question, a tentative knock sounded and Lord Chaswick peered around the door. "Don't mind me. I'll only be a moment, ladies." He stepped inside, crossing to his wife. "I've been called to Knight Hall to meet with Greystone this morning. We've some business to discuss, and I'm not sure when I'll be back."

"Would you mind staying a moment, Chase? Miss Faraday has found herself in a rather complicated situation."

Surely she wasn't going to tell Violet's woes to the baron!

"With Mr. Cockfield," Bethany added.

Lord Chaswick's eyes widened.

"And I think we ought to do something to help," she continued.

"Please, you mustn't concern—" Violet tried to stop them. This was already humiliating enough!

"But of course, what is it?" he asked.

"She's fallen in love with him."

Mortification washed through Violet and, at this point, she said goodbye to her dignity and closed her eyes with a soft moan.

"With Mr. *Cockfield*?" Lord Chaswick asked.

Bethany nodded. "But I'm afraid there may have been some sort of misunderstanding… Would you mind…?"

"No!" Violet burst to her feet. "Oh, no. You mustn't!"

But Lord Chaswick held up both hands. "Miss Faraday, please trust that I would never do anything to embarrass you." He rubbed his chin. "But perhaps I could… unearth some truths. All sorts of nonsense going on over there."

At such a true statement, Violet stilled. *Nonsense, indeed!* Hearing it acknowledged had Violet dropping back into her seat. She swiped at her eyes. She'd felt as though something was terribly off since the day she arrived. What lie had Simon been living?

Chaswick frowned and then lowered himself to his haunches in front of her. "I am going to do my best to clear up a few misunderstandings. Will you trust me to do this?"

Yet another man who wanted her to trust him. Violet glanced over at Bethany, who nodded encouragingly, and then back to Lord Chaswick.

"But first, could you tell me what happened?"

"Must you hear all of it?"

"The general details at the very least, if I'm to be of much help." And then he tilted his head. "Are you up for that?"

All eyes in the room watched her expectantly. Could

matters be any worse than they already were? "I don't suppose it will hurt," she conceded.

Her heart squeezed at the possibility of returning to Knight Hall and discovering Simon gone. But if Chaswick could find the truth for her, at least she would have that.

And then she would return to Blossom Court early. Her only regret would be missing Greystone and Diana's wedding.

She would live out her life with only half a heart. Because losing Simon was going to be so much more painful than losing Christopher.

Because the love she had for Simon was bigger than herself. She was simply going to have to find herself again. And she would.

She stared down at one of her palms. There was a profound affection crease at the end of her heart line, which meant she would have a deep, lifelong love—most likely marriage. She'd read the lines a million times, hoping for the impossible.

Greystone deserved a happily ever after. Posy deserved one. As did the ladies seated around her.

Violet exhaled. *But so do I.*

We just don't always get what we deserve.

"The details are quite simple." Violet narrated her story as concisely as possible. "I realize it isn't at all proper, for a lady to attach her affections to a servant—to the butler." By now, she'd been through two handkerchiefs—her own, and one that Diana had handed her. "But I do love him. And I wouldn't have cared what people said about that."

"Well." Lord Chaswick swallowed hard and finally rose. "I find that rather admirable."

"As do we," Bethany added. "Will you go now, Chaswick? Will you speak to them?"

"I will." And then he turned back to Violet. "But promise me one thing, Miss Faraday?"

"I suppose that depends," she answered, hating to sound ungrateful.

"Wise woman." And then he grew serious again. "Don't make any decisions, don't go anywhere, and for God's sake, stay away from Lord Captain Thompson until after I've returned. Can you do that?"

"I've no interest in Captain Thompson," she answered.

"So you'll be here when I return?"

"I will."

She would not run away even though her feet were itching to do just that. She would wait.

She would see this through.

"MAY I remind you of the terms of our bet?" Greystone poured scotch into two tumblers. "If you forfeit, I win the dubious distinction of selecting your future duchess. My choice, of course, is Violet."

They had been over this numerous times. Simon rubbed the back of his neck. After instructing the underbutler to step into Simon's duties for the day, Simon and Greystone had been locked in disagreement for what felt like hours now. Failing to arrive at any sort of resolution, Greystone brought out a decanter of scotch. "Violet says tea fixes all of life's troubles, but I respectfully disagree."

"Indeed." Simon accepted the glass gratefully. But did he? Agree, that was? Because he'd much prefer to be taking tea with Violet that afternoon rather than belaboring the details of this ridiculous but binding wager.

"Would it make a difference to know I would have chosen Violet for you to marry even if you hadn't ruined her?"

"She isn't ruined. And I'm going to marry her regardless." Simon placed his empty glass on the table beside him. "But a lost wager is not going to have any part in my decision to marry. Violet deserves better than that."

If she'll have me.

"Then let's play a game of vingt-et-un. You win, and you've fulfilled the terms of the bet. I win and...?"

"No."

No more bets with Greystone.

The door to the study swung open and Chaswick, Westerley, and Spencer entered without ceremony.

Westerley shifted a suspicious glance between them, Spencer crossed his arms, and Chaswick... all but glared at Simon.

"I could release you from the debt altogether," Greystone said without acknowledging any of the arrivals.

"You've got to be joking," Spencer protested.

"Not at all. His reasons are not inconsequential. Quite significant ones, in fact. And as he's unwilling to fulfill the forfeit, I don't see any other way out of it." Greys set his jaw. "Bit of a conundrum."

"So, I understand." Chaswick sent Simon a knowing look. "Miss Faraday is at Byrd House presently."

"What the devil is she doing there?" Simon's heart skipped a beat. He hadn't even realized she'd left the house. *Why had she left without telling anyone?*

"Is she alright?" Blast and damn, was she really considering Thompson? Simon stood abruptly. "What all do you know?"

"I know a few things. But first, I'm interested in hearing where you stand in the matter."

"Where I stand?" Simon grimaced, remembering the conversation he'd overheard between Violet and Thompson earlier. "Does that even matter if she accepts Thompson's offer?"

"Why would you think she'd take him back?"

"Because she didn't refuse him."

"She isn't interested in him." Chaswick smiled, looking rather like the cat who'd caught the canary. "Miss Faraday is concerned with only one gentleman this afternoon, and she is thoroughly convinced he's a butler."

Simon narrowed his eyes. "But she didn't refuse him —Thompson."

"That's because she isn't even considering him."

Simon froze upon hearing this. He was an idiot!

Violet had promised to trust him. So why would he presume that she would suddenly be interested in a title?

"Let's have a new wager—dispense of this altogether," Greystone suggested again.

At this point, Simon was willing to give Greystone whatever he wanted—Heart Place, if necessary.

"But that would ruin all of the side bets. We can't have that." This from Westerley, who'd been quiet up until then. "Because, speaking for myself, failing to honor a wager, even one such as this, would plague me for life. I doubt you'd feel differently, Blackheart. It's the one thing that is truly ours."

"True," Spencer said, frowning. "And a wager is a wager."

"But love is love. You do love her, don't you, Blackheart?" Chaswick pinned his gaze on Simon. "Because if you do, I think I know how we can satisfy all involved."

"I'll do anything," Simon admitted. "Because I do, I love her with all my heart."

EXPOSED

"We have been instructed to have you at the statue of Achilles at precisely six this evening," Bethany announced. "If you wish to hear Mr. Cockfield out, that is."

Violet glanced at the clock on the mantel. Already, it was half-past four.

She wasn't sure what she'd expected, but it hadn't been this.

Why a public place?

"He wants to see me?" She dropped her gaze to her gown, which was wrinkled and might have a spot of tea on it. And then she touched her hair and face. "I'm all splotchy!" Once the tears had begun, despite the other ladies' attempts to keep her cheerful, they'd returned on and off for most of the afternoon.

Bethany studied her with a frown. "Nothing a little lavender water can't repair. And one of Diana's gowns should fit you nicely. Don't you think, Diana?"

"Absolutely. I have a juniper evening dress that would suit

your coloring perfectly." Violet's future cousin-in-law rose. "But we haven't much time."

As it turned out, Violet depleted every last minute preparing for the meeting—what with a hasty bath being drawn, some hair styling, and a hint of paints insisted upon by Tabetha.

At twenty minutes until six, the person staring back at her in the looking glass barely resembled the one who'd sat feeling sorry for herself all afternoon. Curling tendrils had been arranged to fall around her face and shoulders, the swelling was mostly gone from her eyes, and the pallor she expected wasn't as noticeable with just the hint of rose dabbed onto her cheeks.

Violet smoothed the bodice of the gown, an off-the-shoulder design made up of a luxurious silk. "This seems more appropriate for a ball." She bit her lip. "It's almost indecent!"

"Precisely," Diana quipped and then handed her a lace wrap.

"The carriage is waiting, and I don't think this is a meeting you'll want to be late for." Bethany had changed into a different gown as well. She and Lady Tabetha would come along with her, but Chaswick had ordered his two younger sisters to stay home.

When Bethany had begun to argue on their behalf, her husband had leaned in and whispered something that effectively silenced her protests.

Protecting his innocent sisters from having to watch the devastation of Violet's heartbreak, most likely—if that was how all of this played out in the end.

But Violet was not entirely without hope. When she felt that dread in her belly, or the urge to flee for Blossom Court, she reminded herself of Simon's plea very early that morning —to trust him.

"I suppose I'm as ready as I'm ever going to be." Was one ever ready for something like this?

Bethany led Violet outside and all of them climbed into the carriage. At the very least, Violet wasn't going to be left alone in the aftermath. She had friends, and that alone bolstered her courage.

The carriage jerked into motion, followed by Lord Chaswick and Mr. Spencer on horseback behind them.

"I feel like the guest of honor at a funeral procession," she said.

"You do look rather like you're going to your own execution." Lady Tabetha pinched her lips together, but then laughed anyway. "We should have used more rouge."

"*Tabetha*," Bethany hushed her sister but then studied Violet. "Although you do look a tad pale. You aren't going to be ill, are you?"

Violet shook her head. "One minute, my heart feels like it's going to beat right out of my chest, and the next, I forget to breathe. I do wish Chaswick could have just told me what he discovered."

"It's going to be fine." But even Bethany was tapping her fingers against her thumbs at a frantic pace. The next time Violet glanced outside the window, the carriage was pulling up to the park.

And across the lawn, she could see the statue. The giant sculpture had been erected to honor Wellington and depicted a young man who was supposed to be Achilles. But although the resplendent figure had a sword and shield and a cloak draped over his shoulder, his only other covering was a fig leaf.

And standing at the foot of the monument was Simon, waiting for her.

"He's here. He's already here." Her voice was little more than a whisper, her mouth suddenly as dry as the Sahara.

The door swung open, and she was surprised to see Greystone, dressed to the nines and looking a little sheepish but also... proud?

"After all this is over, I'm going to owe you a Herculean apology." His words ought to have sounded ominous, but they held more of a promise as he assisted her out of the coach. "But for now, trust that I wish you nothing but happiness, and no matter what you decide, I support you wholeheartedly."

Violet stared over at her very handsome cousin, and then, nodding, took his arm. "I wish you all weren't being so secretive."

Greystone squeezed her hand. "You look beautiful, by the way." He urged her around the horses in the direction of the statue.

At the edge of the clearing, Violet noticed that Greystone and Simon were not the only people who'd come. Lord and Lady Westerley were standing near two other coaches, and had been joined by Bethany and Chaswick, as well as Mr. Spencer and Lady Tabetha.

Violet swallowed hard, feeling, oddly enough, like a bride.

Thoughts such as that were bound to lead to disappointment. She shook her head and then stared at the ground.

"Breathe," Greystone said from beside her.

Violet nodded, knowing they must be nearing the statue now. And when she could no longer help herself, she lifted her head.

And there he was.

Simon looked... magnificent. And although his jaw ticked,

giving away some nervousness, he looked perfectly comfortable wearing a fine linen shirt, expertly tied cravat, black coat, and an evergreen waistcoat. She noticed that his tan breeches were tucked neatly into a shining pair of Hessians.

Her butler, she decided, might just as well be a prince.

She lifted her gaze to meet his, and her heart fluttered... Butterflies...

And tingling filled her, because the look in his eyes was nothing less than love.

He stepped forward, one hand extended, and again, the sense of Greystone giving her away shook her.

"Violet," Simon said.

She'd gone far too long without hearing his voice.

Greystone pressed a cool kiss to her cheek. "I'll be right over there if you need me," he said softly and then, with a nod in Simon's direction, strolled to where the other couples waited... watching.

Her gaze shot back to Simon. A moment of clarity hit her. She would always be looking for Simon. No matter where she went or what happened today. Because her heart wanted to be whole.

"You came," he said.

Despite being freshly shaven, and... had he had his hair cut? He was her same dear Simon. The man who'd crawled out of her bed in the early hours that morning.

"Are you going to tell me what all of this is about?" At last, she would have her explanations. "You are not my cousin's butler."

He shook his head. "I am not. I don't suppose I'm a very good substitute for one, either." He lowered his face and stared straight into her eyes. Violet swallowed hard.

"I don't mind that. I just want the truth."

"And you'll have it. But first, my love, I owe you an apology for something else."

The breath Violet inhaled was a shaky one. "Go on."

"I asked you to trust me without telling you why. And then I imagined you were seriously considering Thompson's proposal. That wasn't fair of me. Trust needs to go two ways."

She nodded. "Christopher is my past, and that's where he'll remain." Was Simon to be her future? Violet reached up to touch his cheek. "I meant what I said last night."

"You love me." It was not a question but words that sounded almost reverent.

"Yes." She wouldn't turn back now. "But..." She dropped her hand, what she'd overheard that morning rearing up to shake her confidence. "You don't want to marry me."

"You were in my office—the butler's office—when Greystone and I spoke." Simon clasped both her hands in his. "You should have listened longer."

"I was afraid to hear worse. You see, that's the plight of an eavesdropper—hearing things one doesn't really want to hear."

"I never want to hide anything from you again." His eyes were shining now.

"What would I have heard, had I stayed longer?"

"You would have heard me tell your cousin that I wanted my offer to come from my heart. I didn't want any other forces at play when I asked. And I need your answer to come from yours. I want you, more than anything, Violet. You're the person I need when I'm happy, or when I'm tired, or for a million other reasons just because you are you. I'm not making any sense, but... I've never *needed* another person in my life. Not the way I need you. I love you, Violet." His eyes were shining as he dropped onto one knee, staring at her in earnest. "I pray you feel the same. Marry me? Make me the happiest of men?"

"Yes," she answered, and then blinked... and then laughed. "You foolish man." Shaking her head, she tugged at him. "Of course, I'll marry you. Come up here."

He drew her into his arms this time. But rather than seal their proposal with a kiss as she'd expected, he grew serious again.

"There is something else..."

"I will love you anyway," she said. A person had no control over who they fell in love with. She hated the idea of thieving, or anything criminal, but she... trusted him.

She would demand explanations—eventually, but she didn't need them now. She was simply happy not to have to live her life without him.

"Do you know how incredible you are?" A dazed sort of amazement lit the light blue flecks in his eyes. "Unbelievable."

"I believe in you." She shrugged. It was the unvarnished truth. But then she smiled. "I don't know how, or why. I just... do."

He didn't say anything but instead swallowed hard. And then...

"My name is Simon Cockfield, but it is not my full name. I am Simon Benjamin Alexander Harold Cockfield, Duke of Blackheart, but also Marquess of Rowland, Earl of Webb, Viscount Hill, and heir presumptive to a number of other titles."

Violet blinked and then glanced around as though someone was, indeed, pulling a prank on her.

"That day at Heart Place, I was showing you my own home. I... made love to you on my own bed."

Her gaze flicked down to his hands. His own...? "The

watch, it was on the dresser in Blackheart's chamber." She shook her head. "You did not steal it?"

His eyes widened a moment. "No. It belongs to me. I didn't think twice about taking it. But you noticed. And you…"

"I hope you don't think less of me, but I loved you anyway." Violet stood, remembering… his beautiful horse, his ease on a ballroom floor, the respect he seemed to receive wherever he went. "I was going to have to have a talk with you about curtailing such habits in the future."

Simon laughed but all she could do was shake her head. Was she sleeping? Was she dreaming?

"I didn't realize…" she was dumbfounded. How had she not put it all together?

"Are you angry?" Simon was watching her closely. "Initially, it was refreshing, spending time with you the same as any other gentleman could. Having you joke with me, challenge me. I especially enjoyed it when you put me in my place."

"I never meant—" She wanted to cover her face but couldn't, not with Simon's arms holding her.

"But as I came to know you, as I came to love you, I wanted you to know all of me."

Violet tilted her head, realizing… "You took me to your home…"

He nodded. "I was caught between lying to you and making good on a promise."

"What sort of promise? Why would you pretend to be the butler at Knight Hall? I don't understand."

Simon tightened his arms around her.

She would have married me as a butler!

And now he owed her the explanation for all of it. He exhaled. "I cannot imagine the presence of these fine gentlemen here today has gone unnoticed."

He'd never been one to stall, but this part was going to be… a little awkward.

"It has not," she answered, waiting patiently for the explanation that was long past due.

"I accepted a particularly foolish wager last March." He winced sheepishly. "And without going into a good deal of detail, what's relevant is that I lost."

Violet nodded. "To Greystone?"

"Yes."

"You set your title aside for a… bet? And please, don't skip the details on my account. I'm most curious as to how this came about." Then, pressing herself against him, she stared at him like a schoolteacher might stare at one of her students who had misbehaved.

He couldn't help smiling. She was just so… Violet.

"The details are less than gentlemanly," he admitted.

"Of course they are."

She deserved to hear all of it. Resigned, Simon prepared to rehash the bet he'd entered into at Westerley Crossings last March. "I'm going to preface my explanation first by telling you that, at the time, we'd consumed copious amounts of scotch."

"I see."

"Yes, well…" Simon cleared his throat.

"And that bet was…?"

"That Westerley could convince Miss Jackson—now Lady Westerley—to marry him, and that he could accomplish this in less than twenty-four hours." He winced at the sound of that. Simon had known better than to bet against Greys. The man rarely lost, if ever.

"I take it she did not accept his suit so easily?"

"No, I believe it took him closer to a week." Simon had been quite disappointed.

"And might I know the terms of this wager?"

"If I was wrong, then, for the duration of the Season, I would be honor-bound to perform the duties as Greystone's—"

"Butler," she finished for him. She wasn't scolding him—yet.

"The terms were that my identity remain a secret. And aside from a few necessary exceptions, I couldn't tell anyone who I was. Which wasn't problematic, until... you came along."

"Me?" But she appeared rather pleased at the notion. And the sun, which was very low in the sky, shone a golden light on her face.

Simon halted his explanation to steal a kiss, a kiss that left both of them a little breathless.

"You would make an excellent spy. Whenever I turned around, there you were, watching me, catching me dealing with my steward, or one of my sisters, always thinking the worst." He grinned.

"I thought you were going to corrupt poor Posy!" she accused. "And how was I to know?" But then she smiled, but with a crease between her eyes and shaking her head. "All of this was for a silly bet?"

"Honor dictated that I fulfill the terms. I had to follow it through." Simon squeezed her. "And if I forfeited, your cousin would win the distinction of selecting the woman I am to marry. This was the part of the wager I regretted most of all."

Violet grew serious, watching him closely. "And he selected me?" She frowned.

"He tried, but I wouldn't allow it. I have proposed to you because I wanted to. The decision was all mine."

"But then how…?" She blinked at him. "You are really… Blackheart? The Duke of Blackheart."

"Yes, and as to how, well, the terms of the bet have been renegotiated." Simon glanced over his shoulder and absently noticed that shadows partially hid the details carved into the statue. Hopefully, the setting sun would provide him the same sort of cover. "This is what I was discussing with Greystone most of the day. I offered him Heart Place, but he refused. I was willing to do anything…"

"But it would have been dishonorable." Violet showed her understanding. "Honor, once forfeited by a gentleman, is nearly impossible to get back."

"Yes." But he would have done so, if necessary. As it was, he was going to have to sacrifice his dignity instead.

"Trouble was," he explained. "Greys and I were not the only ones with wagers."

"Go on now!" Mr. Spencer interrupted, shouting across to them. "Enough with the stalling!"

Violet glanced over to where the others waited, and then back to Simon.

"Westerley and Greystone bet that I would concede before the end of the Season, and Chaswick, Spencer, and Mantis, now the Earl of Crestwood, bet that I would not. The losers of their collective wagers would sprint through the park…" He cleared his throat, covering his mouth with one hand. "Unclothed."

Violet's brows raised, and then she darted her gaze to the statue and back.

"Without so much as a fig leaf." Simon winced.

"And if your bet with my cousin was renegotiated, or if Greys released you from the terms, it would ruin their wager," Violet guessed.

"Yes, so, this afternoon, Chaswick proposed an alternative."

"And that was?"

He reached up and untied his cravat.

"Oh Simon, no!" Her mouth fell open. "So... you... must... without...?"

He unbuttoned his jacket and, after struggling for a few seconds, shucked it off his arms. "I only hope you'll forgive me some day. Because I told them I would do anything so that I could marry you freely." He unbuttoned his waistcoat and then added, "I'll understand if you wish to make a hasty departure with the other ladies now."

Violet wasn't moving, however, but stayed at his side, shaking her head with a wide smile. "Oh, no, Simon. I wouldn't miss this for the world."

He leaned forward to press his lips to hers.

Of course she wouldn't.

"I'm going to support you in all things, beginning now," she said, laughter in her voice. "Besides, if I leave, who will hold your clothes for you?"

EPILOGUE

"**G**ood morning, Vi. I see that Blackheart got the announcement turned in on time." Greystone glanced up from the paper, the morning sun slanting onto the table promising an unusually blue sky for the day.

"I requested additional copies." Posy handed one over to Violet. "I can still hardly believe that in all that time Mr. Cockfield was working here, he was actually a duke. How positively wretched of him to fool us like that." But Posy was grinning. "But I suppose I'll have to forgive him since Aunt Violet's engagement notice is on the front page!"

Violet met Posy's gaze, feeling closer since they'd talked late last night. They'd gone to Greystone together, who hadn't been all that surprised. It wasn't necessarily going to be easy, but Posy was going to be just fine, with or without Miss Mallard. Because she had family that loved her.

Unconditionally. And nothing could change that.

"I'll have to clip the article for my journal." Violet lifted the paper, which was still warm from the iron.

Duke to Marry.

She smiled to herself, amused at having been left out of the headline.

The Duke of Blackheart, it read, *who has been suspiciously absent from this season's flurry of festivities, has exclusively announced to this columnist that he intends to wed the Marquess of Greystone's cousin—Miss Violet Faraday of Yorkshire. No date has been set as of yet, but trust* yours truly *to bring you the latest word as soon as the happy couple settles on one.*

The great question being, will it be before or after Lord Greystone's nuptials?

If the columnist had any idea, he would have news indeed.

"That rascal didn't fool me for a second," Aunt Iris declared for the twentieth time since Greystone had made the announcement. "It was quite obvious to me your butler was not at all who he claimed to be. The first time I saw him, I said to myself, that Mr. Cockfield is nobility. And I'm sure Violet saw the same. She would never have formed an attachment with him otherwise." She glanced at Violet. "Well done, my dear."

"Aunt Violet fell in love. It's as simple as that," Posy said. "Just like Greystone and Diana."

But another article had grabbed Aunt Iris's attention, and she was holding the paper close to her face, twin spots of pink on her parchment-like complexion. "Did you see this? Not you, Posy. Greystone, look on page four. What is becoming of this city? Unless it's simply a lie made up to sell papers."

Violet flipped to the page in question—as did Posy.

Another Tribute to Wellington?

"Witnesses have reported," Posy read. "Seeing a gentleman racing through Hyde Park, unclothed, in the vicinity of the Achilles statue on the night of May first. The tribute occurred at approximately seven in the evening, and the villain wore nothing but a black masquerade mask. The man's identity is unknown but Bow Street Runners are seeking information so he can be tried for such a blatant crime. At this time, however, there are no known suspects."

Violet pinched her lips together, trying not to smile.

"Oh my," Posy said.

Greystone clucked his tongue, but Violet couldn't even look at him. She'd either burst into laughter or combust from embarrassment.

Or perhaps both.

A stout gentleman entered, somewhere around the age of sixty, and walked around the table to refill their empty and half-empty cups. Mr. Smithery performed the duties of butler with much greater skill than Simon had, although he lacked Simon's style.

And good looks.

The afternoon before, while strolling through the garden with her fiancé, Violet had lamented this very fact to him.

"Miss me, eh?" And at her answer, he'd comforted her in the very best way and then had promised to bring her tea in bed—their bed—after they married.

Violet pulled her fan out of her sleeve and waved it below her face. "Is it hot in here?" she asked no one in particular. It wasn't the first time she'd felt overwhelmed by... all of it.

Because falling in love with Simon Cockfield was one thing, marrying the Duke of Blackheart quite another.

"I hadn't noticed. Is Blackheart taking you driving this afternoon?" Greystone asked.

She kept right on waving her fan. "He is. But first, we've plans to go... shopping this morning." The ruse was all part of a last-minute decision agreed upon by her and Simon. Reluctant to take anything away from Diana and Greys's wedding plans, but also too impatient to wait for their own, they'd agreed to marry by special license.

Today—Violet shivered—was her wedding day.

And as most of their relationship had been conducted secretly, aside from a very public and unusual engagement, they'd decided a private ceremony was appropriate.

"I'm just going to pop upstairs." Violet allowed Mr. Smithery to pull back her chair. "So that I'll be ready when the carriage arrives."

Simon had asked if she minded the groom seeing her before the ceremony if she thought it would be bad luck. When she'd hesitated, he'd told her not to worry.

So she hadn't.

Because the line in her palm had not been wrong after all.

And according to Simon's lifeline, she was marrying a man who valued family and relationships greatly.

After checking her hair, unable to sit in her chamber, Violet went downstairs early and slipped outside just as a gleaming black coach pulled up to the house. She expected to ride to the church alone but was pleasantly surprised when Bethany peered out the door.

"You needed witnesses," Bethany explained, looking fresh and pretty in a mint cotton gown. "And when I heard Black-heart discussing it with Chaswick, I insisted it be the two of us."

"Of course." Violet climbed in and steadied herself with the leather strap as the coach rolled onto the street. The ceremony was scheduled to take place at St. George's, which was just a short drive away, and yet they seemed to be traveling in the wrong direction.

"Where are we going?" Violet reached across to open the small door to the driver's box but Bethany stopped her.

"He's been instructed to deliver us at precisely nine o'clock, so we're circling the park first."

"I wouldn't have minded waiting." But Violet leaned back and smiled at Bethany. "It was in the papers," she said, staring forward.

"The announcement? I saw that."

"No, the other." Violet smothered a grin with her gloved hand. She would never forget watching her proud Mr. Cockfield leisurely remove his waistcoat and cravat, not showing any embarrassment, but instead, grace that matched Achilles himself. When he'd lowered his hands to unfasten his breeches, however, she had dragged him behind a nearby tree. "Surely not everything?"

He'd smiled wickedly. "I've been told I may leave my boots on."

She had covered her eyes and turned her back.

"If I'd thought this through properly, I would have brought Dane along," he'd commented while shuffling out of his breeches, handing them to her from behind.

"Dane?"

"Mr. Dane, my valet."

Her butler, Violet took a moment to marvel, employed a valet.

"Do you need help?" She kept her eyes focused in front at her, ironically, on the statue.

"I think I've got this. With or without the boots?"

"Er… With? You don't want to hurt your feet." She couldn't help but giggle at the image of him wearing his boots and nothing else.

"Damn breeches… Why do they make these so tight?"

"If you take your time removing your boots and then putting them back on, you might have cover of darkness."

Violet had become more nervous for him with each passing second.

"Ah, no, I've got it."

"You are... ready?"

"Only for you, Violet." His voice held both sincerity and laughter.

She turned and met his eyes—dark, warm eyes that were filled with love. In the setting sun, his shoulders and torso gleamed golden, with the perfect smattering of curling black hair across his chest and trailing down—

"Violet?" His voice brought her gaze back up to his face. "Will you take these?"

He had handed her his breeches and with a wink, her fiancé, who was also, incredibly, not a butler or thief or criminal, but the Duke of Blackheart, took off running to the sounds of hoots and hollers from his friends.

He had suffered that ultimate indignity so that he could marry her. And so that they could do so freely.

Today! He was marrying her today.

Violet stared out the window at the park and blinked away tears. But these tears were tears of joy.

He had told her he did not want a wager to taint his proposal.

He had done it for... *them*.

"If it makes you feel better, Violet, we covered our eyes." Bethany's voice brought her back to the present. Bethany was trying not to laugh.

"You did not." Violet knew better. "You all watched."

And what a sight it had been...

Bethany feigned innocence but then burst into giggles. "Oh, but it was indeed too tempting to miss."

Violet agreed wholeheartedly.

The two ladies shared a moment of silent appreciation, and then Bethany turned serious. "You are happy?"

"I am," Violet answered without hesitation.

And she was. She was enthusiastically, deliriously, one-hundred-percent happy. Simon could be maddening and mysterious and arrogant, but he was also compassionate, understanding, generous, and oh, so very charming. Regardless of whether he was a butler or a duke, he was *the one*—the person who owned the other half of her heart.

The carriage rounded the corner and rolled toward St. George's. Again, violet peered out her window and this time, laughed right out loud when she saw the group of suspiciously familiar-looking people mingling outside.

"He wanted it to be a surprise." Bethany sounded as pleased and excited as Violet was.

"It's perfect." Violet could barely speak.

Although she had agreed to marrying without any fuss so as not to take away from Greystone and Diana's nuptials, seeing these faces filled her heart.

"You aren't mad, then?"

"Of course not." How could she be, when so many people cared about her and Simon? "I'm not sure there would even be a ceremony without all of you."

"We are all somehow connected, aren't we?" Bethany said.

"We are."

Lord Chaswick and Greystone approached the carriage, looking dapper and pleased. Violet blinked away fresh tears. This was a moment she had given up on for herself.

Magic. Her own happy-ever-after.

She removed her handkerchief from her sleeve and dabbed at her eyes.

"None of that," Bethany said, her own eyes looking suspiciously bright.

After a watery smile and a kiss on the cheek for good luck, Bethany stepped outside, and then Greystone peered in, reaching his hand for Violet's.

"You didn't think I'd miss this, did you?" he asked, looking proud and oh, so very lovable.

She'd lost her only sister and her parents long ago, and Greystone had lost his parents as well, but the two of them had made do with one another—and Aunt Iris and Posy. They'd become a different kind of family.

And now, both of them were on the brink of expanding it.

"I'm so very glad you are here," she told him.

"You are ready? You haven't changed your mind about him?" Greys smiled. "Because I'll take you back to Knight Hall if you have."

"Oh, no. I am ready. I've been ready for a lifetime. And oh, Greys, I love him so much. I would have married him regardless," she said.

Greys nodded slowly. "Then let's put him out of his misery, shall we? I do believe he's waiting at the altar now."

Violet took her cousin's hand and allowed him to lead her inside.

To Simon.

SIMON HAD ALWAYS THOUGHT he'd be sick with nerves when this moment arrived. The moment he stared down the church aisle, watching for his bride.

Instead, he felt only anticipation.

And when the organist struck up and Violet appeared with

Greystone beside her, heat radiated in Simon's chest. Marrying her brought him... joy.

He'd hoped to marry for love, a great love, but had never believed it would happen. Because any woman who married him, he'd always known, would have come to him first knowing she'd become the Duchess of Blackheart. He'd not thought it possible to separate his title from his person.

He hadn't even realized he would want to do that.

But Violet had fallen in love with... *him*.

As she walked gracefully toward him, she glowed—partly from the rays of sunshine slanting across the sanctuary but also from within.

Unexpected emotion thickened his throat.

She wore a simple but elegant gown—one that suited her perfectly. Halfway to the altar, she glanced toward the pews where the guests he'd invited sat, smiling as though to welcome them all.

She'd agreed to marrying in secret, but he'd sensed a hint of sadness. Of course, she'd wanted the people she loved to be there. So, with but one day to plan, he'd invited the people who cared for both of them—those who would wish to witness this ceremony, not for their own status, or so that they could boast to their friends, but because they were happy for the two of them.

Her gaze locked with his and he forgot everything but his bride.

Joy. *Unadulterated joy.*

Joy at knowing she would be the person to go through life with him.

As his wife.

His duchess.

Losing that bet was the best thing that ever happened to

him. But, damn, he was going to have to thank Greystone for that—despite the undignified dash they'd insisted he make.

Which, in all honesty, had been incredibly fair of them. Fair, considering all he'd been willing to sacrifice otherwise.

"Nervous?" Westerley asked from beside him.

"No," Simon shook his head, his gaze not wavering from Violet. "Were you?"

"Surprisingly, I wasn't either. A little in awe…" his friend answered.

And then she was beside him, and Greystone was placing her hand in his.

"Dearly beloved," the bishop began.

Simon faced his bride, allowing her to see all the love he felt in that moment.

Because that was precisely what she was. His dearly beloved.

BONUS EPILOGUE

 rescent Park

Two and a half years later

"Guests will be arriving any hour now." Violet wrung her hands together. "I've inspected all the rooms. The kitchen has everything they need, except for the turkeys, of course, which won't be delivered until Christmas Eve. The decorations are dusted—"

"You've taken care of everything." *And then some.* Simon took both of her hands in his and squeezed.

His wife had been caught up in the preparations for weeks now, but now that the day had arrived, she was second-guessing everything.

They hadn't entertained a great deal since their marriage,

aside from family and close friends. But having recently completed the renovations to the Manor at Crescent Park, Violet had suggested it was time.

And so they'd decided on a Christmas house party.

"Breathe." Simon widened his stance, so she had no choice but to meet his eyes, and then pressed his forehead to hers. "Everything is perfect." He kissed her. "*You* are perfect."

This woman, Simon had learned, had more capacity to love than he'd thought possible for one person. Beginning, but not ending, with Simon and their six-month-old twin sons, she always managed to also love and support his sisters and brothers, her cousin and niece, and all of their families, as well as an abundance of friends who made up an essential part of their lives.

"Sometimes," she whispered in his ear, "I'm almost too happy."

With an audible sigh, Violet wound her arms around his neck.

And then, his very proper wife nibbled at his earlobe.

"You say they'll be here any hour?" Simon's hands roved over his wife's bottom. "That means we have time…"

Even if Violet had somehow missed some small detail, their servants, who were some of the finest people in all of England, would take care of it.

His staff was the best because he paid more than any other employer—and they deserved it. He also took steps so that they didn't have to sacrifice having families of their own in order to work for him—unless they wished to do so.

Simon had only unfastened a few buttons at the back of her dress when sounds of approaching vehicles filtered through the windows of their bedchamber.

They froze, neither willing to move out of the other's embrace. "How much are you willing to wager," Violet finally said, "that the first to arrive are Bethany and Chase?"

"I'll not be swindled so easily." Because Violet only wagered when she knew she would win. And Simon was still smarting from the last one he'd lost—having bet the twins would be girls.

Although, of course, he hadn't lost at all. Every day with his wife and sons was a win.

When the carriage sounds halted outside, Violet dropped her hands from around his neck with a disappointed sigh. But then she leaned forward to kiss him.

"Tonight," she said.

"If you aren't too tired." Because she spent so much energy loving on their boys, and she'd not hold back in showering their guests with attention this evening.

"I won't be." She met his eyes in the mirror over her vanity, smoothing her gown as she did so.

"Nor will I," Simon stared back at her, and then very deliberately smirked.

"I never should have told you what that does to me," Violet scolded, shaking her head. "Now, I'll be thinking about it all afternoon."

His wife did not hesitate in telling him what she liked. And for some reason that he didn't quite understand, Violet had confessed to loving "the smirk."

"Just giving you something to look forward to," Simon promised, taking her by the hand.

"Wicked, wicked man." She leaned her head back, resting it against his chest. And then she added, "My dear Mr. Cockfield."

"I aim to please," he growled near her ear. "Miss Faraday."

"DIANA AND GREYS are right behind us!" Bethany announced as her husband assisted her out of their carriage. She rubbed her back with a grimace as she did so. Despite being seven months into her confinement, she'd insisted the drive was short enough to endure and convinced the baron that they absolutely must come to the party.

Because it was Christmastime.

A nanny exited behind them, holding their daughter, Gwendolyn, and Violet couldn't resist welcoming the little cherub with a kiss.

Out of the corner of her eye, Violet noticed Simon greeting his friend heartily. He'd protested at first that she would plan such a large party, but he would enjoy sharing the holidays with the people who meant the most to him.

"Let's get you out of this wind." Violet took Bethany's arm. "Mrs. Purdy will show Nanny to her room in the nursery."

"And I need to see the babies!"

"But of course," Violet had planned on looking in on them again anyway.

Party or not, she had no intention of neglecting Benji and Alex.

"We've fixed up an entire floor for all the children." In addition to the small nursery the twins shared, across the hall from Violet and Simon's chamber. "I'm excited to see how the boys respond to having other children about." Violet spoke proudly of her two sons—both spitting images of their father.

Alex had been first, Benjamin five minutes later.

"I don't know how you did it… Twins!" Bethany said.

"I don't know how I did it either," Violet agreed. "How are you feeling with this one?"

"Aside from the heartburn, surprisingly well. He kicks more than Gwennie did."

"So you think it's a boy?"

"I don't know why, but yes. For some reason, this one has my husband's personality. Even now, it's as though he hears your voice and is protesting that he cannot come out and socialize." Bethany laughed. Because Chaswick's outgoing charm was almost legendary.

"With that in mind," Violet patted Bethany's arm as they climbed the curved staircase to the upper floor, "I am ordering you to rest for all of this afternoon."

Violet had Bethany comfortably ensconced in a luxurious suite just as more carriages sounded from a distance. "Pull the bell, Bethany, if you need anything," Violet ordered from the door.

"I'm fine."

"Promise me," Violet put on her stern face.

"Very well. Now go." Bethany shooed her away and Violet dashed down the stairs just in time to meet up with Simon at the front door.

"She is very, very pregnant." Simon slid his gaze toward the stairs. "I am surprised Chaswick consented to traveling."

"Never, ever tell her that. But as the house party was partly her idea, she didn't give him much choice. Not to worry, though, love, the baby isn't due until February." Violet and Simon stepped outside just as Greystone's carriage pulled to a halt.

"You are here!" Violet announced.

"Finally!" Diana grinned as she exited the carriage, looking even more fashionable than Greys. Diana had not had an easy time in society, but her persistence had paid off, and the ball she'd hosted in London last spring had been declared a resounding success.

A full-on ballet had been performed for the guests while supper was served. Those who hadn't been scandalized declared the Marchioness of Greystone to be the hostess of the decade.

Because Diana had been one of the dancers.

"I'm so glad you are here. Bethany is upstairs already." Violet brushed a kiss along the younger girl's cheek.

"She is well? The traveling wasn't too much?"

"She's fine. I'm the one who insisted she rest." Violet reassured her. "She was determined not to miss seeing everyone together for the holidays."

"She does seem to enjoy Christmas more than most," Diana said.

However, Violet was prevented from showing Greys and Diana upstairs, as more carriages appeared, followed by... more carriages.

And before long, guests were shaking hands, a few squealing and welcoming one another with varying levels of exuberance. Servants, nannies, and governesses rushed in and out of the house to assist the arrivals. There were even a few dogs amongst them.

"The two of you are saints for doing this," Lady Crestwood told both Violet and Simon. After spending over a year at her husband's country estate, partly in mourning but also because of the birth of their son, the countess and Mantis had finally reentered society last spring. Simon had been thrilled to have his sparring partner back, and Violet happy to become reacquainted with the quietly dignified woman, whom she'd met briefly in London while Simon had been playing butler.

They had brought not only their infant son, but were also accompanied by the earl's younger half-brother, and Cordelia, the earl's twin sister, a magnificent woman with blond hair and warm brown eyes.

Next to arrive was Collette, who had surprised all of them with her marriage to the Duke of Bedwell. She'd met him at Miss Primm's Private Seminary for the Education of Ladies, the school where she'd been hired to teach, and the two had wed before the first term ended. As the duke's mother had died the year before, they had brought his sister, Lady Fiona, with them as well. Simon had also invited Bedwell's half-brother, a handsome dark-skinned gentleman, Mr. Rowan Stewart.

And upon meeting him and making introductions, Violet had felt the seeds of matchmaking take root.

"I'm going to seat Mr. Stewart beside Cordelia," Violet whispered into Simon's ear.

"Whatever you wish, my love," he answered, grinning but shaking his head.

More guests arrived: Posy and her friend, and Aunt Iris. And then Lord and Lady Westerley, along with their daughter, followed by Tabetha and her husband, Mr. Spencer. Simon's sisters and their spouses were some of the last to arrive, and his brother, Lucas, who was one of the kindest people she'd ever met, along with his wife, Naomi, and their daughter.

Although most of the guests were already acquainted with one another, a few introductions were necessary, and with all the conversation, nearly an hour passed before everyone made their way inside.

And when the large front door closed behind them, Violet remained outside with Simon, holding his arm and staring down the drive. "That is everyone, is it not?" She relaxed her shoulders, mentally going through the list of their guests.

"I'm not sure the house could hold one more person." Simon's arm settled around her waist.

"But you don't mind," she said, turning to stare up into his midnight gaze. "I never thought I'd have a holiday like this." Her voice caught. "I never expected to be part of such a large family. I have your sisters, your brother, and their families, and Greys and Diana and Posy, but also all of our friends." Violet was so glad that Simon's friends had been there for him after his parents had passed. She was grateful for all his friends, period. Lady Westerley had christened the lot of them as *The Cocksure Gents*.

And it had somehow stuck.

Violet breathed in this moment. The scent of winter hovering in the air, the breeze cooler now than when they'd first stepped outside.

She closed her eyes, resting in her husband's arms.

Every day with this man was precious to her.

"Fate has been more than good to me." She inhaled. She had never needed a grand house, or a title, or fancy gowns, and dozens of servants. All she'd ever wanted was love—this kind of love. The love of her dreams. "You and the boys are all I'll ever need." She smiled. "Mr. Cockfield."

She touched her husband's jaw, marveling to be so utterly… blessed.

"And you, my love," Simon kissed her, "are my very own happy-ever-after."

— The End —

316

I trust that you enjoyed the Regency Cocky Gents as much as I have! Make sure you haven't missed any...

Lord Westerley and Charley **COCKY EARL**
Lord Chaswick and Bethany **COCKY BARON**
Stone Spencer and Tabetha **COCKY MISTER**
Peter Spencer and Miranda **COCKY BROTHER**
Mantis and Felicity **COCKY VISCOUNT**
Greys and Diana **COCKY MARQUESS**

CONTINUE THE JOURNEY WITH ME!

TO READ about Collette's match with the Duke of Bedwell, be sure to pick up *Trapped with the Duke*, BOOK ONE of my next series, **Miss Primm's Secret School for Budding Bluestockings**

His proposal, as honorable as it was, was also somewhat maddening. She had not been born to be a duchess. She'd been born to be a secret.

BETHANY GRINNED and then grew serious again. "You don't have to give him your answer right away. If you think waiting will help, ask for a week, or longer. Because marrying him will change your life one way or another. And it's for life. If you hate it, you'll be trapped with the duke forever, but there is always the possibility..."

"Of what?" Collette insisted.

"That marrying him, that being with a man who loves you, and one you love in return, frees you to be the person you've always been meant to be."

REGENCY COCKY GENTS

A NEW ANNABELLE ANDERS SERIES

Cocky Earl

Jules and Charley

Cocky Baron

Chase and Bethany

Cocky Mister

Stone and Tabetha

Cocky Brother

Peter Spencer's Story

(Formerly Mayfair Maiden)

Cocky Viscount

Mantis and Felicity

Cocky Marquess

Greystone's Story

Cocky Butler

Blackheart's Story

THE DEFIANT DAMSELS SERIES

Lady at Last

Penelope's Story (Viscount Danbury)

Lady Be Good

Rose's Story (Viscount Darlington)

Lady and the Rake

Margaret's Story (The Marquess of Rockingham)

ABOUT THE AUTHOR

Married to the same man for over 25 years, I am a mother to three children and two Miniature Wiener dogs.

After owning a business and experiencing considerable success, my husband and I got caught in the financial crisis and lost everything in 2008; our business, our home, even our car.

At this point, I put my B.A. in Poly Sci to use and took work as a waitress and bartender (Insert irony). Unwilling to give up on a professional life, I simultaneously went back to college and obtained a degree in EnergyManagement.

And then the energy market dropped off.

And then my dog died.

I can only be grateful for this series of unfortunate events, for, with nothing to lose and completely demoralized, I sat down and began to write the romance novels which had until then, existed only my imagination. After publishing over thirty novels now, with one having been nominated for RWA's Distinguished ™RITA Award in 2019, I am happy to tell you that I have finally found my place in life.

Thank you so much for being a part of my journey!

To find out more about my books, and also to download a free book, get all the info at my website!

www.annabelleanders.com

Made in the USA
Las Vegas, NV
30 October 2021

33403305R00194